The Heroine of Auschwitz

A heartbreaking and gripping WW2 tale of love, loss, and courage during the Holocaust.

By Mark deMeza

The Heroine of Auschwitz

First published in 2025

Copyright © Bebetter Publishing 2025

All rights reserved.

The rights of the author have been asserted in accordance with Sections 77 and 78 of the Copyright Designs and Patents Act, 1988. No part of this book may be reproduced (including photocopying or storing in any medium by electronic means and or not transiently or incidentally to some other use of this publication) without the written permission of the copyright holder except in accordance with the provisions of the Copyright, design and patents Act 1988.

ISBN: 978-1-7384541-2-9

This book is a work of fiction. Names, characters, businesses, organisations, places and events other than those clearly in the public domain, are either the product of the author's imagination or are used fictitiously. Any resemblance to actual persons, living or dead, events or locales is entirely coincidental.

DEDICATION

Dedicated to all those who fight evil and oppression.

AUTHOR'S NOTE

My previous novel *The Thirteenth Child* followed the story of the fictional Kisch family who lived in Amsterdam in the 1940s under the oppressive occupation of the Nazis. It was based on my discovery that eleven of my Dutch Jewish ancestors were transported by the Nazis and murdered in the infamous extermination camps in Sobibor and Auschwitz.

The Heroine of Auschwitz continues the story of the surviving Kisch family members as they arrive at Birkenau, the massive extermination camp built when the main Auschwitz I camp was overflowing with prisoners. The events within the book are derived from factual events. Through my in-depth research, I have created a work of fiction that depicts life in Birkenau from late 1943 until early 1945. I have changed the chronology of certain historical events to smooth the narrative flow of the novel but have endeavored to maintain factual accuracy.

This period was dreadful for prisoners in Auschwitz and Birkenau, even by their usual standards. In reality, there were beacons of light in the darkness, but they were exceptionally rare. I hope the experiences of the Kisch family and the other prisoners in this work of fiction reflect this.

Mark deMeza
Spring 2025

PROLOGUE

The Polish town of Oswiecim lies about sixty-four kilometers west of Krakow. After the Great War, several brick barracks were constructed on the outskirts of the town, their purpose being to accommodate transient groups of soldiers. Having lain empty for several years, the site then became a base for the Polish army.

The region fell under Nazi control when Poland was annexed by Germany in 1939, and, early in 1940, the SS converted the base into a concentration camp, which became known by its German name, Auschwitz.

The intention was for the camp to be constructed by the prisoners themselves, who first arrived in May 1940, a group of thirty Germans, so-called professional criminals who had been transferred from the Sachsenhausen camp near Berlin. In June, the first of many transportations of Polish prisoners of war arrived at Oswiecim railway station.

During 1941, the Auschwitz camp was extended to include extermination facilities comprising a gas chamber and incineration room, which enabled the Nazis to murder approximately 340 people a day. In the early stages, most victims were Poles and Soviets because the Nazis' plan for the mass extermination of the Jews (the Final Solution) had not yet been conceived.

In mid-1941, the Germans launched Operation Barbarossa, the invasion of the Soviet Union. Reichsführer SS-Heinrich Himmler visited the camp and, in anticipation of the arrival of significant numbers of Soviet prisoners of war, ordered the construction of a second camp in Brzezinka, three kilometers from Auschwitz. In fall 1941, 10,000 Soviet prisoners arrived to build the camp. By the following spring, the first section of the new camp (B1), comprising seventy-eight brick barracks, was completed and all the Soviets were dead, mainly because of overwork and mistreatment.

This second camp also became known by its German name, Birkenau.

As a consequence of the Wannsee conference in January 1942, when the Final Solution was agreed by the Nazis, a further 220 barracks were constructed (B2). To save time and money, these new barracks were built of wood and were completed toward the end of 1943, using the slave labor of captured prisoners of war.

During 1942, the gassing and incineration operations in Auschwitz were transferred to two converted farmhouses in Birkenau, known as the Little Red House and the Little White House. As the transportation of Jews was accelerated by the Nazis, a further four crematoria were built, each combining gassing and incineration operations. These were designed and built in conjunction with German industrial corporations to optimize the extermination process and were all in operation by the middle of 1943.

In the period from early 1941 to the middle of 1943, the Nazis increased Birkenau's extermination capacity from approximately 124,000 to 1,600,000 human beings a year.

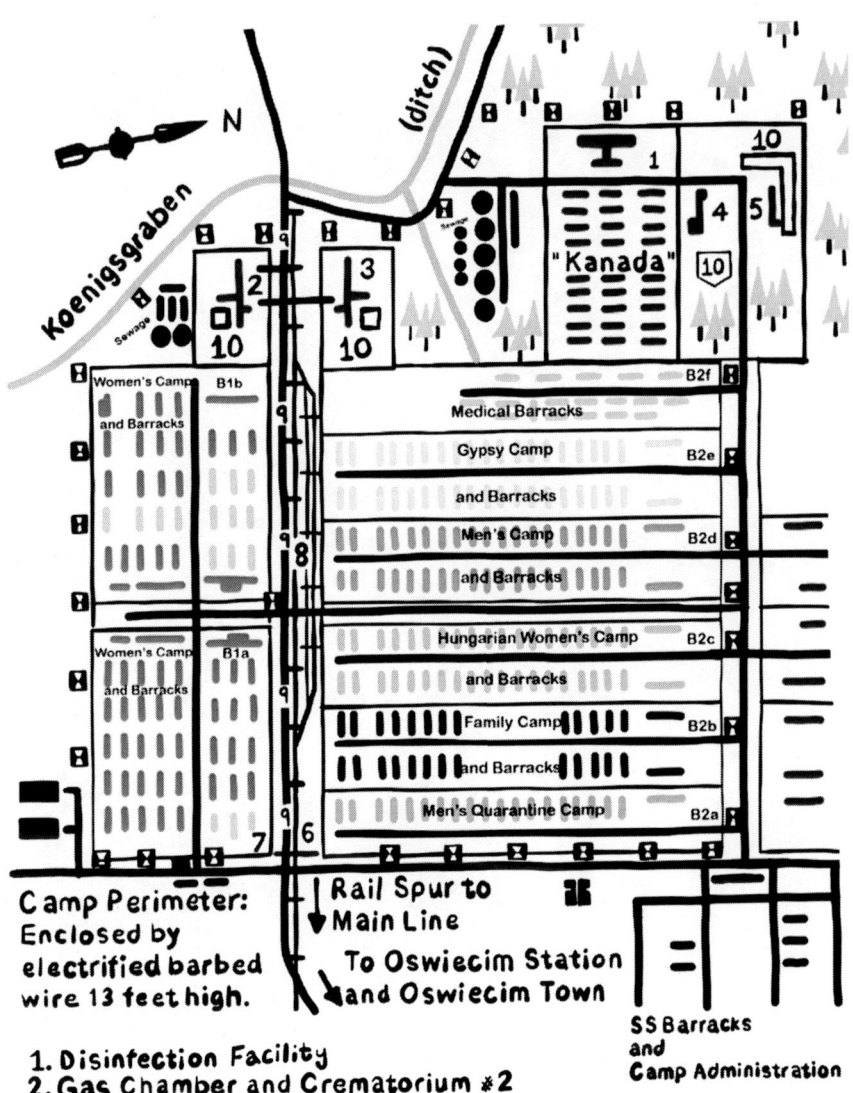

MAP OF BIRKENAU

1. Disinfection Facility
2. Gas Chamber and Crematorium #2
3. Gas Chamber and Crematorium #3
4. Gas Chamber and Crematorium #4
5. Gas Chamber and Crematorium #5
6. Main Guard House
7. Medical Experiments Barrack
8. New Railroad Platform
9. Lagerstrasse
10. Ash pits

GLOSSARY

Birkenau Camp – the whole Birkenau facility as shown on the map. Birkenau was divided into sections, each fenced off with barbed wire, such as the men's camp, the women's camp, etc.

Lagerstrasse – the long, wide stretch of land running vertically between sections B1 and B2 on the map (reference 9). This area was open ground until the "Rampe" platform was built and the railway line was extended into the camp during the first half of 1944.

Barracks/Block– a single-story, brick or wooden building to house prisoners or perform a camp function (washroom, latrine, etc.).

The Prisoners

Kommando – a work group of prisoners laboring in a particular area, such as on farms or in factories.

Sonderkommando – a work group selected for special activities, such as working in the crematoria, gas chambers, or on the railway ramps when transports of prisoners arrived.

SK – camp nickname for a Sonderkommando.

Sonder – camp nickname for a prisoner working in an SK.

Kapo – a prisoner appointed to lead a work group. Kapos were identifiable by their white armbands, which included their rank.

Blue stripe – based on the blue-striped uniform he wore, the nickname for a member of a work group, reporting to a kapo.

Oberkapo – a kapo with responsibility for several kapos.

Block elder – a kapo, the most senior prisoner in the barracks, often a career criminal.

Block manager – a kapo responsible for the smooth running of each barracks, especially for roll calls and discipline.

The SS Captors

Commandant – SS-Obersturmbannführer – Head of Auschwitz and all its sub-camps.

Reporting to the Commandant –

> Roll call leader – SS-Rapportführer – responsible for roll calls (usually twice a day).
>
> Barracks leader – SS-Blockführer – responsible for an individual barracks in a section.
>
> Work group leader – SS-Kommandoführer – responsible for the various prisoner work groups in operation within the camp or its sub-camps.
>
> Senior Guard – SS-Sturmbannführer – responsible for eight to ten guards.

Camp guard – SS-Schütze – the lowest rank in Birkenau. Guards represented approximately 75% of all SS staff.

BOOK ONE

WINTER 1943/44

ARRIVAL

CHAPTER ONE

November 1943

The rusty cattle car door screeched shut, and they were plunged into darkness. The dullness of the day cast weak tendrils of light through the two small, glassless, barred windows.

Rachael took up position a meter from a window, not to benefit from the light but because she had been told it would provide a much-needed, albeit occasional, source of fresh air during the journey. She remained on her knees so she could hug her brother tightly, kissing his face and tousling his hair. His warm tears trickled onto her cheeks. A wave of joy and relief raced through her body.

A hand reached out, silhouetted against the window light, as if waving.

"What was that?" an anonymous voice asked.

"I found an old margarine wrapper in my pocket," came the reply. "It would've stunk if I'd kept it there, so I threw it out the window."

"You fool," somebody exclaimed. "The camp supervisors specifically said it's forbidden to throw *anything* out of the truck. They say, in the past, some people tried to leave messages on scraps of paper."

"There's nothing written on it," the voice replied. "It's just a piece of paper."

In the dark, she could hardly see, but Rachael sensed the nervousness gripping her Dutch compatriots. SS instructions were to be obeyed, no matter what. Since the Nazi invasion of the Netherlands in May

1940, they had learned that disobedience of SS orders led to severe repercussions.

She heard noises on the railway platform outside: the camp supervisors shouting at the other Dutch Jews who were still boarding and the incessant rapping of their batons on the steel sides of the trucks; the barking of the SS dogs.

The quiet within the truck was broken by a clunk as the metal locking arm of the door was released, and the sliding door screeched open. Rachael saw the shadow of a supervisor scurrying away, replaced by the shape of a SS soldier, pistol held in one hand, a piece of paper in the other.

"Who threw this out?" the soldier shouted. There was a nervous shuffling within the cattle car, but no response.

"Who threw this out?" the soldier repeated more loudly. Still no response. "If the person who threw this out doesn't make himself known at once, I'll shoot every one of you!" As if to emphasize his point, he waved the muzzle of his pistol at the prisoners.

Somebody brushed past Rachael.

Although the cattle car was crammed, those around him shuffled to one side to make space. The man who had discarded the margarine wrapper stepped forward.

"It's only a margarine wrapper," he protested. "There's nothing written on it."

"It's forbidden! Nothing's to be thrown out!" the soldier shouted. "Are you stupid?"

The man made as if to speak, but before a word passed his lips, the soldier pointed his pistol and let off a shot. There were screams in the dark, and the prisoners gasped. The man peered down at his stomach, an expression of faint surprise on his face as he watched his blood spreading across his shirt like ink on blotting paper.

The man collapsed to his knees, head bowed and holding his wound with a hand. He held his free arm up, fingers stretched out as if reaching for something outside, past the railway platform, past the transit camp fences and into the wide-open spaces beyond.

The soldier bent over the edge of the cattle car, and Rachael could make out his features. She shivered at his cold, emotionless expression. The nearest Jews stepped back in fear, making those already squeezed at the back gasp for air under the crushing weight of their compatriots. Only a few of them saw the soldier raise his arm again, but they all heard the roaring gunshot rattling the rotten wooden timbers of the cattle car. There was a meek thud as the body of the man slumped to the floor.

The soldier moved his face to within millimeters of the dead man and looked down disdainfully. Rachael thought he was about to pull the body off the car, but he pushed it inward to move it away from the metal grooves the sliding door sat in.

The SS man turned to walk away but before doing so threw the scrap of margarine wrapper on top of the body. "You! Close and lock that door. Now!" were his parting words. Two camp supervisors rushed forward and slid the door shut, casting the truck into near darkness.

Silence reigned until Rachael heard the gentle shuffling of feet, and squinting in the gloom, she saw shadows moving around. The occupants of the cattle car were spreading out, taking up their original positions across the truck floor.

*

Once the train was moving, whispered conversations started up inside the truck. Relatives who had been separated while boarding were reunited. Passengers discussed the trivia of the everyday: the harsh winter chill; the aches and pains of the elderly; the scarcity of food; the health of relatives.

"Do we have toilet tissue?" a man asked loud enough for the other occupants to hear.

"I've got one roll," came the reply. "I don't know how long it'll last."

"There's an empty barrel here, underneath the window," a woman said. "I assume that's our toilet."

Soon after, a scream pierced the air as a young boy discovered his foot was surrounded by the pooling blood of the dead man. This event seemed to bring the occupants back to the grim reality of their situation.

"Are we going to Auschwitz?" It was a child's voice.

"Nobody knows," came the reply.

"We know," another man's voice struck up defiantly.

"Shh!" a woman said. "Don't upset the children with your...with your nonsense."

"Wherever we're going, the Nazis are sending us to a labor camp where we'll be manufacturing products for German industry. It'll be hard but meaningful work, and as long as the Nazis need us, we'll stay alive." There was a reassuring tone to this deep, measured voice, which calmed the mood of the Jews.

All the while, Hannes clung to his sister, his face buried in the warm folds of her coat. She wrapped her arms tightly around him, doing her best to cover his ears and muffle the voices within the cattle car.

During the following hours, the occupants of the cattle car had to squeeze around each other to make their way to the water barrel, which was placed in the opposite corner to the toilet barrel. They sipped out of cupped hands before returning to their places. There was less traffic around the toilet barrel, although the smell of urine in the enclosed space quickly grew stronger. Rachael advised her brother to hold his nose and breathe through his mouth. The ten-year-old was temporarily diverted by this newly discovered technique for eliminating odors.

When her brother complained of aching feet, she suggested he sat on his suitcase. This prompted others to do the same, and their burdened legs were given some respite.

Occasionally, the train came to a halt, sometimes at a station, when one man near the window would peer out and call out the location—"Hoogezand," "Winschoten," "Nieuweschans."

"Nieuweschans. We're on the Dutch border," somebody remarked. "Nearly in Germany."

It struck Rachael that she had never left the Netherlands before.

Sometimes, the train stopped for no apparent reason, seemingly in the middle of nowhere with no station in sight. Once, they did not move for hours, until a single train passed them from the opposite direction. As soon as it had gone by, the cattle car lurched onward.

Whenever or however the cattle cars stopped, the doors never opened. Not once.

"Bremen." "Berlin." "Breslau."

"We're almost in Poland."

It was dark in the truck, so they could not read their watches. They crudely measured the passage of time by the frequency with which day slipped into night. They had seen nightfall three times since their departure from Westerbork, with no food, except for items they had brought with them. Those who had brought no food begged the others to share. Some were successful, some were not. The sliding door remained shut.

The exit from the Netherlands had been an event that prompted discussion among the occupants, who reminisced about the people and places that were left behind or debated their ultimate destination. However, their imminent arrival on Polish soil was met with stony silence.

In the intervening period, the prisoners had been subjected to increased deprivation and degradation. The drinking water had significantly diminished before the end of the first day and had been rationed for use by the ill, older adults, and children only. By the middle of the second day, the barrel was empty. No food had been provided. The small portions of bread and cheese that had been smuggled onto the train in camp were soon consumed.

No matter how much the occupants had tried to resist, after twenty-four hours in transit, almost everybody had emptied their bowels at least once. The stench became almost unbearable. Rachael would crane her neck toward the window to catch a mouthful of clean, cold air, but she felt guilty that Hannes could not enjoy it as well. He was not tall enough, and she was too tired to lift him up.

During the hours of daylight, the proximity of the occupants to one another gave them a modicum of physical warmth and created a kind of camaraderie. But the October nights of Germany and Poland were colder than most of them had ever experienced, and they seemed to shrink into themselves, as if hibernating, away from their neighbors.

On the third morning, there were shrieks and moans of lamentation as they discovered those who had not survived the night. These continued during the day.

From time to time, Rachael would kneel, soaking her torn stockings on the wet floor but able to address her young brother face-to-face.

"Be strong, Hannes," she would repeat. "Wherever we're going, being strong is the best way to survive. Think of Mama and Papa, and when we might see them again. Then this horrible, smelly train will feel like nothing." He hugged her tightly.

He was only ten years old, she thought. How could he conceivably grasp their situation? She missed her parents, but Hannes was a child and would be severely affected by their absence. After the sheer elation of being reunited, Hannes had soon lapsed into a silent melancholy.

She had barely slept, drank, or eaten for over three days and was so fatigued the world seemed distorted and confusing in her mind. Her senses were numbed; she could hardly feel her body, and even the stench of feces seemed to have receded. She wondered if she was dreaming, until a sudden lurch of the train would jolt her back to reality, and her aching limbs screamed and her nostrils were filled with that indescribable smell.

CHAPTER TWO

November 1943

The train ground to a halt early on the fourth morning. Rachael knew this stop was different. Outside, dogs were barking and snarling incessantly. Men were shouting and running along the platform right outside the door.

A weak light seeped through the cattle car window, not enough to dispel the darkness within.

"At last, we're here!" somebody gasped.

"Yes! Fresh air, and a chance to stretch my legs!" another sighed.

"Maybe some food before we start work tomorrow?" somebody else added with cautious optimism.

Rachael heard the bustling activity outside, which confirmed the other cattle cars were being opened. The barking and the shouting grew louder and louder, until there was a solid thud on the outside of their own car, accompanied by the ear-splitting, high-pitched screeching of the door bolts being released.

By her side, Hannes moved closer to her, squeezing himself tightly against her.

A cloudy, gray morning greeted them as the truck door slid slowly open, but after three days of darkness, they were blinded by the daylight. They shielded their eyes for protection. Rachael looked down and saw brown, dirty puddles all over the carriage floor. Seeing them clearly for the first time made her nauseous, so she raised her head to look away.

"Out! Out!" somebody shouted. "Everybody must get out as quickly as possible. Form into lines. Two lines for men, three lines of women and children!"

Rachael climbed down from the cattle car, trying not to touch the filthy floor as she did. She made to help Hannes down, but he shook her off, so she turned her attention to an elderly, frail lady sitting next to her brother. Rachael gently took her forearm and lifted her off the truck and onto the platform, noticing her black fur coat, which had once been elegant and smart, was smeared in brown filth.

Rachael was relieved to feel solid ground beneath her feet, rather than the rocking and lurching of the train, but it was mayhem on the platform. People were climbing off the cattle cars and then strolling around aimlessly with their belongings in hand.

"Everybody leave their belongings behind!" the voice shouted.

Rachael took in her surroundings, but there was little to see. A concrete platform ran along the length of the train. A line of men in shabby blue-and-white-striped uniforms was standing on the edge of the platform, holding wooden sticks in their hands. The contrast between these shabby men and the small number of SS soldiers, who strode along the platform in their shiny black boots, pristine gray uniforms, and with rifles held by their sides, could not have been starker. A few blue stripes wore white armbands with the word *kapo* stitched onto them. These men looked healthier and wore coats over their uniforms. They, like the SS men, were walking along the platform with a certain swagger.

The men dressed in blue stripes advanced with their sticks raised, demanding the prisoners drop their belongings. Those who did not react immediately had their knuckles rapped. The initial chaos barely eased as the Jews made their way from the train, having to negotiate the discarded cases and bags and desperately trying to avoid the blows raining down from the blue stripes.

Rachael clenched her brother's hand, petrified that if she let go, they might lose each other. A few elderly people fell to the ground among the bustling melee, but despite the threats of the stick-wielding guards and the pushing created by the forming lines, there was always at least one prisoner who took a risk and helped them back to their feet.

Rachael found herself on the outer edge of the women's line and came face-to-face with a snarling, blue-striped guard, who raised his wooden stick to hit her. She cowered, raising her hand above her head and, placing herself between the man and Hannes, moved on before he could strike.

Several meters farther on, the next blue stripe possessed a less threatening demeanor, neither shouting nor waving his stick aggressively, merely pointing toward the midpoint of the train where the fronts of the lines were forming. "Men and women in separate lines," he said. "Two lines of men, three lines of women and children. Orderly lines of men and women!"

"What do we do?" Rachael pleaded in her best German accent, leaning forward and pointing at herself and her brother. "We must stay together!"

"You're Dutch?" the man replied.

"Yes!" Rachael responded.

"You're Dutch, and your spoken German's almost perfect," the man said and, leaning forward as much as he could amid the noise, whispered to her, "Tell nobody, but don't go on the trucks under any circumstances. When the SS officer asks you, tell him you're fluent in Dutch and German. Tell him about every meaningful skill you've got. And how strong and healthy you are. The same applies to the boy. And you're going to have to convince the SS he's sixteen."

The man stood up straight and shouted, "Move on! Move on! Three lines for the women and children, two lines for the men!"

Rachael guessed there must have been twenty cattle cars in their train from Camp Westerbork. Several blue stripes waded into the lines to retrieve discarded cases and bags and carry them to the edge of the platform. A separate group of blue stripes took these belongings and threw them into four large piles along the length of the train.

"What about our fragile belongings?" a voice muttered. "I've brought a mirror, some bottles of medicine. Everything'll be destroyed."

A young girl, her blond hair cascading from beneath a light-blue beret, and standing in the row ahead of Rachael, turned to her mother. "Mama, the man in the uniform said we'd be given our bags back later. But most of them are brown like ours. How will they find them in that great big pile?"

Rachael could not see the mother's face, but she detected the uncertainty in her voice when she replied to her daughter. "I'm sure they'll find a way, sweetheart. I'm sure they will."

To Rachael's right, a middle-aged man with a long, graying beard and black hat was persisting in carrying his black leather suitcase. He walked past two of the blue-stripe guards without them reacting. A nearby SS soldier pushed one of the blue-stripe kapos in the back with his rifle butt and pointed at the bearded man. The kapo moved forward, raised his stick, and brought it down on the man's shoulder with such ferocity that it made a swishing noise like a whip.

The man screamed.

"All belongings must be left behind!" the blue-stripe kapo shouted, glancing over his shoulder at the SS soldier before continuing. "You'll be reunited with your property after you've had a disinfecting shower."

The bearded man was not progressing, so the line of male prisoners started backing up behind him.

"You heard, Jew!" the SS soldier shouted. "Drop your case and get moving!"

The bearded man remained perfectly still, looking straight ahead, gripping his case. The kapo raised his arm and struck again, so ferociously Rachael felt the ripple of air on her face as the stick swept past. For the briefest moment, the Jew flinched before regaining his composure, biting his lip to conceal his pain.

The kapo raised his stick to strike again, but the SS soldier recognized the obduracy of the Jew and shouted, "Never, under any circumstances, allow anybody or anything to disrupt the ramp selection process. Obstacles must be removed."

The kapo grabbed the bearded man by the lapels of his long, black coat. Although the man was only of medium build, the kapo had difficulty pulling the uncooperative prisoner out of the tightly packed lines. The kapo possessed a wiry build, and weeks of deprivation had made him even thinner. After several attempts, he successfully dragged the Jew out of the line.

"Now move!" he screamed at the others. Those who had fallen behind quickly shuffled forward to catch up. As Rachael and Hannes passed by, they observed the bearded man standing alone on the concrete ramp, like a statue carrying a suitcase.

"Put the case down!" the kapo demanded. There was no response. The guard positioned himself directly in front of the Jew. "Put the case down!" The kapo's face reddened. The man looked straight through him, unblinking. Another thrash of the stick had no effect.

"For God's sake, leave the case!" one prisoner pleaded.

"It's for God's sake I'm doing this," the bearded man replied.

"What the hell do you mean?" the kapo asked, pushing the end of his stick under the man's chin, forcing him to raise his head.

The man turned his head and looked at the kapo. "I'm a rabbi. The objects in this case permit me to communicate with God. And God can communicate with me. We simply can't be separated," the rabbi replied calmly.

The kapo was taken aback. "You must leave your case. You'll be reunited soon."

The rabbi shook his head.

Without the kapo noticing, the SS soldier drew near. "What the hell's going on here?" he demanded.

"This Jew says he's a rabbi, sir," the kapo replied, removing his blue-and-white-striped cloth cap. "He's refusing to leave his case because of some religious stuff in it." He bowed his head and took a step backward, taking a swipe at the rabbi's arm as he did so.

Without warning, the SS soldier drew back his leg and planted his shiny black boot in the back of the rabbi's knee. The effort required made him grunt. The rabbi cried out in pain and crumpled to the floor, sliding the case underneath his body.

"I'm not as patient as your Jew friend here," the soldier scoffed. "I'm going to ask you one more time. Believe me, I'll only ask once. Leave the case and get back in line."

The bearded man, on his knees and head bowed, placed his arms on the floor to create a protective shield around his case.

"To make this labor camp run efficiently, everybody must follow orders without question," the SS soldier shouted, addressing the Jews who were passing by. "The repercussions for not following orders are severe.

"You!" The soldier pointed at a nearby blue stripe. "Remove this man from the platform!"

The blue stripe grabbed the prostrate rabbi by his coat collar and tried to drag him away but was too weak. The soldier looked around angrily until the kapo himself stepped forward, and with some effort, these two gradually pulled the rabbi clear and toward the edge of the ramp. The rabbi neither complied nor resisted, remaining quite immobile with his hands tightly gripping his case.

A single-story wooden shed, recently whitewashed, ran alongside the platform for a distance of thirty meters. The SS soldier spoke to the two blue stripes in a hushed tone, after which they maneuvered the rabbi around the corner of the building. Turning her head, Rachael lost sight of them. The SS soldier turned on his heels and followed. Moments later, a gunshot rang out, succeeded seconds later by a second.

The two blue stripes scurried out and took up their places on the platform. When the SS man returned, Rachael watched him replacing his pistol in its holster before stopping, placing a hand in his trouser pocket to retrieve a pristine white handkerchief and stooping to wipe his boots. He folded the handkerchief before tucking it back into his pocket. It was stained red.

"Let this be a lesson to you all," the soldier said. "Always follow orders in Birkenau. Work hard and behave yourselves. It's simple."

Moments later, an SS officer appeared. The silver-plated death's head badge on his dark-gray cap seemed out of keeping with the smartly presented, pleasant face that looked out from beneath its black brim. He placed his hands on his hips and with chin raised spoke to the prisoners. "Welcome to Birkenau. Please form into lines as requested."

There was a certain trustworthiness in his voice, and the lines of Jews were soon formed: five lines stretching from the rear of the train to the center and five from the front to the center.

The pleasant-looking SS officer stepped forward. "Listen hard!" he said. "This railway platform is almost two kilometers from the labor camp. It's been a tiring train journey for you, I know. We'll provide transport for those people who don't feel able to walk that distance. Perhaps those of you who are a little older, or mothers and their young children, or those with a walking impediment, would rather take a free truck journey to the camp instead."

As the officer finished speaking, a soldier who had taken up position between two cattle cars halfway along the train raised his arm and shouted, "Carriages disengaged!" The steam engine hissed, and the train edged forward. A gap appeared where the two cattle cars separated, revealing six open-topped trucks lined up on the other side of the train, their engines growling, and each accompanied by three more blue stripes.

"*Don't* delay!" the officer ordered. There was little movement among the prisoners. "For those Jews who decline the offer of a free ride and then can't keep up when walking to the camp...well, you've already been shown the consequences."

After these words, some people made their way through the gap and toward the trucks. The blue stripes placed wooden steps at the rear of the vehicles so weaker prisoners could climb aboard more easily. This encouraged more prisoners to step forward.

Many Jews took time to hug their loved ones.

"There's no need for long goodbyes. You'll soon see each other again," the officer said, watching them. "Hurry!"

"Those of you who think they're physically able to walk to the camp, please stay in line."

Within twenty minutes, the six trucks had departed, and those left behind had been told by the SS guards to await their return. The guards knew full well the trucks were nowhere near fulfilling their tasks for the day.

Each one was tightly packed and, with only a couple of benches to sit on, most of the occupants were forced to stand. Tightly packed again, Rachael thought. The Dutch had just spent three days being tightly packed. At least it was in the fresh air, and the waving children appeared to be enjoying the novelty of a free ride in an open truck.

"Can we go in a truck?" Hannes asked eagerly.

"Not today," Rachael answered, the words of the blue stripe ringing in her head.

While the Jews stood waiting, an SS soldier walked along the women's lines. He stopped next to a woman standing near to Rachael, the one who had been reassuring her daughter earlier.

"How old are you?" the soldier asked.

"Fifty-five," she replied.

"You can travel by truck," he said. "You'll slow the rest down if you walk."

"But my granddaughter!" the woman pleaded.

"She can go with you," the soldier said. "We don't wish to separate women from their children and grandchildren."

The woman left the line and led her granddaughter through the space between the cattle cars.

CHAPTER THREE

November 1943

SS-Hauptsturmführer Josef Mengele locked his office door and passed through the nearby southern gate of the Roma camp, saluting the guard on duty. He made his way eastward along the wide Lagerstrasse toward the main Birkenau entrance, a wide, single-story brick building with an arched gateway, above which an office was located with windows on all four sides offering an elevated view across the entire camp.

Mengele could never fathom the freezing temperature of this place. Looking at a map, anybody could be forgiven for thinking Auschwitz had a climate similar to many German cities and towns. However, even in October, the cold permeated his uniform and his woolen undergarments and made his bones quiver. The wind whipped across this expanse of flat land and was so biting he could barely keep his eyes open. It did not help that no matter what he did, his office in the shabby wooden barracks could not be warmed.

The doctor walked only a few hundred meters and already wished he was back in his office, partially protected from the cold. He had taken part in many selections and had always performed his duty whenever his name appeared on the roster. But he no longer enjoyed the selection process, pointing one way for the truck transport and the other way for the march into camp. Thousands of people standing in front of him, his finger or stick granting life or death sentences. Left, right, left, right, left, right. It was a mundane and monotonous task, but of course, he fulfilled it as an order given by the SS leadership. Particularly when there were large numbers of trains arriving, Mengele believed his selection duties became a hindrance to his vitally important anthropological experiments.

Mengele preferred it when his presence at the selection was voluntary. He could arrive and depart as he pleased and could make a more considered evaluation of the recent arrivals. He would walk up and down the lines of Jews and Roma people, stopping each time he saw a potential subject for his experimentation. Occasionally, he would tap somebody on the shoulder and beckon them to step out of the line so he could examine them from all angles. He might prod them with his stick or ask them about their backgrounds. When he had become a medical doctor with an avid interest in anthropology, he had never dreamed he would lead radical experimentation aimed at proving differences between certain races and classes of human beings.

On arrival in Birkenau, Mengele had been appointed Lagerführer, the leader of section B2e, the Roma camp, where he held responsibility for six SS officers and a group of SS guards. This camp was the only section in Birkenau where men, women, and children were allowed to live together. Otherwise, males and females were strictly segregated.

There were thirty accommodation barracks in the section, which housed enough Roma people to provide the doctor with most of his patients. When he was not present for selections, he would remind the SS officer on duty to make sure dwarfs and twins were sent to barracks 32 of B2e. Pregnant women and mothers with babies were also useful for his research.

As he passed through the arch, Mengele saluted the two SS guards on duty. Although he was beyond the barbed wire fences and watchtowers that marked the boundary of the camp, his thoughts were very much on his experiments. This train was the only one planned for that day, so it would not be much of a distraction for him. But the Auschwitz commandant, SS-Obersturmbannführer Höss, had recently informed the officers of the plans for the Hungarian Jews. Even those with experience of the largest camps in the Reich's network fell silent when Höss revealed the estimated number of arrivals. Four to five hundred thousand. Transportations of this magnitude would push every operation within Birkenau to its absolute limits, and that would mean Mengele himself would have to spend significantly more of his valuable time on platform selections, gas chamber duties and hospital supervision. Away from his experiments.

Mengele continued straight on, and as he approached a sharp, ninety-degree bend in the road, the railway platform came into view. Two trucks crammed with Jews had already driven past him in the opposite direction, so he knew the selection was well underway. As he reached the front of the train, he noticed how orderly the process was. There was no aggressive barking of the dogs, nor shouting, nor waving of rifles and battlements. Apart from two gunshots that were fired, he had heard nothing. He mused how well-behaved the Dutch Jews were, and that had been the case for every single transport. They made an interesting comparison with the Poles or Soviets, who were unruly and angry and appeared to be more willing to sacrifice themselves on the railway platform. It was a pity this was one of the last transports from the Netherlands. He had heard there were almost no Dutch Jews left.

The doctor walked to the side of the train and made his way between the men's and women's lines.

"Make way, please!" he said politely to acknowledge the civility of the new arrivals. He casually waved his stick from side to side to widen the gap between the two sets of lines and walked slowly so he could look to his left and right and glimpse every prisoner.

Mengele was disappointed when he failed to spot any twins or dwarfs on his way to the midpoint of the train, where he cordially greeted the other SS men on selection duty. Taking a position several meters in front of the three lines of women, the doctor held his baton behind his back, set his feet into a wide stance, and stuck out his chin to watch the selection.

The lines of men were shortening appreciably faster than the women's. The SS officer who was selecting from the women's lines had himself only recently arrived in the camp, and he was certainly taking longer than his colleagues. Mengele also noticed this officer was selecting an unusually high number of Jews to enter the camp for hard labor. The SS target for this part of the selection process was for an average of three-quarters of the prisoners to be sent by truck for special treatment, with only a quarter being selected for labor.

The new SS officer was awkwardly conscious of his shortcomings and became visibly flustered. Mengele thought him too young to be chosen for this role and wondered why more experienced men had not stepped in.

The doctor approached the SS officer and tapped him gently on the shoulder. The officer was startled and, swinging around, grabbed his pistol. Mengele placated him with a polite smile.

"I can see you're new to the selection process," the doctor said. "I've been involved in many, and I'll gladly demonstrate how you might complete the task more efficiently."

"By all means, sir," the officer replied, stepping back and gesturing for Mengele to take his place.

Two SS soldiers were standing between Mengele and the end of the women's lines. Their role was to bring the prisoners to the doctor one by one, and, once selected, to move them away in the correct direction.

Mengele addressed these two men. "You must move these Jews more quickly," he said. "Give them a push. Use your stick. You'll soon find things run more smoothly." As he spoke, he took his baton from behind his back and held it in his hand with about thirty centimeters of it showing between his fingers. He continued, "As soon as the point of my baton touches the Jew, you move them away, and the next one should be ready to step forward. I suggest one of you brings them to the line, the other takes them away. Let's see how we get on, shall we?"

One soldier took a woman from the line. She moved slowly, cautiously, so the soldier pushed her forcefully with his hand. "Hurry up, you filthy old Jewess!"

The woman, who was about fifty years old and on her own, had barely come to a halt in front of the doctor before the end of his baton tapped the left shoulder of her green winter coat. "Right," Mengele said.

The other soldier shoved her toward the gap between the railway cars, where a blue stripe escorted her to the crowd waiting for the trucks. In the few seconds it took for the soldier to return, another woman was ready to be taken to the trucks.

Rachael was approaching the front of her line and watching the doctor perform his duties. Standing there with his baton darting around, he looked like the conductor of a symphony orchestra. His expression was serious, but his eyes were wide and energetic, and Rachael was sure of one thing. The conductor was enjoying himself.

Mengele's voice continued like rapid fire. "Right, right, left, right, left, right, right, right…"

"Don't take the boy!" a voice whispered in Rachael's ear. "You've got a chance of going left, but not with the boy."

"He's my brother!" Rachael protested. "I must look after him."

"I know it's difficult," the blue stripe continued, "but I'm telling you, one left and one right is much better than two right."

"Rachael," Hannes interjected, "if we go left, will we get a free ride on one of those trucks?"

The front of the line was almost upon them, and Rachael was bewildered and distraught, but she saw the urgency in the blue stripe's face.

Then Rachael and her brother were standing in front of the SS doctor, his baton poised in the air.

"I've studied and spoken German for over ten years," Rachael blurted out, struggling to keep her composure. "Surely, the camp would benefit from somebody who's a native Dutch speaker and also speaks German fluently. My brother's ever so strong and runs as fast as a cheetah. And with his small fingers, he can carry out intricate tasks with tremendous dexterity."

Mengele's baton paused in midair. Another SS soldier, who had been watching the process from a short distance away, stepped forward. "Excuse me, sir. I understand an administrator in Kanada has been sent for special treatment, so they're looking for a German speaker. We find so few good German speakers among the Poles and Soviets, but the Dutch are excellent. And reliable."

The doctor barely registered the soldier's comments. But on closer inspection, with her deep-red hair, blue eyes, and pale skin, he considered her a potential specimen for anthropological research and experimentation. If the boy came along, so be it. He would find a use for the boy, he was sure.

The baton touched the lapel of Rachael's coat as the doctor spoke. "Left." Holding her brother's hand as tightly as she could, she walked over to join the people gathering at the side of the platform.

It took barely an hour for the Dutch Jews to disembark, form lines, and be selected. As Mengele made his way back to his camp office, a group of blue stripes was moving piles of belongings from the railway platform to create larger piles ready for collection by the trucks. Three kapos were racing back and forth, striking the blue stripes at random to keep them scurrying in fear. Two SS guards were standing to one side, talking and smoking cigarettes. From time to time, they would shout at the kapos, pointing their rifles menacingly.

Having the same route to camp, those prisoners selected for hard labor were walking ahead of Mengele. The doctor estimated there were two or three hundred of them. He was pleased that, thanks to his intervention, the selection targets would have been met. Three SS guards walked to the rear of the prisoners, rounding up stragglers like zealous sheepdogs.

The trucks carrying the other prisoners continued shuttling into the camp full and returning empty. Rachael watched them passing through the arched gateway and driving in a straight line along Lagerstrasse until the gray clouds on the horizon seemed to reach down and they disappeared.

As Rachael's group passed through the entrance, they had to make way for another truck entering the camp. This one held no Jews but was piled high with their belongings that had been left on the platform. It was followed by more, all heading in the same direction.

"Look!" someone shouted. "They're taking our cases for us to collect later!"

Some people cheered, but Rachael remained silent, sniffing the air. There was a smell, a little like railway engine smoke, but denser and more pungent, and, as the group of prisoners ventured farther into the camp, the stench grew.

*

Rachael had heard of Auschwitz and Birkenau, but she, like the rest of the Dutch Jews, knew little about them. In her mind, she had assumed Birkenau would be like Camp Westerbork in the Netherlands. But even from a distance, the camp looked massive in comparison. To the left of the arched entrance and beyond Lagerstrasse, there were rows upon rows of barracks. But to the right, the barracks seemed to stretch forever until they were swallowed up by the morning mist.

How many barracks had there been in the Dutch camp? she asked herself. Certainly, less than fifty. Birkenau had to be hundreds. That SS officer had mentioned Poles and Soviets were already there.

And German Jews. And with this last transport, all the Dutch Jews were in Birkenau. But how did they find enough work for them? Whether hard labor or otherwise. How did they feed them? She knew how Westerbork operated but could not conceive how Birkenau could function on such an enormous scale.

Suddenly, her legs felt heavy.

"What's wrong, Rachael?" Hannes asked. He was watching her and noticed her head dropping.

"It's nothing, Hannes," his sister replied. "I'm just a little tired after that awful journey." She forced a smile and picked up her shoulders.

"Don't worry," her brother added. "We'll get a good night's sleep tonight."

The area immediately inside Birkenau was wide and stretched into the distance. To both left and right, scores of barracks were confined within endless runs of barbed wire fences, twice the height of a prisoner and supported by concrete posts. The wire was wrapped around white enamel insulators to carry an electric current. There had been no electrified fencing in Westerbork.

From behind the wire, a few prisoners watched the new arrivals. There was a blankness in their expressions, a listlessness that Rachael found disquieting.

The gate was locked behind them. Rachael sensed that a good night's sleep did not lie ahead.

CHAPTER FOUR

November 1943

"I'm tired," Hannes complained. "When will we go to our accommodation and have something to eat? I'm starving. And I really need the toilet."

The Jews had been standing by the camp entrance for half an hour while the SS officers who had escorted them from the platform completed and exchanged paperwork with the SS officers inside the camp. Then they started walking along Lagerstrasse.

Having yearned for fresh air and free movement after three days in the cattle car, Rachael felt heavy legged and understood the strain on her brother's young legs.

The trucks continued trundling in and out of the camp.

"The others are ahead of us," Hannes said. "If we aren't quick, they're going to be first in the food line! And I'll wet myself."

One of the four SS soldiers leading the new prisoners raised his arm and shouted, "Pay attention! You'll be passing through this gate on the right. You're going for a shower to get you clean after a long journey, so you'll be ready for work in the morning." He turned, walked up to the gate, unlocked it, and swung it open. "It's not too far. Don't lag! Anyone who lags will be severely dealt with."

The icy wind lashed the prisoners' dirty faces, and they wrapped their coats and jackets tightly around their shoulders. This road was much narrower than Lagerstrasse, too narrow to allow a truck to travel along it. The two roads formed a crossroads in the camp.

Behind the barbed wire on each side, Birkenau was split into individual, smaller sub-camps, also surrounded by electrified fences. Rachael was so close to the fence she heard the incessant humming of the electricity surging through the wire. The barracks seemed to be almost within touching distance, as were the prisoners standing outside. A few clotheslines were strung between two barracks, on which blue-stripe uniforms and gray aprons were hanging, together with some tattered civilian clothes.

"Where are you from?" somebody called from among the marching prisoners.

In an instant, one of the kapos pounced upon the speaker, an elderly man of slight build and a gray wispy beard.

"Never speak unless spoken to!" the kapo screamed, dragging the man out of the line and forcing him to his hands and knees before striking him viciously with his stick. He grabbed the prisoner by the collar and thrust him toward the barbed wire fence. "This is what happens when you don't follow orders!" The kapo lifted the man so that only his toes were touching the ground. He took a step forward before pulling the man to him, so close their faces almost touched. With all his might, the kapo pushed his arms out and then let go. The man crashed against the fence.

The old Jew jolted as the electric current shot through him, his limbs jerking like a mad puppet. He screamed with a mixture of surprise and pain. Desperately struggling to free himself from the barbs, he only snagged other parts of his clothing, and the louder and more agonized his screaming became. Until he fell silent.

The SS guard leading the line shouted out, "Any of you lot contemplating escaping over the fence has seen a simple demonstration of what will happen to you."

The prisoners shuffled on, leaving the lifeless body of the man hanging from the barbed wire like a macabre scarecrow.

Rachael endeavored to stay alert to her new surroundings. She was counting the barracks as they passed by on the right, but she was as tired as she had ever felt, and her mind lost track. In the end, she guessed there were some eighty to a hundred individual barracks, separated by the wire into three sections.

To her left, the layout and number of barracks looked similar, and when they had entered the camp, there were barracks on both sides of Lagerstrasse. Could there be four sections in Birkenau, almost four hundred barracks in total? she thought.

Rachael counted her steps and concluded each wooden barracks was about thirty to forty meters long. She remembered well the blocks in Westerbork with their three-tiered steel bunks and two prisoners sleeping on each level. Two hundred occupants per barracks made sense. She calculated the Birkenau capacity in her head and came to eighty thousand. That's way too many, she told herself. Her mental arithmetic must be failing her. She took her hands out of her coat pockets, and the cold air numbed her flesh. She looked down and, like a child, used her fingers to check her calculations. Her estimate was still eighty thousand, and whether the estimate was right or wrong, it was near enough and led her to a simple conclusion. This was a massive labor camp. Camp Westerbork held only ten thousand prisoners. The arrival of a thousand Jews from Amsterdam would be barely noticeable.

The Dutch Jews had suffered dreadfully after the invasion of the Netherlands by the German army in May 1940. To Rachael, it was beyond doubt that conditions in Birkenau would be worse than those in Westerbork. The only uncertainty was how much worse. She knew a battle lay ahead of her and her brother, and to survive, she would not only need her German-speaking skills but also the knowledge of camp administration she had learned in Westerbork and the resourcefulness of working with the Dutch resistance.

*

A feeling of unease swept through Rachael as they passed through the next gate and turned left. They were walking parallel to Lagerstrasse. The watchtowers that loomed over them marked the perimeter fence of Birkenau, and the barrel of a machine gun was poking out of each one.

"We're going in the same direction as the trucks!" an unknown woman said excitedly. "This is a shortcut for the walkers. This path's too narrow for the trucks, so they've gone a different way! We're going to see the others!"

Others murmured in agreement.

A strange smell filled Rachael's nostrils. Sweet, sticky, and oily, it was almost tangible.

A few prisoners started coughing. Although it was bitingly cold, the fresh air had been invigorating, but now Rachael's mouth felt dry, and a cloying sensation at the back of her throat made her gulp. She coughed and coughed again loudly to clear her throat, but without success.

"Look!" a male prisoner shouted, his finger pointing straight ahead.

At first, Rachael could not work out what he was pointing at. Another fence and gate lay ahead, and clusters of trees beyond them. Between the trees and the leaden skies, there was nothing.

Suddenly, a burst of bright orange light flashed above the tree line like a sparking match. But when Rachael watched intently and her eyes became accustomed to the light, she spotted plumes of dark smoke billowing into the air, barely distinguishable against the dark sky. Another flash of orange followed, which she recognized as a flame. The flame and smoke were coming from the mouth of a black chimney, which was protruding from behind the treetops.

It dawned on Rachael that it was the smoke that was causing them to cough. When she looked closely, she spotted specks of black dust landing on her palms. As they walked on, the number and size of the specks grew until she was convinced her every breath was sucking them into her lungs. Several prisoners nearby had covered their mouth and nose with their hands, and when Rachael did the same, her coughing eased.

The smell had grown more pungent, like burning meat, and even when her mouth and nose were covered, she could not dispel it.

The fifty prisoners were walking toward the chimney and with every step grew more apprehensive. The SS guard leading the group, a middle-aged soldier with sunken eyes and oversized ears, sensed the unrest and turned to the prisoners.

"No talking!" he shouted. "You've been warned! You've been selected for hard labor, so you don't need to worry about the chimneys…for a while." He struck the nearest prisoner viciously with his stick. Like Pavlov's dogs, the kapos and blue stripes followed suit and set upon the prisoners with their sticks.

"Rachael, what does he mean?" Hannes asked. "What does he mean about chimneys?"

Rachael thought for a few seconds before answering. "I don't know, Hannes. But like the man says, it's best we do as we're told. We don't want to get hit by that big stick, do we?" She was relieved that this answer seemed to placate her brother.

The prisoners arrived at the next gate and fence, which marked another section. They filed through, and the gate was locked behind them. Rachael had seen no trees in the other sections, yet here there was nothing but trees. Two groups of birches stood on either side of the path. They were mature and sparsely populated, allowing Rachael to catch glimpses of light between their trunks. There was another stretch of barbed wire fencing, behind which stood several wooden barracks. But no chimneys. She saw no more chimneys. She was relieved.

The trees towered above them, so even the top of the chimney they had watched earlier was hidden, but the black smoke seemed to have grown darker as they approached, and its ever-increasing stench hung in the air as reminders of its proximity. Rachael looked down and watched layers of black particles gathering on her palms. She rubbed the coarse grit between her fingers, scouring her skin.

The prisoners walked less than a hundred meters before the tree line ended and the area opened up before them, revealing a single-story brick building on their left. This building was approximately the same width as the other barracks but was appreciably longer. There were windows along the length of the building, except for its center section, which possessed none whatsoever. On its roof, there were two chimneys, not one: one was billowing smoke with intermittent sparking flames; the other lay dormant.

"Come on, quick!" the SS guard suddenly shouted, starting to run. The other SS guards, kapos, and blue stripes started whipping the prisoners in a near frenzy. "You can see the disinfection block from here. Once you've showered and received your uniforms, you'll be taken to your barracks and given a nice bowl of hot soup," he continued. "Hurry!" The prisoners responded immediately, but the blows continued unabated. Rachael shielded Hannes with one arm and herself with the other but received a painful blow on her elbow. It was only when they had passed through the exit gate that the beatings stopped and the prisoners slowed to a walking pace.

Rachael had caught only a fleeting glimpse of the brick building, spending most of the brief dash with her head down and arms shielding herself and her brother. As the large-eared guard locked the gate behind them, Rachael looked back, wondering what had caused the sudden urgency.

The pathway bent through ninety degrees as it passed the building and led to the exit gate. The kapos and blue stripes had been positioned on the outside and rear of the path, forcing the cowering prisoners to face inward to their left. Rachael caught sight of another on the other side of the path, identical to the first, with two dormant chimneys.

Whatever these buildings were used for, the SS did not want them to be seen, she thought.

The disinfection building had been constructed recently, which was evidenced by its clean, red brickwork and glossy paintwork. The other buildings in Birkenau possessed a dirty and shabby appearance. Most of them appeared to have been designed with as few windows as possible. The disinfection block was T-shaped, with several large windows running along its length. There was one small chimney. This was the biggest structure she had seen in the camp.

The prisoners were herded through a doorway at the top edge of the "T" and into a large, unfurnished room, which was empty apart from a single wooden chair and a ring of blue stripes and gray-coated female guards standing around its edges.

"Move inside!" the kapos shouted. "Spread out! Don't block the doorway! Move along!"

The SS men entered once all the prisoners were inside. The large-eared soldier climbed on the chair, whipping it with his stick several times before raising his arms to speak.

"We must maintain a safe and hygienic environment if our workers are to remain fit for work. We'll eliminate the dirt and disease you've brought with you. Every worker must be subjected to the disinfection process. Every piece of clothing, every item you're wearing, and every millimeter of your body must be cleansed."

The soldier was an awkward-looking man, and he wobbled nervously on the chair before righting himself and continuing. "You're now in the undressing room. Take off ALL your clothes and leave them in a pile. Put all your other belongings in a separate pile. That includes wallets, purses, jewelry, rings, necklaces, hairpins, and anything else you're carrying. This must be done immediately, without fuss."

There was a stirring among the prisoners. Rachael noticed the perplexed look on her brother's face as his eyes darted around the room. She had seen him naked many times while he was growing up, but he had never seen her naked. In fact, she doubted he had ever seen another human being without clothes on. Yet here they were, hundreds of strangers being forced to undress in front of each other. Men and women of all ages and backgrounds. The room offered no privacy whatsoever.

Nobody moved. The SS soldier climbed down from his chair and struck a middle-aged woman wearing a black fur hat across her back with his stick. She flinched and cried out in pain.

"You Jews must learn to follow orders without question," the soldier said. "As you've already experienced several times, disobedience leads to severe consequences in Birkenau. So do as I say and get undressed!"

There was a rustling noise as the prisoners removed their clothes and placed them on the floor. Jewelry and other metal objects jingled like festive bells as they struck the concrete floor.

The woman who had been struck by the SS soldier was rubbing her shoulder to relieve her pain and was not yet undressing.

"This is unacceptable!" the soldier shouted. He grabbed the woman by the coat and dragged her out of the room and outside. Before any of the prisoners had grasped what was happening, a single shot rang out. Moments later, the soldier returned. He approached a nearby female guard and held out his hand. She took the black fur hat off him and placed it on the floor behind her, nodding without expression.

"Is there anybody else who refuses to undress?" the soldier asked.

Rachael removed her shoes and coat, hoping that her brother would follow suit. But he stood motionless.

"Hannes, you must undress!" she said in a tone that was empathetic but firm. "Look at them. Everybody's getting undressed, and so must you. And me." Her brother glanced around slowly, his mouth half open. While he was distracted, she grabbed hold of his coat, pulling it swiftly over his shoulders and away from his body before depositing it on the floor.

Slowly and methodically, Hannes unbuttoned his shirt and continued to undress until he was stark naked, shivering in the cold, his hands clasped in front of his genitalia. His head was bowed, not daring to look around, but he was so cold, he shuffled gingerly toward his sister, who grabbed his head and pulled him to her. Hannes threw his arms around his sister's midriff. He felt the comforting warmth of his sister; she felt the cold shivering of a frightened little boy.

When most of the prisoners were undressed, a door opened at the far end of the room.

"Pick up your clothes and belongings and go at once into the next room!" the SS guard barked. "Your clothes will be disinfected. They're as filthy as you are." These orders were repeated by the kapos and blue stripes as the prisoners ventured timidly through the doorway. Several guards leered at the naked women as they passed.

Beyond the door was the long corridor with large windows that Rachael had seen from outside. Several bulky metal doors were set in the opposite wall. Some of these were closed, some were open. A line of blue stripes was waiting and, seizing the clothing of the prisoners before any could complain, threw them into the cavities that lay behind the open doors.

The blue stripes were everywhere, Rachael thought. She had expected to see members of the SS swarming everywhere, but the SS guards were scarce and the officers more so. It was these prisoners in shabby, gossamer-thin clothing who performed the work, cowering under the pitiless glare of the kapos and SS.

The corridor was warmer than the undressing room. When a blue stripe opened a metal door, she heard the hiss of steam, and a waft of warm, humid air touched her face. She closed her eyes to enjoy the moment before the bitter cold returned.

"How will we be able to find our clothes again?" Hannes asked.

"Well," his sister replied. "If you were watching carefully, you'd have seen our clothes being put through the fourth door along. So when we've had our shower, and the clothes are washed and dried, we'll come back to the fourth door to collect them." She thought her explanation sounded plausible to a ten-year-old, but in truth, she did not believe they would wash, disinfect, and dry their clothes by the time they had showered.

"That's good," Hannes said. "That's my favorite jacket. It's got lots of pockets to put things in."

While the blue stripes were depositing the clothes in the disinfecting chambers, the guards were driving the prisoners onward. "Keep moving! This corridor isn't big enough for you all. Get into the next room!"

The corridor exit was flanked by two waist-high wicker baskets, each guarded by a blue stripe demanding the prisoners deposit their remaining possessions inside. An SS guard stood watch.

"It's just a toothbrush!" a woman protested.

"*Every* item must be placed in the basket!" a blue stripe insisted.

"How will we clean our teeth with no toothbrushes?" the woman replied.

"One more word out of you, and I'll have your teeth pulled out," a nearby kapo growled. "Then you'll not need a toothbrush!"

There was a sharp decrease in temperature in the adjoining room, but Rachael hardly noticed. She was thinking of the wicker baskets. Her clothes and belongings were gone, and she was sure she would never see them again. She did not mind about the everyday objects; it was the personal items that bothered her: the photographs of the family; the ring that her mama had given her on her eighteenth birthday, which would not pass to future generations. Every trinket, however small, tied her to her roots, her family and friends, her community, her religion, her country. It had all been thrown unceremoniously into a wicker basket. The Nazis had rendered her naked, physically and psychologically. She was overcome with doubt, like a tiny star floating in the vast emptiness of space.

She looked down at her naked brother, not knowing if he was shivering because of the cold, his fear, or both. And at that moment, she was reminded that no matter how she felt, she must do everything in her power to protect her brother, come what may. He was all that was left for her.

*

As Rachael and Hannes passed into the next room, they were greeted by a metallic whirring noise. Two women wearing gray uniforms and five blue stripes were shaving the heads, armpits, and genitals of the prisoners.

"Boy! Come here!" a blue stripe shouted, and for the first time since their arrival, Rachael was separated from her brother. She had to stand in line with several women waiting to be shaved.

By the time Rachael reached the front of the line, her brother was gone. She looked for him in every direction, causing the shaving machine to scour her scalp as its blunt blade skimmed over her head. She bit her lip when it clipped the upper part of her ear and drops of blood dribbled down her neck.

It seemed like only seconds before her head was shaved and the gray-skirted woman was demanding she raise her arms to give the blade access.

Rachael looked down. The long red hair she had cherished from an early age, and which had been admired by so many people, was lying in uneven clumps around her feet like straw scattered on a stable floor. A blue stripe was crawling on all fours, picking her hair up and throwing it into a linen sack he was carrying. Rachael instinctively moved her hands to protect her modesty in his presence, but the barber shouted at her to keep her arms up. The man moved off to the next prisoner without paying the slightest attention, and with that, her beloved red hair was gone.

The barber pushed her away and beckoned the next prisoner. Rachael ran her fingers over her scalp. It was like a poorly maintained lawn, bare in places with irregular patches dotted around.

The next woman was holding a bucket of green, oily gel, which she was scooping into the outstretched hands of the prisoners with a rusty ladle.

"That's the disinfectant," she said. "Spread it all over your body and wash it off in the shower."

A blue stripe shepherded Rachael into the shower room, which comprised eight sets of four-headed showers. There were no partitions between the males and females.

"Get in!" the blue stripe shouted, prodding her in the back with his stick. She stepped forward and under the freezing cold water streaming out of the showerhead above, which battered her scalp like a thousand needles and cascaded down her face. Her lips opened wide to allow drops to tumble into her desperate, parched mouth. It was painful and refreshing at the same time. She swallowed hard, and her throat felt clean, clear of the black dust. There was a bitter aftertaste in the water that made her gag, but it did not prevent her from gulping as much as she could endure.

"Stay there!" the blue stripe screamed, using his stick to slap her on the bare backside to stop her walking away. "We don't want you to bring diseases into the camp. You people need to be fully disinfected before you leave."

Rachael remained under the flowing water, her eyes smarting from the gel she had spread over her head. Finally, the blue stripe gestured toward the exit, grabbed the next prisoner by the forearm, and pushed him into the shower.

Rachael was shivering uncontrollably. She had been cold earlier, but the addition of the cold shower was almost unbearable.

The next room was like the undressing area, the prisoners standing around waiting, except whereas before they were clothed and dry, now they were naked and wet. The prisoners were looking around, hoping to find towels to dry themselves. But there were none.

Rachael could not see her brother, but the room was full, so she started searching for him. It was like walking among ghosts, white lifeless figures with blank eyes and silent, open mouths, anonymous in their bald nakedness and with their hands still covering their private parts. Her skin crawled when her arm brushed against a stranger's body, and she saw in their face the same revulsion and horror she felt.

But there was no sign of her brother. He must have passed into the next room. Ignoring the nauseating feeling, she squeezed through the crowd with determination to reach the next doorway.

The corridor was the mirror image of where they had handed over their clothes and valuables. Sturdy metal doors and lines of blue stripes and gray aprons lined the way. They were emptying, rather than filling the chambers, removing the disinfected clothes and placing them in separate piles of underwear, shirts, skirts, socks, aprons, jackets, and shoes. Another blue stripe stood by each pile, handing out the items of clothing to the prisoners as they passed, paying no attention to their shape and size. Ever-watchful kapos were present to keep the process moving.

"But these aren't my clothes!" a man wearing nothing but a pair of metal-rimmed spectacles exclaimed. "They're much too small! My clothes went into the second chamber along, not this one," he added, pointing to an unopened metal door.

"You'll take what you're given!" a kapo retorted, striking the man with his stick, which was little more than a gnarled piece of wood. A trickle of blood ran down the prisoner's back. A thin welt appeared, like a red stripe across his shoulder blades. "You can't get your clothes back. They're being disinfected and the chamber's full of gas," the kapo added. "You should be grateful to have any at all."

By the time she had reached the end of this corridor, Rachael had received some random clothes and a pair of black leather shoes with a gold-colored buckle. The clothes looked passable in the circumstances, but they stank of a disinfectant that made her eyes water.

The kapos forced the prisoners into the dressing room, where they hurriedly put their clothes on. They had barely spoken since leaving the undressing room, as if their shame and humiliation prevented it. Once dressed, the prisoners began conversing.

Rachael discovered her gray blouse was stained, but it was at least thick and warm. Her apron was much too big for her, but the black leather shoes and pock-marked socks were a good fit.

When she glanced around, Rachael almost laughed at the absurdity of these people dressed in the clothes of others in every shape, style, and size. There were Jews who were short in stature and whose arms and hands were engulfed by the sleeves of oversized shirts and jackets or had to hold their trousers by the waistline to prevent them from slipping down, and conversely, larger people burst out of tiny clothes. They were like clowns in a grotesque circus. The lady who had owned the black hat was staring down at a shabby headscarf nestled in her hands. All the women were given headscarves.

But there was still no sign of Hannes.

As they filed out of the disinfection building and back outside, Rachael caught sight of the smoking chimneys and, looking down, watched the specks of black soot gathering on her freshly washed palms.

"Get in line! Now!" The abuse from the barking blue stripes continued.

Four sets of tables had been arranged in the open space at the front of the building, each one manned by four blue stripes, and it was in this direction the prisoners were being corralled.

Another line with an uncertain end, Rachael thought.

She could not determine what was going on, but as she shuffled forward, she heard cries and yelps, and her fear resurfaced.

When Rachael reached the front of the line, a blue stripe was standing waiting, holding in his palm scraps of paper no bigger than his finger. He handed her one and gestured for her to move on. Before she did, she looked down and saw there was a number on it, nothing else, just a number, scribbled in black ink.

The second blue stripe was sitting down behind the table, a discolored white rag in his right hand and a glass jar containing a murky liquid in the other.

"Left arm," the man said, grabbing her wrist and twisting it so the inside of her forearm was showing. He dipped the rag in the jar and brusquely rubbed it over her arm. The liquid on the rag made her skin tingle. The blue stripe pointed at the next man, sitting directly beside him and who was slouched over the table, holding a metal pointed instrument in his hand. A bottle of dark-blue ink stood nearby.

Rachael offered her arm, but the man shook his head.

"Number," he said, snatching the scrap of paper from her hand and placing it on the table next to the ink. "Arm."

The man was of slim build, but Rachael was surprised how strong his grip was as he pinned her wrist to the tabletop. Her natural reaction was to resist, but it was pointless.

"Keep still!" the man continued. "It'll hurt less." He dipped the instrument into the ink. Rachael felt a sharp pain as its metal point pierced her skin, followed by a stinging sensation as the ink entered her body. Before she had fully grasped what was happening, the sharp point pierced her skin again. Rachael winced but remained silent. She winced a little less each time the needle pierced her skin. When he was finished, the number was tattooed clumsily but legibly on her forearm: 57619.

The final blue stripe, who was also seated, picked up the scrap of paper that lay on the table by his neighbor and checked Rachael's tattoo before asking her to confirm her name, date and place of birth, which he duly added to a list of names in a leather-bound ledger lying on the table before him. For his last task, he threw the paper into a wicker basket at his feet.

*

Once tattooed, the prisoners with their throbbing arms, damp bodies, and ill-fitting clothes had no time to loiter. A young SS soldier was standing on an upturned wooden crate. He had pale skin, and wisps of ginger hair stuck out from beneath his cloth cap. He spoke in a high-pitched voice.

"Women that way!" he shouted, pointing to the right of the disinfection building. "Men that way," he added, directing their attention to the left and the gateway they had recently passed through.

Rachael was desperate to find Hannes, but there were five or six times more men than women, and the lines of men were already moving away. She stepped out of her own line to look for her brother, but a blue stripe struck her on the arm, sending a searing pain through her body and obliging her to return. The suffering was not worthwhile, as there was no sign of her brother, and only a couple of minutes later, she lost sight of the departing men as they passed through the gateway.

To Rachael, it seemed to be only moments ago when she had been in the shaving room with her brother by her side. When they had become separated, she had searched for him with some hope of spotting his blond hair before despondently realizing he would have the same shaved head as the other men. And then the men were gone, and that ray of hope was extinguished. Her head and shoulders slumped as the fatigue and hunger that she had been ignoring during her search overwhelmed her.

I'm alive, so he's alive, Rachael reassured herself. She was on her way to a women's camp and Hannes would end up in a men's camp. She knew males and females would have been forced apart at some point, but she would find her brother. Her anxiety eased somewhat, although the fatigue and hunger remained.

Heads down, the women trudged along the path, stragglers being continuously harangued by the blue stripes, and with the barking orders of the kapos ringing in their ears. Rachael noticed the path widening, and when she looked up, she recognized Lagerstrasse opening out before them, running in a straight line to the camp entrance in the distance.

Two trucks passed them, empty.

A sickening sensation swelled in Rachael's stomach, more than the pangs of hunger, as she realized they had come full circle. Of her Dutch compatriots, who had taken truck rides in that very direction, there was no sign whatsoever.

Two SS soldiers were leading the women. Rachael knew attempting to speak to them would be fruitless and would certainly lead to a beating. The same would be true of the kapos. Her only chance lay with a blue stripe. She slowed her pace and allowed herself to fall back several rows, glancing at the blue stripes who were walking alongside, hoping to catch sight of an encouraging expression. Instead, they cruelly sneered at her or waved their sticks menacingly.

Rachael fell back several more places until she spotted a blue stripe who was not aggressive. He was walking with his head bowed, not engaging with the prisoners at all. This was the man who had given her advice on the railway platform earlier that day. He had a round face, dark eyes, and a small, thin-lipped mouth. Tufts of dark-brown hair poked out from beneath the rim of his blue-striped cap.

Rachael maneuvered herself so she was walking right beside the blue stripe.

"Where are the rest of the Dutch from my transport?" Rachael asked out of the corner of her mouth, her head bowed.

There was no reply, so she repeated the question. The man responded in a voice she barely heard.

"Don't ask questions. You'll just get beaten...or worse," he said nervously.

"Please tell me!" the young woman urged. "Are they in the same part of the camp as the rest of us?" She wondered if Hannes would be with the Dutch men or stranded with nationalities he would not understand.

"Don't worry about them," the blue stripe said. "Just look after yourself. In Auschwitz, it's a full-time job keeping yourself alive without worrying about anybody else." She watched him through the corner of her eye. His lips parted slightly as if he were about to speak again, but he did not.

"Please!" Rachael pleaded, hoping to coax a few more words from him.

"They're gone," he replied.

"Gone?" she asked, bewildered. "To another camp?"

"Up the chimney, and God willing, up to heaven," the blue stripe answered, raising his head skyward.

Rachael had seen the two buildings with chimneys. As she followed the gaze of the blue stripe, she saw the billowing black smoke and sparking flames.

Suddenly, her senses sharpened, cutting through her fatigue like a knife. She swung her head around and saw two more chimneys either side of the path behind them. Both were surrounded by a tall wattle fence. With her head bowed, she had not noticed them as she passed.

Her eyes panned across the horizon, and six chimneys were jutting above the tree line.

Rachael swallowed the cloying smoke, which spiraled down her throat and into her lungs. Holding up her palms, small dust specks gathered, quickly forming a layer of black on her hands, like a shroud. She was filled with revulsion as the full horror dawned on her.

"All of them?" she asked the blue stripe.

"Every single one of them," he replied before moving away from her, preventing any further opportunity for her to speak.

Rachael looked up. The ominous smoke seemed to separate into millions of individual black specks that spread out, saturating the sky and obliterating the remaining daylight.

CHAPTER FIVE

November 1943

The entire Birkenau camp was placed under curfew during the selections from the arriving trains. Prisoners did not leave the camp to work in their kommandos and did not leave their barracks either. It was silent as Rachael and the rest of the new arrivals entered their camp, which lay on the right of Lagerstrasse, about halfway along.

Here, a proportion of the barracks was constructed of brick rather than wood, having been built earlier when there were fewer cost constraints. They had suffered less wear and tear from four years of exposure to the Polish climate. Thick walls protected their occupants from extremes of heat during summer but maintained interminably freezing temperatures during winter.

"This is B1, the women's camp," the ginger-haired SS man said. "There's to be no contact between male and female workers. There are two sets of electrified barbed wire fences to keep you away from the men in B2." The soldier pointed across Lagerstrasse.

Rachael stared across the stretch of ground between the two lines of fencing, wondering how she would find her brother among so many barracks. If he was there, she would locate him, she promised herself. Her eyes flitted across the horizon, taking in the camp entrance, the low wooden barracks, which from this distance looked like rows of coffins, and finally the sparking chimneys to her left.

At least she had walked in a full circle around the facility, she thought, and had an impression of the layout and enormous scale of Birkenau.

The Dutch women passed along a pathway that split their camp into two. They approached a brick barracks, which had a doorway halfway along its length.

Rachael noticed how low the single-story barracks were. The tops of the doorframes were only centimeters away from the tiled roofs. There were several large windows along the building and one narrow chimney, much shorter than the flaming ones.

Two men were waiting in the doorway of Barracks 19. Both were wearing blue-striped uniforms, but the taller of them wore a woolen coat with a green inverted triangle stitched to its breast pocket and a white armband. The other man, standing to the side and behind and with the same armband but a red triangle, was clasping a bundle of papers to his chest.

Inverted triangles represented the backgrounds of the kapos: green signified a criminal, red a political prisoner, pink a homosexual, and purple a Jehovah's Witness.

The ginger-haired soldier approached the men and thrust some papers into the hands of the taller man, who immediately passed them on without looking.

"Forty-seven," the soldier said. "Make sure they're all registered in time for tonight's roll call. It's forecast for rain, and I don't want to stand around for hours getting wet." He turned and marched away. The women followed the two kapos into the building.

A narrow corridor of whitewashed bricks led inside. It seemed inconceivable that the temperature inside could be lower than outside. It was as if the brickwork had absorbed every day of cold, not giving any concession to the warmth of summer but devouring every icy moment of winter.

"You see those two rooms?" the tall man said, pointing at two doors flanking the barracks entrance. "One's mine. I'm Kaminski and I'm the block elder." He pointed at his white armband. "I'm in charge. You do what I say and work hard, then you may survive..." Rachael saw he had the word *kapo* written on his armband. The women already in the barracks wore the familiar yellow star on their clothes.

"The other room belongs to the block manager, Lisowski," he continued, pointing at the smaller man who had followed them inside. "He works for me. And guess what? You do exactly what he says as well. Disobey either of us, and you'll be sent up the chimney."

The women murmured restlessly, but the block elder struck his wooden stick so hard against a bunk it broke in two. They fell silent.

"Pick up one blanket each and find yourselves a roost," Kaminski ordered, pointing at a pile of filthy linen stacked on the floor outside his room. "Four people to every bunk."

Each roost was hemmed in on three sides by whitewashed brickwork. The top two bunks were made of wooden slats covered with a thin layer of straw. The bottom bunk was the floor itself, a mixture of mud and straw flattened by the bodies of sleeping prisoners.

Lisowski spotted Rachael examining a top bunk. "It's usual for the new arrivals to sleep on the floor. By all means, take one of the top two, but when the others come back from work, be prepared to be chucked off. They leave their blankets as markers."

Most of the higher bunks were occupied by three or four prisoners or covered by filthy, threadbare blankets. The newcomers picked up their blankets and walked around, looking for a spare place. Some prisoners who were working later that day on the night shift were asleep. The others sat on their bunks, nodding or shaking their heads to indicate whether a berth was free. There were few spaces readily made available, except for those on the floor.

Three Dutch women chanced upon a vacant space at the same time. They each put forward their respective arguments why they should prevail. This was carried out politely at first, but shouting ensued when no consensus could be reached. Rachael was shocked when the trio started shoving each other, screaming and shouting, and tearing at each other's shabby clothing.

"Stop!" Kaminski bellowed. He had returned after visiting his room to collect a replacement stick. "Though it gives me enormous pleasure to watch Jews descend into the gutter where they belong, scrapping like the wild animals they truly are, fighting in the barracks isn't allowed. The punishment for this is that there'll be no dinner today. That's a punishment for you all, not just you three. Your next meal will be breakfast."

The prisoners groaned in unison, and insults were shouted at the three protagonists, who distanced themselves from the empty berth. A few minutes later, one of them returned and cautiously climbed into the bunk.

Rachael crawled on all fours, examining the earth beneath the bunks. The whole barracks stank of stale sweat, rotten food, and feces, but she discovered the smell was significantly worse at ground level. It was also worse at one end of the building, so she selected the driest, smoothest, and cleanest patch of ground farthest away from the stench and put her blanket down. She then sat down on the bunk above.

Within fifteen minutes, the forty-seven women had taken up places within the barracks. Two of them were sitting on the same bunk, glaring at each other. Of the rest, some had placed their blankets on one of the two upper bunks, but the majority had taken a berth on the bare floor.

Kaminski rapped his stick on a brick partition wall to gain their attention. "I'm not telling you the house rules. You'll find out soon enough." There was an empty bucket at his feet, and he kicked it forcefully across the floor. It rolled several times and came to a halt, covered in wet filth. "There'll be no access to the latrines or washrooms until morning. So if you need to go, you've got to use the bucket. I suggest you go sooner rather than later. In the dark, it's not so easy to find, and if you knock it over, it makes a big noise…and a big smell." He paused and laughed. "Having traveled in the cattle cars, you should be used to this."

The block elder returned to his room and closed the door behind him. Lisowski followed suit.

*

Rachael looked down at her watch. Of course, it was not there. She had deposited it in the basket in the disinfection building. The weather was dull and dark, and it was easy to think dusk was falling. They had arrived at dawn, which seemed like hours ago, but how many exactly she could not say. She rubbed the pale band of skin that showed where her watch strap had been and realized none of them knew the time anymore. They had lost their freedom, their families, their belongings, and their time. What did they have left?

Some women, no longer able to combat their fatigue, went to sleep. But for others, the trauma of the last few days overcame their need for rest, and they talked among themselves or took up conversations with the other occupants of Barracks 19.

Rachael could not sleep. Rain began falling in a steady drizzle. She was looking through a dirt-encrusted window, water streaking down it. Through the wet and dirt, she stared out across the camp, wondering where her brother was.

A large group of women approached from the direction of the chimneys and were driven into the women's camp by kapos and blue stripes. As they passed each barracks, several of them would leave the line and go inside. When they reached Barracks 19, ten prisoners entered, going straight to their bunks and ignoring the new arrivals.

The last four years had prematurely aged many people, so it was difficult to judge their ages. Rachael watched a woman who looked in her late twenties, and whose clothes were in a much better condition than most of those around her, climb onto the bunk above. She wore a woolen headscarf rather than the shabby gray pieces of thin material given to the Dutch women earlier that day. She had a stylish blue coat, only spoiled by a stripe of red paint daubed across its back. The woman had an olive complexion, wide dark-brown eyes, and round cheekbones.

It occurred to Rachael there were three types of women in Barracks 19. The majority were dressed in plain gray uniforms or ill-fitting, shabby clothing she had watched being handed out in the disinfection building. But while the new arrivals genuinely yearned for food and water, these prisoners had advanced well beyond that point. Their eyes cowered in the shadows of their recessed sockets, and their skin was almost transparent, draped over protruding cheekbones and so fragile, it cracked like thin ice on a pond. Short clothes revealed lower limbs devoid of muscle and flesh.

Rachael had heard the phrase "I'm dying of thirst" many times during her life in Amsterdam, but now she understood how ludicrously inappropriate it was. These women were truly dying of thirst.

The second group included the woman in the bunk above Rachael. Apart from the clothing, these women appeared cleaner than the others. They were starving and downtrodden, but not as severely as the others. A residual spark of life flickered within them, while the rest walked around like ghosts.

The third group was the new arrivals, somewhere between the other two groups, wearing the clothes of the ghosts but in better physical condition. Rachael asked herself what the reason for such a stark contrast between the women was and how she might appear after a few months in this hell on earth.

A few of the prisoners gathered around a brick oven and chimney, which stood in the center of the barracks. They used their threadbare blankets to wipe off the rain and ease their shivering.

"That chimney couldn't warm the rats, never mind us," one of them complained.

Rachael wondered how anyone could survive a freezing night in this place with drenched clothes and a damp blanket.

The rain and black clouds brought the night on. There were no electric lights inside, just the searchlights on the watchtowers scanning the camp and intermittently illuminating the interior of the barracks. The features of the prisoners faded, replaced by silhouettes. Rachael was relieved she couldn't see their traumatized faces. They had become shapes, no longer human beings.

A light flickered as Kaminski strolled out of his room, carrying a candle. He raised it up, and its trembling flame created grotesque shadows on his face.

"Just to remind you," the block elder said. "There'll be no food this evening."

Kaminski entered the block manager's room and closed the door. In the silence of the barracks, men's laughter could be heard from within, and the clinking of glasses together with the clanging of metal dishes.

"Has anybody got any water?" a woman asked.

"We've got no water," the reply came. "And we aren't allowed out…"

"But my mother's sick," the woman pleaded. "She's got a fever and is so weak. I think she's caught typhus."

A series of unknown voices continued the discussion.

"If she's got typhus, there's no point wasting water on her."

"Don't be so cruel!"

"I'm not being cruel. It's just a fact."

"Poor soul! God have mercy on her."

"God's mercy's in short supply in Birkenau!"

"God have mercy on us all."

"I'm surprised your mother hasn't been selected."

"She speaks German, so they gave her a job in Kanada," the first woman replied. "Everything was fine until the kapo was replaced. The new one's an asshole and set her working outside like a farmyard animal." The woman sobbed. "In a few days, she's been transformed."

Rachael leaned toward the shadow in the upper bunk. "What's Kanada?" she whispered.

"Kanada's where the belongings left on the railway platform are taken, sorted, and then sent to Germany," the shadow responded.

"Why call it Kanada?"

"Kanada's a land of plenty, full of riches, and somewhere we dream of living in," the shadow replied. "The Kanada sheds contain the possessions of thousands and thousands of prisoners. Jewelry, money...everything of value that's brought here can be found in Kanada. In Birkenau, it's the land of plenty. But few dare to steal from there. If the SS find out, it's a bullet in the back of the head, or worse."

"I'm Dutch and speak German," Rachael said.

The shadow moved closer and whispered, "Well, you'd better hope the woman dies tonight and the SS gives you her job."

"I couldn't possibly!" she protested. "Anyway, I already have a job in Kanada," she added, recalling the comments of the guard on the train platform.

Rachael was suddenly struck by the reality that she herself had probably replaced a woman who had died of typhus or some other dreadful disease or malnutrition. She shuddered at the thought.

When the dying woman coughed again, Rachael cried out, "Please, can someone give the poor woman a drop of water?"

"Don't worry! It's your first day," the shadow remarked. "It's dog eat dog in Auschwitz. You'll soon learn to grab every opportunity you can. Every breadcrumb. Every drop of water. Every simple job instead of a hard one. Every blanket with one less hole in it. Grab them all and perhaps you'll stay alive for one day more...if you're lucky."

There was a pause until the shadow added, "By the way, my name's Elke."

"I'm Rachael."

"Have you found a bunk?"

"Yes, on the floor."

"It's too cold to sleep on the bare floor. The rain will find its way into the barracks, and you'll wake up wet and covered in mud. You can sleep on this bunk with us. We share whatever body warmth we've got. It's a tight squeeze for five, but—"

"I couldn't!" Rachael interrupted, balking at the prospect of sharing a confined space with four strangers.

"Birkenau will change you," Elke said. "In a few weeks, a new Rachael will emerge, a Rachael who'll do and say things the old one would never have dreamed of. Remember! Grab every opportunity."

Rachael stooped and crawled under the wooden roost. The previous occupants had rolled the ground flat, but it was as hard as concrete and cold as ice. She laid her blanket down for insulation and comfort, but it failed at both. She tried lying on her back and on her side but found no respite. After three days in the cattle car yearning to lie down, she asked herself whether standing up would be a better option. As Elke had warned, rivulets of water were seeping through the wall.

Rachael thought of her brother and where he might be. She was an adult who had experienced the world. He was only a child, and she was harried by the thought he might be alone and frightened. She realized she, too, was alone and rolled out from under the bunk and stood up.

"Elke, does that offer still stand?"

"Of course. Squeeze up everybody! We've got another one coming on board."

The young Dutch woman climbed onto the top bunk and lay on her side with her knees protruding beyond its edge. She was uncomfortable, but the sound of the women's breathing helped her relax until eventually fatigue engulfed her and she fell asleep.

CHAPTER SIX

November 1943

A gong was ringing in the distance, but Rachael did not stir until Elke pushed her off the bunk.

"Hurry!" Elke urged. "We must be ready for roll call. There was no roll call last night, so this one will be worse than usual." She grabbed Rachael by the hand and led her out into the light. "Follow me!"

It was mayhem outside. Women were streaming out of every barracks in B1. Beyond the barbed wire, the men were doing the same in B2.

"Latrines first!" Elke said. "They'll be almost clean now but indescribably filthy in a few minutes." Elke was of a similar height to Rachael, but her blue coat gave bulk to the slight body beneath. She darted among the thronging women, squeezing through narrow gaps when possible. Rachael barely kept up, but without her new bunk mate, she knew she would be lost.

Elke pointed at a barracks as they ran past. "That's the washroom," she said.

"There's nobody waiting," Rachael gasped.

"Everyone's going to the latrines first," Elke replied.

Sure enough, a horde of women was crowding the entrance to the next barracks. Elke and Rachael joined them, pushing and shoving like the rest.

It was only then, while crammed together and barely moving, that Rachael saw Elke clearly for the first time. Close up, a few strands of dark-brown hair escaped from beneath her blue headscarf. Her skin seemed even darker in the daylight and reminded Rachael of the colorful pictures of exotic women sunning themselves on Mediterranean beaches that she had seen in glossy magazines. Elke must have been striking once, Rachael thought. Once.

"Where are you from?" Rachael asked.

"That's a long story," Elke replied. "A story for another day."

*

The stampeding feet had churned the rain-sodden ground into sickly, thick mud. Rachael heard it squelching and hoped it would not seep inside her shoes. The smell and the claustrophobia were as distressing as that within the cattle car, she thought.

The women inched their way toward the latrines block. A gong rang out again.

"Ten minutes gone," Elke gasped, her chest constricted by the pressure of those around her.

"Ten minutes," Rachael said. "What does that mean?"

"Thirty minutes left," Elke replied.

"To do what?"

"To go to the toilet, have a wash, have breakfast, tidy the barracks, and be in line for roll call."

"What if we're late?"

"You don't want to know," Elke warned.

The two women finally squeezed their way into the latrines block. A few of the women had resorted to fighting to gain entry, while the weaker ones had simply given up.

From the outside, the latrines and washroom blocks had the same appearance as the wooden barracks Rachael had seen the previous day, with no windows on the walls but skylights on the roofs and a doorway on each gable end. With people in front of her, the first thing she noticed on the inside was the roof. There was no ceiling, just the crisscrossing of the wooden beams. As she moved forward, she covered her nose. It was only about a quarter of an hour since the sounding of the first gong, but the stench was as strong as the cattle car had been after three days, and it grew stronger with every step forward.

The mass of women ahead of her thinned out, and the interior came into view. It was one open room. Three rows of concrete toilets, one on each side and one down the center, ran the length of the barracks. Each toilet section contained eighty open holes. Rachael knew this because, while waiting, she counted the number of women sitting there, so tightly packed they were frequently touching.

The women sat down on the cold, bare stone without fuss and exited hurriedly via the far door.

"I assume there's no toilet?" Rachael asked, remembering her experience in the cattle car.

"That's a *luxury* we've been deprived of," Elke replied in an ironic tone. "If you ever find any paper, don't tell anybody. They'll beat you up and steal it from you."

When the two women reached the front of the line, Elke turned to Rachael.

"You know where the washroom is," she said. "I'll meet you back in our barracks after the washroom." With that, she scurried away, sitting herself down halfway along the room.

"Get a move on!" somebody shouted behind Rachael, shoving her forward. She spotted a woman leaving a hole along the central section and, to reach it first, had to barge past another woman who had spied it at the same time. Rachael was swiftly learning that Dutch good manners would count for nothing in Birkenau.

She finished in the latrines as soon as she could. Nobody had toilet tissue, and the stink from the cesspit below was unbearable.

As Rachael approached the washroom barracks, women were pouring out of it. On entering, she saw a metal trough on either side with another down the center of the building, each with faucets positioned every two to three feet. A few women were standing there, twisting and turning the faucets and striking the pipework with their hands, but without a drop of water flowing. Like those before, they gave up and left the washroom. Rachael looked down at her hands and wondered what dirt and bacteria were clinging to her skin right then. At least she had had a shower the previous day, she thought. But what would it be like if the faucets were not repaired soon?

The gong was ringing as Rachael reentered Barracks 19.

"Another ten minutes?" she asked, seeing Elke in a line that snaked around the interior of the building.

"Yes, we must hurry," Elke replied. "We've only got twenty minutes left. Quick, stand by me!"

"Oy!" a woman behind them shouted. "Get to the back of the line. No jumping in!"

"Give her a break. She's new!" Elke shouted back with equal vigor.

"Stop gossiping back there!" Kaminski yelled, careening around a corner with his stick poised to strike. Seeing the woman opening her mouth to reply, he thrashed her across the shoulders. The woman winced but only let out a muffled moan once the kapo had disappeared.

The women shuffled forward in silence until they reached Lisowski's office where a blue stripe was standing in the doorway, behind a steel barrel, out of which he was ladling a liquid into the bowls of the waiting prisoners. He was proceeding at such speed he often missed the bowl and splashed the women's hands. A puddle was forming on the floor and seeping across the rock-hard ground.

"Keep moving!" Kaminski shouted. "Breakfast ends in five minutes or when the barrel's empty, whichever comes first. We won't be late for roll call."

Some new arrivals murmured their disapproval. Kaminski grabbed the nearest by the collar of her gray dress and dragged her outside. Three loud thwacks of his baton were heard, followed by silence.

Kaminski came back inside accompanied by two kapos wearing white armbands, who made their way to the rear of the line and forcibly removed several of the women.

"But we had no dinner yesterday evening," one woman complained.

"Well, you'll have to learn to do things more quickly if you want to eat," the block elder sneered.

"What's that?" Rachael whispered to Elke, nodding toward another steel barrel, which contained a dark-brown steaming liquid.

"It's supposed to be tea or coffee," Elke replied. "One thing we know for sure is that there's no tea or coffee in that barrel. It's as bitter as hell. We think it's made of weeds or herbs that grow in the region."

"Then why drink it?" Rachael asked.

"One day soon, Rachael," Elke replied, "you'll be begging the kapo to give you an extra spoonful."

"It looks too revolting to drink," Rachael remarked.

"It *is* too revolting to drink," Elke said. "But drink it you must, otherwise, you'll starve. Every crumb and every drop of food needs to be consumed. And as quickly as you can, before it gets stolen."

Once outside, Rachael stared down at the ladleful of brown liquid swilling around in her metal bowl. It looked disgusting and smelled of rancid vegetables, but it was hot, and cupping her hands around the bowl, she felt the warmth permeating her frozen fingers. She closed her eyes and contemplated the warm sensation as the liquid coursed down her throat and into her body.

The first sip made Rachael's whole body shiver, its bitterness more biting than any tea or coffee she had tasted before. But I must, she thought and took one long gulp, which consumed half the contents of her metal cup.

"Here's a tip," Elke said, pouring the residue of her drink into the palms of her hands, rubbing them together and massaging her face, neck, and ears.

Rachael watched, aghast. "What on earth are you doing?"

"It might look and taste disgusting," Elke replied, "but it's hot and wet, and there's probably fewer bugs and diseases in it than the mud and shit we live in. Whenever there's no water in the washrooms, I always do this."

Rachael poured the remaining liquid into her cupped hands and used it to wipe the dirt off her fingers and from under her nails. When she raised her hand to her face, the smell of rotten vegetables was noticeable. She closed her mouth, held her breath, and wiped her face.

The gong sounded. Ten minutes left.

Suddenly, music started playing. Rachael looked at Elke in bemusement.

"It's the camp orchestra," Elke said. "Every day, the work groups leave the camp to the sound of classical marches! The SS prefer Strauss or Beethoven to be played. Tchaikovsky has fallen out of favor. Next to speaking German, being able to play a musical instrument is the best talent a prisoner can possess."

"But why?" the Dutch woman inquired.

"The SS say a lusty march lifts the spirits of the prisoners as they approach the day ahead. The prisoners say the marches are deafening and intended to block out the sound of the SS and kapos beating and shooting them."

The roll call yard was a strip of land between the last barracks and the barbed wire fence next to the women's camp entrance. There was a slight slope because of soil having been dumped on one side when a ditch had been dug. To Rachael, used to the orderly process in Westerbork, the yard was nowhere near large enough to perform a well-organized roll call and was hopelessly inadequate for the mayhem unfolding before her.

In order to reach their places, the women were crossing the yard in all directions, bumping into each other and occasionally coming to a standstill. The ten kapos raged around them, striking out with their sticks and roughly handling the women to ease the congestion.

It was clear to Rachael that the behavior of the kapos had changed. Earlier, they had been supervising the women and meting out targeted beatings. Now, their batons were continuously in motion, arcing in the air like windmills, striking whoever was nearest and using their boots whenever a woman fell. Kaminski, Lisowski, and a third kapo, who were studiously examining their paperwork, were the only kapos not acting aggressively, although they kept glancing nervously toward the camp gate.

As lines formed, Lisowski and the third kapo stepped forward. Between them, they examined the tattoos of each woman and cross-checked them with their documentation.

"Where do I go?" Rachael asked.

"All the newcomers form a line at the far end of the yard," Elke answered. "My line's right here... But you must hurry. You're on the other side of the yard." She paused for a moment before adding, "Be careful of Irma Grese!"

"Who's Irma Grese?" Rachael asked.

"You'll find out soon," Elke answered. "Don't look at her and don't speak to her!"

Following Elke, Rachael dodged through the crowd, searching for any of the Dutch arrivals she recognized. There was more traffic in the middle of the crowd, but the kapos were operating around the edges and she wanted to avoid their blows.

Rachael pushed and shoved her way forward until she found herself at the far edge of the crowd, standing behind Elke at the head of a line with the Kanada kapo in front of them. To her left, there were fifteen to twenty lines. To her other side, she shuddered at the sight of bodies piled up right beside them. The sight was dreadful, but somehow compelling. The Dutch woman had not seen a dead body before, except for her Grandpa Ruud. But he had looked so peaceful lying in his coffin. In contrast, the limbs of these women were tangled into contorted shapes, and their skin was drawn so tightly it seemed to pull their mouths into vacant grimaces. They had not died in peace.

Kaminski was a couple of meters behind the kapo, legs apart and arms tucked behind his back, watching. He checked his watch and strode forward.

"If anybody isn't in line by the time SS-Rapportführer Gruber arrives, they'll pay a heavy price!" the block elder screamed. He lashed out at a passing blue stripe, who fell to the ground and frantically tried to regain his feet in the slippery mud, succeeding just before the stick fell upon him again.

The impending arrival of the SS was driving the kapos into a nervous frenzy.

Suddenly, the flurry of cries and shouts stopped as everyone followed Kaminski's stare and looked toward the camp gateway. Everybody stopped moving. Three SS functionaries were walking toward them. They were wearing the familiar gray-green uniforms and caps of the SS, but one of the three was a woman, and Rachael had rarely seen female SS members. Their uniforms were quite similar in color and design except that the woman wore a skirt and had a thick, black cape draped around her shoulders.

This must be Irma Grese, Rachael thought. She had long blond hair, which cascaded to her shoulders and obscured her SS lapel insignia. Rachael thought her well-rounded cheeks and immaculately applied makeup gave her the appearance of a film star rather than an SS officer in a labor camp. While the impact of Birkenau seemed to prematurely age its inmates, the impact on Grese was in complete contrast. She looked like she might still be a teenager, or in her early twenties at most.

A huge German shepherd dog was by the side of the SS senior supervisor, straining on its leash, growling and baring its teeth. The dog looked too powerful for her to hold, but each time it lurched forward, she jerked its leash hard, lifting its front paws clear of the ground.

"Whoa there!" SS-Oberaufseherin Grese urged. There was a steely coldness in her voice not reflected in her delicate features. Rachael thought she detected the semblance of a smile as she tugged the beast's leash.

Lisowski walked hurriedly over to the SS officers and offered Grese several sheets of paper attached to a clipboard. The blonde ignored him and allowed the dog to pull her toward the waiting lines of prisoners. It was Rapportführer Gruber, the roll call leader, who took the sheets.

"These had better be accurate," Gruber warned Lisowski. "It's going to rain this morning, and I'll hold you personally responsible if I get wet."

"They're all here! They're all here!" Lisowski simpered. "Forty-seven new arrivals from the Netherlands yesterday, eight dead overnight, nine hundred and seventy-two in total in Barracks 19. All accounted for."

"Okay, let's get started!" the SS officer said.

Kaminski took a step forward and shouted, "Attention!" The weary prisoners attempted to stand up straight. "Hats off!" he continued, and the women removed their caps or headscarves. Rachael obeyed the commands.

"Irma, would you like to check the bodies?" the officer asked Grese, removing a sheet of paper from his clipboard. Grese always counted the bodies.

"Give me the list, man!" Grese shouted at Lisowski, who ran over to retrieve the sheet and hand it to her. The German shepherd was growling so ferociously the block manager took pains to walk well wide of the dog, stretching out his arm to pass the paper to Grese and avoid its salivating jaws.

"Eight dead, let me see," Grese said, walking past Rachael at a distance of only a few feet. The Dutch woman's head was bowed, but she was drawn to watch Grese as she passed and noticed her immaculately applied red lipstick, contrasting with her smooth, pale skin.

"What's this?" Grese demanded angrily. "The bodies are supposed to be laid out so they can be easily counted. Not piled up like this!"

"Look, Madam!" Lisowski replied. "One, two, three, four, five, six, seven, eight."

"Do you think I can't count?"

"No, no! Of course not, Madam!" Lisowski stammered.

"Then answer my question! Why are the bodies not properly positioned?"

"There were five bodies we knew about." Lisowski appeared to be shrinking in front of her. "But we found three more this morning... at the last minute, Madam."

Rachael remembered Elke's words of warning, but she felt compelled to turn her head to see the events unfolding a short distance behind her. Five bodies were lined up neatly next to each other. The other three had been placed on top without the neatness of the others but were easily identifiable and countable.

"None of the prisoners told you about these deaths when they rose this morning?" Grese asked. "Which prisoners didn't tell you?"

"I don't know, Madam," Lisowski answered.

Grese turned toward the lines of prisoners. "At least three prisoners knew of these deaths but failed to tell the barracks kapos. Step forward if you woke up this morning next to a dead body."

There was an uneasy silence. Unable to contemplate the horror of waking up to discover your bunk neighbor had died during the night, Rachael looked straight ahead. Beyond the barbed wire fencing, two chimneys poked out above the tree line. Both were billowing smoke.

"Those who know me will be aware I'm a patient woman," Grese said. "I'm prepared to let you stand here for as long as is necessary. It'd be much better if the three perpetrators made themselves known. The result will be the same."

The roll call leader walked over to Grese and whispered in her ear.

"Okay, if you insist, Arthur," she replied testily.

Gruber approached Kaminski, and they talked for a minute until the barracks elder beckoned Lisowski over. Gruber handed the clipboard to the block manager. "You two, check these numbers. There's going to be a small selection this morning. We need twenty Jews. I'll do the selecting."

At the mention of the word *selection,* a murmur arose from the women prisoners, which was barely quashed by the threats of the blue stripes.

The SS-Rapportführer walked along the first line of prisoners, farthest away from Rachael's. Occasionally, he would pause and scrutinize the person standing before him and ask them questions. When he reached the end, he spoke. "These can all go to their work groups."

A tall kapo with a white armband and red triangle stitched on his jacket stepped forward and, accompanied by three blue stripes, led the line of women away through the gate and onto Lagerstrasse, where hundreds of men from B2 camp were congregating.

Lisowski passed the clipboard to Gruber, who signed the top sheet, returned the board, and continued to the next line. He stopped several meters along. A woman with short, black hair was standing with her head bowed. Due to the slope of the roll call square, the woman was visible to Rachael. Her body was rocking back and forth. She probably did not even realize she was moving, Rachael thought. The prisoner directly behind her had placed her hand on her back to steady her. The roll call leader spotted this and shook his head solemnly.

"This one!" Gruber shouted.

Kaminski strode over and hauled the woman out of the line.

"Take her to Grese," the SS man added before continuing the selection.

The black-haired woman was barely conscious and offered no reaction to being dragged roughly through the mud. When the block elder reached Grese, he released the prisoner, who fell straight to the ground.

"Is she dead or alive?" she asked.

"Alive," he answered. "Just."

The German shepherd barked ferociously at the woman on the ground, wildly pulling its leash and forcing its owner to dig her heels into the mud to avoid slipping.

"Wolf's so frisky today." Grese smirked. "Although I haven't fed him." She watched the prisoners as she spoke. A small number were returning her gaze, but most looked straight ahead.

"Sometimes I think he's just too strong for me!" She unfurled her fingertips and allowed the leash to slip through her hands. The dog felt the tension in the leash slacken and leaped forward. Rachael looked away in horror, but she could not block out the sound of terrified screaming.

Gruber was unmoved and continued to stroll along the lines. From time to time, he summoned Kaminski, who would remove a prisoner from the line. Each one left with a blank expression and in silent resignation. Every sheet the roll call leader signed, he moved a row closer to Rachael. She hoped he would select twenty women well before reaching her. The sight of the bodies, the sounds of the screams, and the snarling dog petrified her. She just wanted this uncertainty of death to leave.

Rachael had counted the selections one by one. By the time the roll call leader reached the new arrivals, nineteen women had been dragged away.

Rachael could scarcely believe they were being subjected to a second selection in less than a day and hoped the new arrivals would withstand scrutiny. Even after the deprivations of the cattle car journey, they would surely be healthier than the prisoners who had endured the conditions in Auschwitz.

Gruber sauntered along Rachael's row…and did not select anybody.

"Irma, I'm one short," Gruber said. "I've only got nineteen. Perhaps you'd like to help me select the last one?"

"My pleasure," the SS-Oberaufseherin replied.

Rachael stood as upright as she could and looked straight ahead, but she grew aware of Grese's presence beside her. The SS woman was whipping her leather boots, steady as a drumbeat. The dog grizzled in the background.

"Your hair's deep red," Grese whispered in her ear. Rachael felt the warm breath of the blond woman on her ice-cold skin. "Even after those clumsy barbers have done their work, what's left is very striking. I imagine it's very attractive when fully grown and styled." She paused. "And now it's going to end up as a wig for some old hag in Berlin!" She laughed and walked on.

Grese returned several minutes later and stood with Gruber, Kaminski, and Lisowski.

"Well, which do you want?" the roll call leader asked.

"I think I'll take the redhead," Grese replied.

"What's her number?" Gruber asked Lisowski, who scurried over to Rachael, read her tattoo, and scurried back.

A feeling of unimaginable terror overcame Rachael. When she had been a member of the Dutch Resistance, she had thought herself young and resourceful, but the humming of the barbed wire, the snarling of the dog, and the sticks of the blue stripes made thoughts of escape impossible.

She looked around helplessly. Having promised to find and protect Hannes, she was going to fail him after less than twenty-four hours in Auschwitz.

"Number 57619," Lisowski announced.

Gruber held the clipboard up and scanned the sheets. He shook his head slowly. "That's not so easy," he said. "It says here she's fluent in German and she's to be employed in Kanada. In the administration department. Look! It's in writing." He held the clipboard up to prove his point.

"But I want the redhead!" Grese insisted.

"SS-Oberaufseherin Grese!" Gruber said. "They're two short in Kanada, and they'll be expecting this Jew as a replacement. I'm not willing to take the risk of doing otherwise. Not even for you."

"SS-Rapportführer Gruber," she replied in an insolent tone. "You could report that she died during the night..."

"Just take somebody else! It makes no difference," he replied.

"Very well," Grese waved her hand nonchalantly in the air. "Take the next one in line."

Lisowski, like a busy mouse, hurried back to the line and returned with the next prisoner's number. The SS-Rapportführer checked the sheets and nodded. "Okay, take her." He then signed the document.

Gruber turned to Kaminski. "Okay, the roll call and selections are signed off. Take the new arrivals to their work groups. When you've done that, get rid of those bodies."

"Yes, sir!" Kaminski bowed, relieved the roll call had ended. Roll calls were challenging when Irma Grese attended and selections were required. He was not concerned about the distress caused to the prisoners, but the Oberaufseherin had cost him several blue stripes, and even a block manager had fallen victim to her. A good block manager who had been difficult to replace.

"Irma, will you escort the selected prisoners to Block 25?" Gruber asked.

"Of course!" Grese replied. "I'm sure Wolf will enjoy helping me out."

The twenty women who had been selected were huddled in a group near the barbed wire fence. Grese and the dog passed Rachael as she walked toward them.

"Well, that was a stroke of good fortune!" Grese said. "You're the lucky girl with red hair." She stopped and stared coldly at Rachael. "Luck does not last long in Auschwitz. Be warned. Block 25's not far away." She pointed over Rachael's shoulder toward the main camp entrance. "Never forget how close it is."

Rachael stared ahead, but her heart was pounding, and she could hardly breathe. This blond woman, who would have attracted admiring glances in any bar in Amsterdam and who looked young enough to be a recent school leaver, terrified her.

Rachael remained there, paralyzed by fear, until a kapo arrived to take her to Kanada.

CHAPTER SEVEN

December 1944

Whenever Rachael broached the subject of her brother's whereabouts, she was met with surprise and reticence. Surprise that a boy so young had been selected by the SS to stay in camp. Reticence because the women were unwilling to share the commonly held and most logical conclusion that Hannes might have survived the railway platform selection but would not have lived much longer. The SS would have picked him out within weeks, if not days, and sent him to the gas chamber.

Elke was the only prisoner to share Rachael's positive hope for his survival until it was proven otherwise. Elke nodded earnestly while Rachael explained how her brother had received a pedal bike for his seventh birthday in May 1940, and within six months, its saddle was being raised to accommodate his extraordinary growth.

"My father was so frustrated," the Dutch woman sighed. "He bought a bigger bike for Hannes's birthday in May 1942, and the following month, the Nazi-controlled government in the Netherlands confiscated all bikes owned by Jews. Hannes was devastated."

Rachael wiped her eyes. She had been separated from her brother for ten months during 1943 when he was in hiding in Vierhouten with their mother, only to be reunited on the railway platform of Camp Westerbork. The euphoria of their reunion lasted only a few traumatic days in a cattle car before they were ripped apart again in Birkenau. She realized she was clueless as to the whereabouts of her father, mother, and both brothers. Her whole family.

"Be strong!" Elke reassured her, seeing the tears welling in her eyes. "We must keep looking for Hannes. Giving up isn't an option."

"You're right!" Rachael replied, firmly wiping away the last of her tears.

CHAPTER EIGHT

December 1944

Ludwig Albin looked down, and his hands were shaking. This had never happened before. Having spent his whole life working on a farm, he possessed powerful hands with long, wiry fingers and wrinkled, callused skin. But these were hands that had developed because of physical toil, and today, they had been put to use on tasks that had been almost unbearable to watch, never mind take part in. And this was only his second day in Birkenau.

The train journey was long and arduous, lasting two days and nights. His hometown of Gorzov Wielkopolski in northwest Poland was only 500 km from Auschwitz, but the train had crawled along the tracks, stopping repeatedly for unknown reasons, and the doors to their cattle car remained shut throughout. It was nighttime when they arrived. The cattle car was cold, but they were packed so tightly together they drew a trace of warmth off each other.

When the wooden door slid open, their senses were assaulted. First, the freezing wind rushed in like a stinging slap to their faces. Harsh spotlights dazzled their eyes, which had grown accustomed to days of darkness. The sounds of men shouting and dogs barking pierced their ears. The last twenty-four hours on the train had passed in near silence. The songs and hymns that had lit up the first part of the journey had ceased long ago.

Ludwig stood several centimeters taller than most of the passengers and gained an immediate understanding of their surroundings. He wondered about the confusion suffered by those who could see nothing but the heads and shoulders of the surrounding people.

Ludwig watched the blue stripes thrashing any of his fellow Poles who lingered for longer than a moment before shepherding them into the lines that were forming ahead. It was not long before he reached the front and was motioned to approach an SS officer, who, head down, was recognizable by the distinctive silver skulled emblem on his brimmed cap, which intermittently glinted in the beams of the spot lamps. Ludwig had been watching him signaling to his left and right, and how the men had been harried into two separate groups.

The SS officer looked up only to see Ludwig's chin. He needed to crane his neck to take in the Pole's full height. Ludwig thought he saw the officer's eyebrows rise.

"Sonderkommando," the officer ordered to a nearby SS guard, pointing at Ludwig. "Take this one straight to the barracks. They're shorthanded up there, and if you take him now, he'll be there in time for the next shift at six."

Special work group? Ludwig asked himself. He had been born in Gorzov Wielkopolski, whose proximity to the German border meant there had been a strong trading history between the town and its neighbors. Ludwig's father had sold his livestock and produce in German towns and villages, which were more affluent than those in Poland, and his son had accompanied him frequently, gaining a basic grasp of the language along the way.

"Come!" the guard said, brandishing his gun.

The soldier was in his thirties, wore round spectacles with thick lenses, and looked ill at ease in his uniform. Ludwig thought he looked more like a middle-aged bank manager than a member of the infamous SS, which had struck terror into the hearts of the Polish population.

Ludwig was surprised to find himself the only person being led away, leaving the rest behind. The sights and sounds of the platform died away as the soldier and prisoner walked on into the darkness.

The two men had walked for fifteen minutes when the Birkenau camp came into view. Searchlights scanned the area from a line of watchtowers positioned behind the barbed wire fence. A blinding beam came to rest on the pair. The soldier waved his arms in acknowledgement, and the light moved on, like a finger stretching out across the landscape. The men continued.

As the searchlights traced circles across the camp, Ludwig caught glimpses of the barracks; long, low, dark buildings. He thought they looked like rows and rows of coffins laid out end to end across the earth.

The Pole dared not look back, but before the two men passed through the brick archway that formed the entrance to the camp, he did glance back. The railway platform was obscured by trees, and a featureless expanse of emptiness lay between the trees and the camp. SS spotlights darted frenetically across the horizon, and Ludwig imagined the confusion and fear of his compatriots. Sounds were muffled by the distance. Did he hear an engine misfiring? Or was it a gunshot?

Having entered the camp, the guards locked the gate behind the two men. A wide, open patch of land lay before them, stretching to the farthest end of the camp and flanked by barbed wire fencing. Small metal lamps were hung at regular intervals on concrete posts and cast a weak circular light on the ground.

"What's with the personal service?" a guard joked.

"They're desperate for men in C4, so I'm escorting this one now, and he'll be ready for the next shift," Ludwig's guard replied, then shouted, "Watch out!" Ludwig was not paying attention and had stumbled into the soldier.

The SS guard withdrew his baton in a flash and cracked the Pole across the arm. Ludwig did not flinch but pulled himself up to his full height to tower over the soldier. Ludwig was accustomed to people recoiling when his substantial frame loomed above them, so he was surprised that the soldier was completely unmoved and snickered in response.

"Fucking Pole!" the soldier scoffed. "If you weren't going into the Sonderkommando, I'd have put a bullet in your head right where you stand." His eyes bulged, exaggerated by the lenses in his spectacles. Even the timid bank manager can become an arrogant SS villain, Ludwig thought.

The soldier stopped by a gate on the right-hand side of the wide path. An SS soldier was on guard, and another looked down from a watchtower.

The two soldiers greeted one another cordially.

"Any chance of a cigarette, Klein?" the guard asked the bank manager. He was young, in his early twenties, with a pale, unhealthy appearance.

"Here, take a few!" SS-Schütze Klein replied, taking a packet from his pocket and handing it to his colleague. "It was an excellent day in Kanada today!" he added. "A few chunks of stale bread for three packets of cigarettes was a profitable deal for me!"

On the railway platform, the SS soldiers had been screaming and shouting, waving their guns and batons and terrifying the new arrivals. Yet these soldiers were standing around, casually puffing on cigarettes as if they were in a Berlin bar on New Year's Eve. Ludwig watched their smoke drifting into the night sky and yearned for a drag. It seemed like an age since his last cigarette.

A flash of light burst through the darkness in front of them. Ludwig squinted and made out the dense line of trees in the distance. There was another flash, and he saw the vivid orange flame.

"Fire!" Ludwig shouted, pointing.

The soldiers followed his gesture, and both laughed. It took them several moments to compose themselves.

"It's a fire, all right!" Klein mocked. "But not the sort of fire you're thinking of!"

"What is it?" Ludwig asked.

"As a newly recruited member of a Sonderkommando, you'll find out soon enough!" the guard replied.

Ludwig, encouraged that the SS man had at least responded to his question, drew the confidence to take advantage of this increased receptiveness.

"When will I see my family and friends again?" the Pole asked.

"Not for some time," the SS-Schütze replied. "The Sonderkommandos perform special work and aren't allowed any contact with other camp workers. You'll be housed in your own barracks, and with better living conditions."

"Of course," the young SS soldier said slyly, "as a member of the SK, you might see your family sooner than you think!"

"Careful, Schneider!" Klein said, suppressing laughter.

SS-Schütze Klein flicked his cigarette stub away. It sparked as it struck the ground before the SS soldier ground it fiercely under his boot.

"Let's get this one to the barracks," the guard concluded. "Then I can get some sleep before the shift change."

"Sure!" Schneider replied, opening the gate and allowing the two men to pass before locking it behind them.

Ludwig found himself on a much narrower path, a few meters wide and with fences on either side so close they seemed almost within his reach. He heard the buzzing of electricity coursing through the rows of barbed wire, and the barracks on the other side were no longer distant but a few strides away. The fence lamps cast their dirty yellow light to reveal ragged wooden barracks.

Soon, the SS guard turned left and hailed another SS soldier guarding an adjacent gate, who was also smoking a cigarette. There was a plentiful supply of cigarettes in Birkenau, Ludwig thought. They would be a valuable commodity.

During their passage, the bright orange flame continued to spark intermittently, occasionally disappearing behind the taller trees on the horizon, but each time the Pole looked up, the flames were drawing nearer.

Ludwig had hidden his wristwatch in a small pocket stitched under the waistband of his pants. So far, nobody had discovered it and demanded he give it up. He had furtively glanced at it just prior to climbing down from the train when it was three in the morning. Now, he guessed it was probably around four, and those chimneys were constantly billowing smoke. What was going on there?

Once inside Camp B2d, SS-Schütze Klein's attitude hardened.

"Get moving!" he growled.

There were two rows of wooden barracks in this camp, all of which were single story and without windows except for skylights built into their roofs. Apart from a gravel path, which ran between them, the ground comprised uneven, frozen mud, interspersed with the odd clump of grass.

Each barracks stood apart from its neighbor, except for the one they were approaching. Two brick walls, looking conspicuous among the other wooden structures, ran from one building to the next, creating an enclosed courtyard between them. The walls were eight feet high, with a solid wooden gate built into one.

Klain retrieved a set of keys from his pocket, opened the gate, and led Ludwig inside. With no windows and a solid gate, the courtyard was shut off from the camp beyond. One barracks was dark with no access to the courtyard, while light filtered through the skylights of the other and a wooden door was situated halfway along its side. Ludwig could see the efforts the SS had made to keep the SK separated from the rest of the camp.

The guard rapped on the barracks door with his fist. "Smizer!" he called. "Wake up, you lazy Jew! I've got that extra man for you."

Just as the SS soldier was about to strike again, the door was pushed slowly open to reveal a short, stout man wearing a blue-striped uniform under a substantial brown woolen coat. On his upper sleeve, there was a white armband with the word *kapo* stitched on it with black thread, and an inverted red triangle was attached to his coat.

"Sorry, sir," Smizer said. "Come in." The man spoke softly, without emotion. Ludwig wondered if this had been because of his sudden awakening.

Klein strode away, and Ludwig entered the SK barracks.

*

Ludwig bathed in the relative warmth inside the barracks. All he could remember was the biting cold. He clenched and unclenched his fists like a prizefighter, and the numbness in his fingers subsided.

"When did you last eat?" Smizer asked.

Before the prisoner could answer, Smizer continued. "There's some of my soup left. It's cold, but it's more than most'll get."

"What do you mean, 'more than the rest will get'?" Ludwig asked.

"Have your soup first," Smizer replied. "I'll tell you about Birkenau and the Sonderkommando when you're done."

Smizer led him to the opposite end of the building, passing between bunks on either side. The bunks were three high, a good proportion of which were occupied by two to three men. To Ludwig, they appeared to be sleeping soundly on straw mattresses and covered with rough but thick blankets.

A large metal tureen was sitting on a wooden table. Smizer carefully ladled several spoonfuls of liquid into a dented metal bowl and handed it to Ludwig.

"Eat quietly," the kapo whispered. "We don't want the clanging of metal to wake the block elder." He nodded at a closed door behind them and moved toward the center of the barracks.

There were three electric light bulbs hanging from the bare rafters. Ludwig looked down at the contents of his bowl, where obscure lumps were floating in a dark liquid.

The Pole raised the bowl to his lips and took a gulp. He was relieved. It was almost tasteless. The lumps were a sort of mushy vegetable. The liquid held some residual heat, and its tepid warmth filled his mouth, soothing his parched throat and coursing into his aching belly. He quickly gobbled the rest of the soup while the kapo watched.

"I'm the block manager," Smizer said. "It's my job to ensure the barracks are operating efficiently." He smiled wryly. "The SS does like its efficiency. I make sure the daily roll call's accurate and the buildings stay clean.

"My boss is the block elder, Birnbaum, who's currently snoring away in his room as we speak. He's a vicious bastard. Before the war, he was in prison for murder. The SS love to kill Jews, but they love it even more when a Jew like Birnbaum does it. Thank God we're in the SK where we've got some protection from people like him."

"Why's the SK so important?" Ludwig asked. "I've got no special skills."

"Those who are big and strong are assets in the SK," Smizer replied. "They perform the work well and last longer. Robust prisoners who don't think a lot are ideal."

"What does the SK actually do?" Ludwig asked.

"Did nobody explain it to you on the railway platform? About Birkenau?"

"No, I was brought straight here."

Smizer drew in a long breath. "How can I describe the indescribable? The SK teams work twenty-four hours a day, each on a twelve-hour shift. Your shift starts at six." The block manager held up his hands and grimaced like he had a bitter taste in his mouth. "Look! I suggest you try to get some kip. You'll discover soon enough what the SK does. That's far better than any description I can give. Find a space on a bunk. There should be spare blankets."

Smizer turned toward the rear of the barracks but was interrupted by Ludwig.

"Where's my family?" the Pole asked

Smizer desperately wanted to depart but, seeing the man's earnest expression, could not drag himself away. But no words came. His mouth bobbed open and closed silently like a fish. The block manager took a deep breath, bit his lip, looked directly at Ludwig, and slowly yet firmly shook his head.

CHAPTER NINE

December 1944

The sound of clanging metal woke Ludwig up. His mind had been in turmoil, and he thought he might never sleep again, but the stresses and strains of the previous days had finally overcome him.

The prisoners were already moving about by the time Ludwig swung his legs out of his bunk. No one remarked on his sudden appearance. A group of men exited the building with Smizer to return with three large metal tureens containing a dark liquid that looked remarkably similar to the one Ludwig had eaten earlier.

The prisoners started an orderly line close to Birnbaum's room. Some of them chatted quietly, but most stood silently waiting, metal bowls in their hands.

The door to the block elder's room swung open, and a man in his fifties walked out. In contrast to the block manager, Birnbaum was tall and lean. His eyelids were heavy, but his stare was piercing and made those he met feel uncomfortable.

The prisoners were hushed. Birnbaum looked around before addressing Smizer.

"No issues for roll call?" he shouted.

"None," Smizer replied, his voice trembling.

"Good," Birnbaum said. "Get them fed, through roll call, and into work. And quickly! There's an extra transport arriving today, and we can't fall behind." The block elder stepped back into his room, shutting the door firmly behind him.

The prisoners did not need Smizer to prompt them. Two prisoners briskly ladled the breakfast liquid into the waiting bowls, spilling it over the floor and the hands of the men, who licked it off their skin and drank their bowls dry in a few hurried gulps. A third man opened a large canvas bag and started throwing pieces of bread in all directions. The prisoners flung themselves at the food. Not one piece hit the floor before being caught, and the bag was emptied in seconds.

Ludwig was lost and confused and stood by as the others dashed around him. Smizer appeared at his side, holding out a bowl and a fistful of bread.

"Take this," Smizer said. "But be quick."

The block manager looked around and beckoned a prisoner to approach. "This is Ludwig Albin. Arrived on last night's Polish transport. He's the replacement you need."

Smizer turned to Ludwig. "This is Filip Toszka. He's the kapo for the C4 team. Do as he says and you'll probably be alive at the end of your shift. It's the best you can hope for." He paused. "It's the best any of us can hope for."

Toszka was not wearing a blue-striped uniform but dark-gray civilian clothes, which were ragged but presentable. He was of average build, and his clothes more or less fitted him.

His only concession to a uniform was a blue-striped hat. He had a round face and a nose that looked as if it had been broken several times, the result of having been a serious boxer in his youth.

"There's a latrine and washroom in the courtyard," Toszka remarked. "When the lines form up for roll call, stand behind me."

The sky was clear, and the sun had not yet risen when Ludwig stepped into the walled courtyard. Bitter cold banished the sluggishness brought about by his lack of sleep. The watchtower searchlights provided some light as they occasionally swept over the top of the wall.

A washroom and a latrine, both made of wood, had been built against the exterior wall of the barracks. Several of the prisoners were lining up to sit down in the latrines, but Ludwig's intake since arrival had been predominantly liquid and he could urinate without joining a line. The latrine stank but given the number of men in the barracks seemed relatively clean.

The water in the washroom was freezing, but it made Ludwig's skin tingle and energized him. He breathed in deeply, and his chest filled out. He left the washroom with a half-smile on his face. In contrast to the railway platform of the previous night, this courtyard was a tranquil and calming space.

"What the fuck are you smiling at?" a voice called out. "Are you simple or something?"

"Calm down, Paczula," Toszka interrupted, shooing a young man with scruffy blond hair away. "Ignore him," Toszka told his Polish compatriot. "He's extremely emotional. You can hardly blame him."

Toszka led Ludwig away from the washrooms to the other side of the courtyard, where there were no prisoners.

"They say the members of the SK teams enjoy the best living conditions of all the prisoners in Birkenau," the Crematorium 4 kapo said. "Better food, better hygiene, better beds, fewer beatings, fewer deaths. And it's true, we *do* have the best conditions in the entire camp. You're a big powerful guy and might think it's not so bad doing some hard labor and living here in Barracks 13." Toszka looked Ludwig in the eye. "But we pay a heavy price for these physical benefits.

"Today will be the worst day of your life," he continued. "I don't know your story, but I know I'll be right on this." Toszka rapped his knuckles against the wall. "That's why we're walled in. So nobody can be told what work we do twelve hours a day."

Toszka held up his hand to stop Ludwig from speaking. "Don't ask! The SK teams decided we'd never tell new arrivals what goes on there. None of us feel able. No dictionary contains the words that might adequately describe our work. The best way to find out is to experience it. It's the quickest, but most painful, way." He glanced at his watch. "And in sixty minutes, you'll know."

The prisoners lined up in eight rows of twenty-five, two for each kapo. Roll call was well organized, completed by Birnbaum and Smizer under the watchful eye of SS-Rapportführer Müller, the roll call supervisor. Everybody was present and correct, and the SS man signed off the paperwork before the four kapos led the men out of the courtyard in single file.

The prisoners made their way to the B2d exit and turned left, toward the chimneys. The men walked with their heads down, except for Ludwig, whose gaze was transfixed by the tops of the chimney stacks in front of them, flaming orange like sparring dragons.

As the SK men walked on, more rows of barracks stood in a compound to their left, protected by barbed wire fencing. Four watchtowers guarded this section of the camp.

Ludwig felt the air thickening as if he were walking through the thickest smog Warsaw could muster. He wiped his cheek and saw fine particles on the ends of his fingers. The smog thickened, and the constant burning stench grew stronger. It was awful and was deteriorating with every step.

"What the...?" Ludwig murmured. Looking around, the other men were trudging on, oblivious to their surroundings.

The two kapos and their teams approached a fenced area with a gate guarded by two SS soldiers. The camp was a labyrinth of barbed wire, Ludwig thought, and watchtowers were surveying the prisoners' every movement.

A section of fencing that lay before them had been covered with long strips of wicker, creating an impenetrable wall. The birch trees on the horizon grew directly inside the fence and were looming above them, almost completely obscuring the chimneys.

The SS soldiers opened the gate and allowed the prisoners to enter. Overhanging branches flanked the path ahead, which seemed to disappear into the distance like a train swallowed up in the blackness of a tunnel.

They reached the extremity of the woods, the ground opened out on either side of the path, and Ludwig saw the source of the flames, a single-story brick building with two chimneys protruding from its shallow sloping roof. There were four windows in its narrow gable end, but there were only three much smaller windows on its long side.

With the approaching dawn, Ludwig saw thick smoke billowing from both chimneys, which, instead of being carried away on the breeze, seemed to deposit its black dust straight down to the ground below, as if not even the smoke could escape from Birkenau.

This close, the flames were bright enough to make Ludwig recoil.

The Pole was overwhelmed, and it was a shove from the man behind that told him the men were moving on. Toszka was leading them toward this building while the other kapo was heading to the other side of the path. A mere hundred meters away was an identical building with two chimneys billowing smoke.

As the SK team approached, a group of prisoners streamed out of the building, the previous shift returning to the barracks. As the groups passed each other, Ludwig was close enough to see their faces, covered in black soot and drenched in sweat. They were traipsing, exhaustion etched into their features. One man fell to his knees but was immediately pulled back to his feet by three of his colleagues before the kapo or SS could respond.

My God! Ludwig thought. Will I look like that? He drew a crumb of comfort from the fact he was a farmer and would cope better than most with hard labor.

"Come on, hurry!" an SS guard shouted, his wooden baton crashing on the concrete yard beneath his feet. "The crematorium is unmanned! Get in there fast, you scum! You mustn't fall behind your quota! Or else!"

The fifty men of the Crematorium 4 SK team picked up pace and rounded the corner of the building, where sixteen of them darted through the first doorway. Ludwig felt a fleeting blast of stinging heat before the door closed. The rest of the men jogged up to the next door and entered a large room, painted light gray and empty save for rows of benches and clothes hooks, which ran around its perimeter. The words *Cleanliness is Healthiness* were roughly painted in black on the wall.

Crematoria 4 and 5 had been built with a design flaw. The undressing room where Ludwig was standing was in the middle section of the building with the gas chamber and incineration room on either side, meaning the SK team had to drag the dead across the length of the undressing room to reach the ovens. Not only did this involve extra unnecessary work, but new arrivals could not enter the undressing room until the bodies had been removed and the area washed down. The SS kept up the pretense that the Jews were entering a hygienic area.

Ludwig was pulled to one side by Toszka and handed a long strip of steel bent at one end into a U-shape like a shepherd's crook.

"Just do as the rest of us," Toszka said, following several men who had already picked up their crooks and were entering the room to the right. The rest of the men filed through two doorways on the left. The same searing heat roared out of the doors as they were opened, but this time, they were not closed. Some men stripped off their jackets and shirts as soon as they entered.

Ludwig was dumbstruck when he passed into the next room, which was filled with piles of naked bodies. He thought how undignified they looked until he realized the sheer scale of the horrific scene before him. Men, women, children, and babies were so tightly packed that many lay on top of each other. He thought of the cramped conditions he had suffered during transportation, but this room was much bigger than a railway car. There were hundreds of bodies strewn across the floor like discarded rag dolls.

Showerheads were positioned in rows across the ceiling, but they were bone dry. There were three wire mesh cages on each of the two outside walls, attached close to the roofline.

There was no sound except for the SK men moving among the bodies.

"Out of the way!" an SS guard shouted. "You're blocking the door!"

Ludwig stood back in horror as one of the SK team passed him, dragging a body along the floor with the metal crook hooked around its neck. The other SK men were doing the same thing. The emaciated faces of the victims, with sunken eyes and gaping mouths, made him shudder.

"You're a strapping lad," the SS man sneered. "You can do two at a time," he added, and with that placed another metal crook in Ludwig's hand. "Now get moving! The next train's going to be here anytime."

Ludwig stepped cautiously into the room, endeavoring not to tread on any of the dead, but it was impossible. There was not a single speck of floor not covered by at least one body.

"It's too late for them," Toszka said. "There's no benefit in losing your life by showing respect for the dead. You need to move bodies. A member of the SK's most at risk when he's new, and the SS have nothing to lose by killing him. Once you've learned the ropes, you'll be more difficult to replace and much safer."

Ludwig gently lifted the head of a man, his skinny neck fitting easily into the hook. The touch of cold, lifeless skin made him shiver. He performed the same maneuver on another man with his second crook, not able to bring himself to lay a hand on a woman or child.

The Pole allowed a prisoner to pass with his loaded crook, paused for a moment, gripped his crooks tightly and stepped forward. Feeling a slight resistance in one crook, he tugged, and it came free. He exited the gas chamber without looking back, following the others toward the heat.

CHAPTER TEN

December 1944

Ludwig did not know how he reached the end of his first shift in Crematorium 4. Twelve hours seemed like an eternity. The SK team had not spoken to each other except to pass on the barked orders of the SS soldiers and kapos. Their thirty minutes for lunch were spent sitting on the benches in the undressing room where he had first entered. With the gas chamber on one side and the incineration room on the other, conversation seemed futile, almost disrespectful. He felt too disgusted, too sullied to eat the bread and cheese they were given, but his stomach ached, and the surrounding men were devouring their food voraciously, so he succumbed. He ate hastily to assuage his hunger and his guilt.

Inwardly, he laughed at his naivety for having shouted "Fire" on first seeing the flaming chimneys. He should have known. In Poland, there had been rumors of extermination camps, but the Nazis had been so convincing with their stories of increasing numbers of Germans being sent to fight the Russians in the east and the resultant need for foreign labor to man their factories.

Even when they had arrived at the railway ramp surrounded by dazzling lights, barking dogs, and shouting SS soldiers and kapos, the Nazis had kept up the pretense, talking of disinfecting showers to kill lice infestations, of hot soup awaiting them, of the soul-enriching benefits of hard work, of looking after their belongings until the prisoners had been housed, and of providing trucks to ferry the tired and young into the camp. Ludwig had even heard an SS officer asking people to make sure they were carrying their passports because they would be required for camp registration later. He distinctly recalled watching people ferreting among their bags and cases to retrieve them.

But now he knew most of his fellow Poles had been taken directly to one of the four gas chambers and murdered immediately. No doubt, some of them had been lying in the adjacent room when he arrived for his shift at six o'clock that morning.

After less than twenty-four hours in the camp, Ludwig Albin had witnessed the Nazis' propaganda crumble like a child's sandcastle washed away by the incoming tide. How stupid had he been? How stupid had they all been?

*

Upon returning to Barracks 13, the men were given more soup and bread, and also a lump of cheese with a slice of fatty, gristly sausage. The heat in Crematorium 4 had been scorching, and his emotions were so scrambled that, despite the midwinter's night, Ludwig stood outside in the courtyard to eat his meal. A few of the others did the same. Some lit cigarettes, and for the first time since his arrival, Ludwig heard them conversing with one another. It was strangely peaceful in the courtyard of Barracks 13.

The brick walls isolated the SK teams from the rest of the camp, invisible to the rows upon rows of barracks that lay beyond, hemmed in by kilometers of barbed wire, and where thousands and thousands of desperate souls were working, resting, eating, starving, sleeping, awake, talking, contemplating, living, dying.

Ludwig growled. Some men looked at him but said nothing. This is a treacherous and temporary peace, he thought. It's certainly not a peace any other human being can know. The gaping mouths, the pale dead flesh, the cold vacant eyes, the children cradled in their mothers' arms. These were the repeated images he saw and felt in this hushed corner of the courtyard. It was as if he were watching a silent horror movie.

Ludwig had not been keen on reading, but his devout Catholic parents had told him about Dante's *Inferno*, so he was acquainted with the Nine Circles of Hell, each one more gruesome than the last. The terror experienced by the four hundred members of the four SK crematoria teams was equal to anything envisaged by Dante, and Ludwig could not escape the thought that this was not the final stage of hell at all but was the precursor to one or more levels that were even more appalling. What sin had they committed to deserve this?

The Pole bent forward and vomited. The precious food he had yearned for lay on the gravel, barely digested. He remained there, hands gripping his knees.

"It's okay," Toszka said, having seen his compatriot leave the barracks and followed him out. "This happens to us all on the first day. It'll pass. Or at least it'll become less unbearable."

Ludwig lay on his bed that evening with his eyes wide open. The barracks was warm with both brick heaters operational and a bucket of coke on hand to replenish the fire during the night. His straw mattress was primitive but provided enough padding to ease the hardness of the wooden bunk below. He had a gray blanket, which was clean but smelled of disinfectant.

All four hundred SK members lived in this barracks, but with two shifts, only two hundred were present at any point in time. Each bunk was a two-meter-square lattice of planks, which easily accommodated three prisoners without overcrowding. Ludwig located a bottom bunk and took his place without words being exchanged with the other two inhabitants. There was room enough to sleep on his side without unduly inconveniencing the others.

Ludwig could not sleep, no matter what. A farming life was simple and governed by repetitive routines. Thoughts and feelings he had never previously experienced bombarded him. They surged into his mind and departed without resolution before being immediately replaced. His eyes were wide open when the sound of metal dishes clanging heralded the start of a new day.

CHAPTER ELEVEN

December 1944

The thirty buildings in the Kanada facility were called "sheds" but were the same design as the wooden barracks elsewhere in Birkenau, with skylights providing the only source of natural light. The sheds were laid out in three rows of ten, separated by two graveled pathways named Storage Roads 1 and 2, which were wide enough for a truck to drive along.

Instead of bunks, each shed was furnished with two elongated wooden tables, behind which approximately thirty chairs were stationed. The workers in Kanada, who were almost all women, would sit there and carry out their various tasks.

Kanada was situated within the same cordon of barbed wire fencing as the Disinfection Facility. Beyond the wire to the north lay Crematorium 4, so close that Sheds 1 to 5 stood less than 100 meters away from the building and its chimneys. There was a small grove of trees to the south, which concealed the Crematorium 3 compound several hundred meters farther on. The medical camp, B2f, lay along the eastern edge of Kanada with the rest of the Birkenau camp beyond.

One of the SK teams would carry the prisoners' belongings on handcarts if they had come from the nearby crematoria. If the suitcases and bags came directly from the railway platform after selection, they were transported on the back of diesel trucks driven by SK workers.

The SS allocated specific activities to each shed. Rachael was amazed when SS-Unterscharführer Mann had first handed her the list of items to be collected, sorted, and reported. It included watches, rings, necklaces, brooches, gold, silver, diamonds, clothing, shoes, spectacles, hats, books, artificial limbs (living in Amsterdam, she had seen people wearing artificial limbs, but it had been infrequent; in Kanada, Shed 7 was half full of prosthetics, and it was continuously being replenished), alcohol, cigarettes, cigars, hair, hairbrushes, toothbrushes, toothpaste, false teeth, toupees, perfume, suitcases, food, weapons, ammunition, cash. Some categories were subdivided, such as cotton, wool, and silk garments. The list went on for several pages. Rachael paused at the word *hair*, recalling the image of her red locks lying on the floor of the shaving room in the Disinfection Facility.

The administration store, Shed 1, supervised the activities of the other twenty-nine sheds, and within a week of Rachael starting work there, she had seen every single item on Mann's list. She was chilled to discover hair had been removed not only from prisoners passing through the Disinfection Facility but from those killed in the gas chambers as well. In Shed 29, the women would sift and untangle the hair, then pack it into bales, which were sent to Germany.

Once, when Mann appeared to be in an amenable mood, Rachael asked him what conceivable use there could be for the hair, and he answered, "It's for the textile industry. They mix it with other materials to make cloth." Seeing the perturbed expression on her face, he shrugged. "Right now, Germans don't know or care what they're wearing, as long as it keeps them warm, and the original owners no longer need it. German industry's on its knees, and this is free of charge."

Only if you believe murder comes without a price, Rachael said to herself.

"And there's a lot of it," the SS man concluded.

There was a lot. A lot of everything. In some sheds, the belongings were stacked so high they almost reached the skylights, and there was no room to accommodate any worktables. In this wet and cold weather, the SS did not allow any belongings to be left outside, so the sheds were crammed, and the workers' shift quotas were increased.

The Shed 1 workers were provided with two tins: one for gold items and one for other valuables. Periodically, Mann walked alongside the tables carrying a large tin, into which he tippled the contents of the gold tins before returning to his office. He then weighed the gold and passed it to Rachael, who entered the details in the Kanada registers.

The shed supervisors, who were prisoners, worked well together and, after discussion with Rachael, identified the women who had the best aptitude for each task. When necessary, they helped each other, the faster women passing some of their completed work to the slower ones, but the stricter kapos would not allow this practice. It was left to Rachael, as the senior prisoner in Kanada, to amend the daily quota sheets in favor of the stragglers, so SS-Unterscharführer Mann remained oblivious to any individual underperformance.

Those prisoners who missed their daily quota would be beaten or removed from Kanada entirely, and Rachael knew the kapos might become suspicious if no action was taken against a slow worker. She tried to second guess the kapos by moving the worker to a different role in a different shed. The SS replaced the kapos frequently, which made it more difficult for them to identify a struggling worker, but Rachael knew cruel kapos could become sadistic and unreasonable in a split second, and she continuously worried about losing workers.

When reading, Mann wore a small pair of circular, metal-rimmed spectacles, which looked out of place on a man in his early twenties. In the neighboring Shed 2, a group of women was breaking spectacles into separate boxes of metal and glass. In front of them, spectacles lay waiting in piles three feet high that ran the whole length of the table.

Rachael could not reconcile the pair of spectacles perched on the SS officer's nose and the enormous quantity in Shed 2. She shuddered at the memory of her father, sitting in his favorite armchair, looking through the window at the Amsterdam streets below, twisting and turning his spectacles between his fingers as he pondered a clue from his daily crossword.

And her thoughts were led back to Hannes.

*

Rachael could not figure out SS-Unterscharführer Mann. The SS guards she had encountered so far were swiftly identified as either good or evil (most were evil). To her, a good SS guard had a low threshold to reach, that being someone who was not brutal to the prisoners, but Mann exhibited both extremes, behaving with emotionless cruelty one moment and showing compassion the next. This unpredictability made Rachael wary of him.

In Shed 1, Rachael's most important task was to record and summarize the valuables that were collected each day. Because Shed 1 housed items containing gold, silver and other precious metals, Mann's office and the rest of the Kanada administration function were based there as well. The SS officer would leave his office and walk alongside the tables, watching the women intently as they worked. The passengers in the cattle cars would often hide their valuables, and the seams and hems of clothing were popular locations. Each of the Shed 1 women was provided with a small thread cutter to open up garments, and their discoveries were dropped in their metal tins. Mann would stand at the far end of the shed, smiling whenever he heard the tinkle of a gold ring or silver chain dropping into a tin.

Rachael was distraught at the thought of people's hair being harvested off their bodies and converted into clothing material, but she realized the valuables were no different. Every ring could have been a gift from a man to his wife, every watch a present to a husband, every bracelet an expression of love. Now they were meaningless items, tossed into a metal tin, their unique personal histories extinguished forever. She recalled the dainty gold ring given to her by her mama, which had been disdainfully thrown into a basket in the Disinfection Facility.

*

Several weeks into her time in Kanada, Rachael's skills had been put to the test. Faced with several sheds being full to the rafters and inaccessible, she had recommended the reallocation of belongings between the sheds. By doing this, Kanada outputs were increased, and the surpluses were removed. The SS supervisors, kapos, and workers were saved a good deal of time needlessly moving items from one shed to another. Mann was pleased that the outputs were increased and, as a result, promoted Rachael to head of administration in Kanada. Apart from the SS and kapos, she became the most senior person working there. Based upon the way the SS-Unterscharführer treated her, Rachael suspected he thought her senior to the kapos, and she detected some respect, even trepidation in their behavior toward her.

Rachael's predecessor as head of administration had been a nervous woman who was regularly berated by Mann and the kapos for not maintaining accurate and up-to-date records. The woman was relieved when she was reassigned to Shed 12 and was unaware the Shed 1 kapo was in favor of killing her, and it was Mann who interceded on her behalf. Based upon Rachael's suggestion.

Rachael experienced no such nervousness with paperwork and organization. In reality, the change made little difference to her work. Her desk was closer to Mann's office, which meant he was always watching her, but he engaged in conversation with her more than the other women. They would mostly discuss Kanada matters, but he would also update her with camp news.

Her new role included responsibility for the handling of the gold, the most lucrative part of Kanada. Every piece of gold found had to be accounted for. Rings, bracelets, anything. If an item was not solely gold, such as a diamond ring, the women did not stand on ceremony, forcibly separating the precious metal and stone with a hammer. Shed 1 had a target to recover at least two kilos of gold per day; they needed to move swiftly on to the next garment.

Four times a day, Rachael had to complete the most gruesome task in Kanada. The senior SS soldier at each of the four crematoria would enter the shed, carrying a plain-looking sack no bigger than an average handbag, which made a tinkling sound when placed on the table. Every time, it made her shiver.

Prisoners removed their clothes and jewelry prior to entering the gas chambers. These were taken directly to Kanada and were the source of much of the gold processed there. However, there was one more source. When the gas chambers had completed their task, members of the SK team arrived carrying engineers' pliers. They checked inside the mouths of the dead, searching for gold teeth or fillings. Each time they discovered one, they removed it with the pliers. Newcomers to the role would attempt to remove the teeth respectfully, but after several beatings by the kapos, they understood speed was their sole aim. An inexperienced "dentist" who was rushing his work could be understandably clumsy, so when the SS soldier emptied the sack on Rachael's desk, she would be expecting a hideous sight. Lumps of gold were accompanied by teeth not fully separated from their gums, and even shards of jawbone were present.

There was no opportunity to wash the teeth near the crematoria, so they arrived in Kanada covered in flesh and blood.

The melting process required pure metal, so running water was installed in Shed 1. Rachael thought it ironic that the water supply to wash detritus off gold extracted from dead bodies was cleaner and more plentiful than that provided to the living beings in the camp.

The SS hierarchy did not trust the melting of the gold to those people responsible for the crematoria, so they chose SS-Unterscharführer Mann. To that end, a compact brick furnace was built in Shed 1, in a corner next to Mann's office. Each morning, several bags of coal appeared.

The oven was barely bigger than the one her mother owned at home in Amsterdam, so Rachael found it simple to operate. Once filled with coal and lit, it would take around forty-five minutes to reach its required temperature of 1,947°F, depending upon the ambient temperature. The ceramic crucible was the size of a large fist, and the molds produced ingots the size of a small bar of chocolate, weighing one kilo. The SS officer would watch her every move while working with the oven.

Mann told Rachael the gold ingot was the most valuable object in the whole Auschwitz network, and the camp commandant, SS-Obersturmbannführer Höss himself, was informed of the weight recorded every single day. Rachael was nervous whenever the ingots were weighed, as Mann would stand beside her to ensure they tallied with his records.

The gold ingots looked so pure and beautiful, glistening in the light, but seemed so inappropriate given where they had come from.

BOOK TWO

SPRING/SUMMER 1944
GÖTTERDÄMMERUNG

THE END OF DAYS

CHAPTER TWELVE

January 1944

During periods of wet weather, the two roads running between the Kanada sheds became quagmires. However, the SS strictly forbade any dirt from entering the sheds and sullying their contents. There were three latrines, which, compared to those in the main Birkenau camp, were palatial and clean. This made Kanada a coveted place to work.

There was a broad border of grass that ran between the outer sheds and the surrounding fence. The women were occasionally allowed outdoors for a break. They would gather on the southern side of the compound where they would sit in groups and chat, sing or dance, and, for a few precious moments, forget the world around them.

The women never ventured to the northern edge because it was so close to Crematorium 4. Each new worker soon learned about Crematorium 4, but it rarely formed the topic of conversation again. On the southern side, the chimneys were out of sight, and, if the prevailing wind was kind, the stench of the billowing smoke was diminished. If the prevailing wind was unkind, the women would cover their noses with their headscarves and watch the black spots appearing on their skin like a malignant disease. Some returned indoors, but the four crematoria were running for twenty-four hours on most days, and the prisoners became accustomed to the smell and smoke, and some ceased noticing it at all.

The gas chambers were designed to prevent the slightest escape of the fatal gas and also to seal sounds within, but on certain days, especially when the wind whipped across the Polish countryside, muffled noises were carried as far as the nearby sheds. An outsider might not have been able to identify these sounds, but the Kanada workers knew what they were. The desperate pounding of the walls was like tolling bells in a distant valley, accompanied by the strangled cries and screams of men, women, and babies as they clung to life. After a few minutes, there would be silence.

No matter how tightly the workers closed their eyes and covered their ears, the noise soaked into their every fiber, and when it finally stopped, the empty silence of the chambers haunted them.

Sometimes, one woman would start singing, unprompted, and the rest knew what she had heard and would join in. As long as they sang for at least twenty minutes, that would be enough, but they understood why they were singing, and no matter how beautiful the song was, it was tinged with a profound melancholy.

*

The heel of Rachael's left shoe had become detached during the morning, so she made an excuse to Mann that she needed to correct a discrepancy on the Shed 5 paperwork. As long as the weight of gold was reconciled, and there was a report on shed outputs on his desk every afternoon, the SS officer was satisfied.

He did not feel the need to supervise Rachael too closely. He regarded the Dutch people as an exceptionally reliable and even-tempered nation, not dissimilar to the Germans.

The Nazi occupiers in the Netherlands had not needed to install their own government, relying mostly on the existing Dutch civil service structures to do their work for them. Were they trustworthy? Mann would ask himself. A Dutch Jew was a conundrum: a trustworthy nation, an untrustworthy race. He chastised himself for indulging in this needless speculation. Everybody except the Nazi leadership knew Germany had lost the war, and his primary aim was to survive and get away with the little leather bag of gold trinkets that he had hidden—with Zuzana by his side.

Mann nodded his consent with a lack of concern, and Rachael left Shed 1.

The mud, stone, and water of the Kanada paths were frozen into an uneven expanse of brown ice. Rachael picked her way carefully past the sheds. A stumble or fall could cause an injury, and if that led to her absence from work, she could face selection at roll call. Grese would love that, she thought.

The freezing cold was marginally preferable to the warmer weather when the mud would become unbearable and dangerous. Churned up by thousands of feet and mixed with every conceivable source of dirt—rotten food, urine, blood, excrement, oil, glass—the mud looked like dark-brown sludge but was a toxic poison, finding its way into every crevice and recess of the human body and every corner of the camp. An open wound and the mud were a fatal combination. In the race to kill the Jews in Birkenau, infection and starvation ran the SS's extermination process a close second, with the freezing cold and overwork not far behind.

The layer of ice sealed the dirt and infection in, and the entire camp seemed cleaner. Rachael was lucky. She had shoes and a pair of socks and a jacket over her gray uniform, which shielded her from the freezing cold in the barracks at night, but many prisoners had no shoes, or shoes torn to shreds. Their uniforms were tattered, held together by short lengths of thread. Only the lucky few in Kanada and the SK team could keep the cold off.

Having no shoes in Birkenau could be a death sentence. The mud was teeming with bacteria, and the slightest cut from a sliver of glass or piece of wire could lead to a fatal infection. Once, Rachael had attempted to smuggle two pairs of shoes out of the sheds, but Mann had caught her.

"That's forbidden," the SS-Unterscharführer had warned. "It's stealing, and you know the punishment for stealing. I can't afford to lose you." He had looked around furtively and let her keep a pair. "You can take one, but they're only for your use. You understand?"

Rachael had nodded, then carried the shoes back to Barracks 19 and given them to a sick woman in the adjoining bunk who had none. When the woman died two days later, the shoes disappeared, but that did not deter Rachael from regularly smuggling blankets and shoes back to the women in her barracks; she just watched Mann more carefully when she did.

The shoes were stored in Shed 5, a short distance from Shed 1, the door of which was closed to keep the cold out. Inside, the women were working among piles and piles of shoes. The scene might have appeared chaotic at first glance, but each woman had a specific role to fulfill. Some were removing the laces, some were removing buckles, some were separating the leather, while others ceaselessly ferried items to and from the tables, like worker ants feeding a nest.

Rachael entered the shed. Closing the door behind her, she noticed the rise in temperature. Shed 5, like the other Kanada sheds, was well constructed to protect its contents from the elements. It was chilly inside, but the women were working vigorously and felt little or no discomfort.

The young Dutch woman approached Elke, who was the supervising prisoner. The shed kapo watched suspiciously but was fearful of harassing Rachael because she enjoyed the protection of SS-Unterscharführer Mann. He knew that Rachael and Elke were close friends, and the redhead had given him a handful of cigarettes on her way in. All things considered, he thought it best to leave the two Jewesses alone. There were plenty of other Jews to beat up.

Rachael held out the Kanada paperwork to her bunkmate as a pretense of legitimacy to the kapo.

"I need some new shoes," the Dutch woman said.

"Help yourself," Elke replied. "The best ones are in the pile on the left, as usual."

"Thank you," Rachael replied.

"You seem distracted," Elke said.

"Sorry?"

"Are you thinking of Hannes?" Elke recognized the taut expression on her friend's face.

"Yes, I can't get hold of anybody to help me find him."

Elke furrowed her brow. "Why don't you try the man under the tree?"

"Who?"

"Haven't you seen him? In the C4 compound, there's an SK worker who spends a few minutes sitting under a tree. He's been there every day this week. You can't see him from the storage roads, but he's easy to spot from behind the sheds."

"Can a member of the C4 SK really help me?" Rachael asked. "They're isolated in their own barracks and aren't allowed anywhere near the rest of us."

"Who knows?" Elke replied. "It's forbidden to steal belongings, but prisoners do it. The SK teams get to see the victims' belongings *before* we do. If anybody can get hold of enough valuable items to bribe an SS guard, it's a member of the SK. It's forbidden for them to have any contact with the rest of the camp, that's true, but does it happen? Of course it does."

"If I'm careful, nobody in Kanada will see me approaching the C4 fence," Rachael said. "I'll try anything to find Hannes."

Elke nodded.

Rachael made her way toward the shoes Elke had pointed out. From a distance, they looked like an unidentifiable, amorphous brown pile, but as she approached, they took on shape and color as if emerging from a thick fog. The odor of stale, sweaty leather made her wince. And then she was there, at the base of a mountain of shoes, stretching upward at an angle of forty-five degrees until it reached the height of the shed wall.

The young Dutch woman had visited Shed 5 frequently, but this was the first time she had contemplated this pile close up. Rachael considered the innumerable and incomprehensible number of shoes, crushed and lifeless. She was bewildered.

Practical shoes, Rachael reminded herself, bending down. Just find plain, practical shoes. But her mind wandered. She noticed a nondescript brown sandal that reminded her of her papa and days spent by the seaside with her family. The pain and longing for them all intensified.

A flash of red caught Rachael's eye, like a beacon against a blanketing dark sky. She picked up the shoe, open-toed and with a five-centimeter heel, and rubbed the dust off it. Despite its rough handling, its red leather was shiny and smooth. She remembered Meijer's shop on Raadhuisstraat in Amsterdam, with rows of elegant shoes displayed in its window, set against a pristine white linen background, and the pleasure of holding a shoe, the aroma of new leather and the way the shop lights glanced off its polished surface, showing off its vibrant and fresh color. She closed her eyes and saw herself before the war, in her red shoes, talking, laughing, and dancing with her college friends.

She almost smiled but stopped herself. Looking up, she realized every one of the thousands of shoes piled up there belonged to a person, a human being with a story, a story that had already ended.

Whichever way she looked in Birkenau, she could not prevent herself from being reminded of past times. Times which were long gone.

Rachael rubbed her eyes. She had better hurry, she thought, before the kapo lost his patience.

CHAPTER THIRTEEN

February 1944

Rachael's boots crunched through the frozen grass between Sheds 4 and 5. They were good boots, she thought. Almost new, clear of defects and the correct size. Sturdy and well insulated, they would provide solid service. Which was a bonus, given the weather. Of course, they did not match. Finding a matching pair of shoes among thousands upon thousands was an impossibility.

The midday sun took the edge off, but it was too cold to sit down, so Rachael leaned against the rear wall of Shed 5, invisible to the rest of Kanada.

Rachael took in the scene before her, including the two chimneys of Crematorium 4 and their deadly smoke, which she endured daily. An electrified barbed wire fence ran between Kanada and the crematorium, but no watchtower was located there. Anybody who breached this fence would still be within the perimeters of the Birkenau camp, and watchtowers were usually only positioned next to the outer fencing. The nearest watchtower was by the gate from the main camp into the sector containing Crematoria 4 and 5, which was obscured by the small grove of birch trees to Rachael's right. The only other watchtower was on her far left, on the western edge of the camp beyond Kanada and behind the Disinfection Facility and was hidden from her view by the first five sheds.

Crematorium 4 was to her left. It was longer than Crematoria 2 and 3, which they passed every day on the way to and from Barracks 19.

There was an open patch of grass running between Crematorium 4 and the trees, some thirty meters wide. Rachael slowly scanned the landscape. It did not take her long to notice him. The birch trees cast long, dense shadows, but rays of weak sunlight found their way through the canopy and enabled her to spot him, sitting against the trunk of a tree. His knees were drawn up to his chest, his hands on his knees, and his chin resting on his hands. He was motionless.

While supervising in the school playground, Rachael had learned how to whistle forcefully. A shrill, loud whistle was an effective way to catch the pupils' attention. She placed her fingers in her mouth and blew. The man did not move at first, but she gradually increased the power of her call until he raised his head and looked over. Rachael raised her arm, and the man reciprocated. She waved, and he waved back.

When the Kanada camp, C4, and C5 had been constructed, there had been a solitary birch tree standing several meters away from the edge of the woods. Running the concrete fence posts in a straight line left this one tree stranded just inside the Kanada side of the fence. The builders were running to a tight schedule and left it there. The fence was in the line of sight of one watchtower, but Rachael realized that if she could reach the tree undetected, then she would be hidden by the tree's trunk.

At night, it would have been easier. She could judge her movements based upon the searchlights passing the Kanada sheds. From this distance, and in the daytime, it was impossible to know whether the guard in the tower was watching. The watchtower was a considerable distance away, while the tree was just a few meters away. She resolved to take the chance.

Rachael ran toward the tree, but she did not reckon on her new shoes, one of which had a reinforced sole that protruded like a lip. On her second or third stride, the lip clipped her other shoe and sent her sprawling. The distance to the tree was so short that when she came to a halt, she was looking at its gnarled roots.

She lay there for a moment to compose herself. In the background, she was conscious of a noise, like a fly buzzing around her head. The fingertips of her outstretched arm scratched against something hard and coarse, a concrete fencepost. A few centimeters above her hand was a circular white porcelain insulator supporting the throbbing, humming electrified wire. She had seen what the electricity could do to a prisoner.

Rachael carefully removed her hand from the fence post, stood up with her back against the tree, and breathed in deeply.

"Are you okay?" Ludwig said.

Although his words were spoken softly, Rachael was in shock, and he startled her.

"I'm sorry," he continued. "I didn't mean to alarm you." He was standing at the edge of the trees, meters away but secluded from the watchtower. "I thought for a moment you were going to throw yourself into the fence."

"What?" Rachael exclaimed.

"I'm sorry. I didn't mean anything by it. It's just that there's so many people who've nothing left to live for, and they think the only option's going to the fence."

"No!" she said adamantly. "I must find my brother."

"Ah, you see!" he said. "You *do* have a reason to live!"

"And do you have a reason to live?" she asked. The stranger looked big and strong, and his resolute voice reassured her.

"When I started working in C4, I didn't," he replied. "But I had an experience that gave me a reason to live."

"That sounds cryptic," she said.

"Anyway," he said, changing the subject. "My name's Ludwig. And yours?"

"And I'm Rachael," she said, looking at him closely. Standing on the edge of the tree line, he was mainly in shadow, but rays of sunlight found their way through the foliage and illuminated his face. His features were gaunt, which was normal for a prisoner in Birkenau, but he did not appear to be in the same desperate condition as many others. Although his skin was black with dirt, Rachael noticed his eyes were wide and energetic.

The two of them watched each other.

"What brings you to the fence?" Ludwig asked. "I hear Kanada's the land of milk and honey."

"Working in Kanada's fine," she replied. "It's much better than most jobs in Birkenau." She felt the muscles in her belly tighten, trying to suppress the feelings rising within her. "It's my brother!" she blurted out. "I can't find him! We were separated on arrival."

Ludwig's eyes narrowed and softened. "If he was selected on the ramp—"

"No, he wasn't selected on the ramp!" Rachael interrupted. "He came into the camp with me, and we were split up in the Disinfection Facility."

"Okay, so your brother's probably in the men's camp," Ludwig said. There was an assurance in his voice, which gave her cause for some optimism.

"I can guess what brings you here," Rachael said solemnly. "It must be hell in there."

"It's worse than hell," Ludwig answered. "I'd always thought hell was where men suffer unimaginable tortures, but here, we're forced to inflict those tortures as well as suffer them. The scale of the horror's beyond comprehension. We've become emotionless, inhuman creatures. Our bellies are empty, and so are our souls."

Rachael waited. She needed to ask for help but did not wish to pressurize him. He pre-empted her words.

"Strictly speaking, we're not allowed out of our barracks," Ludwig said. "But the SS guards are always interested in smuggled valuables, and a few SK guys have bribed their way into the men's camp for a few hours. I can try to find out if your brother's there."

"Thank you so much!" Rachael exclaimed. "I'll be eternally grateful!"

"Maybe not eternally," Ludwig replied. "We're already too close to eternity in Birkenau."

"I'd best get back to work before I'm missed," he added, rising to his feet.

"You never told me your reason to live," Rachael said.

"That's a story for another day," he replied. "Perhaps we'll talk again?"

"I hope so." She smiled. "You might have news of my brother."

Rachael watched Ludwig skirt around the edge of the trees before walking briskly toward Crematorium 4 and disappearing behind the far wall.

She ran to the rear of Shed 5 and made her way back to the administration shed in time to melt down the day's gold.

*

The following day, Rachael departed Shed 1 at the usual time to carry out her paperwork checks. As she walked down Storage Road 1, her gaze was fixed on the gaps between the sheds, to the Crematorium 4 compound beyond.

As she passed Shed 4, she slowed, turned, and walked between the two sheds. She was pleased when she spotted a shape among the trees. A few minutes later, she was standing behind the birch tree beside the fence, with Ludwig at the edge of the trees.

"It didn't take long for you to come back!" Ludwig said, smiling weakly.

"I'd forgotten to..." Rachael said.

"...to tell me what your brother's called?" Ludwig finished her sentence for her.

"Yes, good guess!" she replied, embarrassed. "His name's Hannes Kisch. He'll know very little German, perhaps a few words. With any luck, Dutch people will be sheltering him."

"And how old?" he asked.

"Well, he's ten years old," Rachael continued. "Tall for his age."

"He's a lucky boy," he said.

"Why?" she asked.

"The SS follow strict age criteria for selection. All children below the age of sixteen are supposed to be selected for immediate gassing. A tall ten-year-old, even one who looks like a good worker, is lucky to survive the platform. Let's hope his luck lasts."

Rachael gulped hard, watching the trails of black smoke drifting above their heads.

"Don't rely too much on Lady Luck." Ludwig said. "In Birkenau, it's safer to expect the worst and leave a crumb of hope tucked away in a dark corner, just in case." He held his hands together and fidgeted. "I don't want to seem pessimistic. I'm just being realistic."

Rachael ignored his words. "He's got blond hair, 'though I guess it's been shaved off now. Oh, and he's got a small scar on his cheek, about the size of a penny and in the shape of a crescent moon...from when he fell off his bike." She racked her brains to think of any other distinguishing features her brother had, but however hard she tried, she could not bring him more clearly to mind. She blinked back her tears, realizing the image of her brother in her mind was already fading.

"I think you're right," Ludwig said. "The best way to find Hannes will be to find the Dutch prisoners. So I'll start there."

As Rachael made her way back to Shed 1, her mood lifted. For the first time since she had been separated from her brother, she believed she was making progress in finding him. Thanks to the man in the trees.

CHAPTER FOURTEEN

March 1944

For a couple of months, Rachael had felt almost clean. The Birkenau mud and feces had been sealed in a smell-free, dirt-free layer of ice. Even the latrines, the primary source of the foul smell in Birkenau, were becalmed. In the camp, the number of hygiene-related deaths decreased while those related to the bitter cold increased.

The brown sludge continued to ooze like volcanic lava, creeping inexorably along the roads and paths.

The women's camp became a quagmire, just like the rest of Birkenau, swimming in a sea of mud and excrement. The women desperately tried to prevent it from entering Barracks 19, but it was futile.

Rachael thought herself privileged. Working in Kanada meant she enjoyed the regular replacement of damaged or worn-out clothing, and the washrooms and latrines were far cleaner. Fresh cool water was always running through the faucets, unlike those serving the barracks, which spat out a few rancid drops from time to time. The women working in Kanada never washed or did their business in the camp unless they had to.

The prisoners knew these favorable conditions were certainly not because of the kindheartedness of the SS hierarchy. The products of the women's efforts were sent to Germany, and the SS wanted to make sure not a trace of dirt would find its way into Kanada and out of the camp.

Rachael was walking along Storage Road 2, which was quieter than Road 1 and where no trucks or handcarts were in sight. Several sheds were so full the workers' tables would not fit inside. These sheds contained items of a lesser value, which were left unattended so the women could devote their time to those of greater worth.

Once a week, Rachael inspected all the sheds, her task being to check their outputs and assess the number of workers required for the following week. If the number of transports was lower, and some women could be released, she would set them working to process the lower value belongings, but the reverse was happening. Since the turn of the year, the number of trains had surged, so twenty trucks were unloading in Kanada each day, rather than ten. Rachael learned from Mann that ten trucks of belongings equated to approximately 1,500 prisoners.

Any further increases would bring the risk of having to leave belongings outside. The Nazis did not want their goods being spoiled by the rain and mud. Rachael did not want any women working outdoors where they would be exposed to greater risks of illness and disease. She thought if she could just hold off for a few weeks more, the weather would become drier and warmer, the women could safely work outdoors, and the SS would be satisfied.

Rachael was nearing the end of her inspections when she noticed the door to Shed 28 was slightly ajar. That shed was full and should have been shut. It contained empty suitcases, which took up a disproportionate amount of room because they could not be stacked efficiently and were waiting to be broken down so the flat leather pieces could be sent away. Although the women could break them down, Rachael thought their manual dexterity was better suited for working with clothes and valuables. She was keen to create some space in this shed and had suggested to Mann they could be rapidly crushed flat by a truck. He had insisted that no trucks were available while reminding her all goods were to be stored indoors.

Rachael squeezed past the door without touching it and silently entered Shed 28. She was on her guard, but there was nothing worth stealing there, and the likelihood was that a worker was taking a furtive nap or had already departed, inadvertently leaving the door open behind them.

The SK men who had been driving the trucks had delivered the suitcases and thrown them haphazardly into the shed. At Rachael's behest, Mann had asked the drivers to leave a space in the middle of the building to allow the women to set up their worktables. What they left was hardly a space, more a thin zigzagging gap meandering through the shed with cases intermittently barricading the way.

Rachael wondered if she should ask Mann to call the SK back to rectify their shoddy work. She was sure the SS man would do it, but he would regard it as a favor she owed him, and the SK truck drivers would know it was she who had made the complaint and would probably make life difficult for her. She could cope with that, but she could not predict the SS's response. The SS could beat, or even kill, an SK driver who made a mistake. This she could not countenance.

As she stood before the mountain of suitcases, she decided to select a team of women to clear the suitcases and make space for some worktables. Even if it took longer than the SK drivers, there would be no repercussions.

Rachael's thoughts were interrupted by a noise. It sounded like a cough. She tensed, staring into the gloomy shed. Nothing moved, and silence resumed. The noise was repeated, only louder. Definitely a cough, she told herself, and coming from within the mounds of suitcases.

Warily, she walked forward, following the narrow gap between the cases. She had progressed twenty paces when the path before her widened into a small clearing where the suitcases had been moved aside.

The Dutch woman leaned forward to listen, but accidentally brushed against the wall of suitcases, making one fall to the floor with a hollow thud. A rustling noise emanated from the gloom. The cases around that side of the clearing were stacked head high. She stood on her tiptoes and peered over.

The weak sun shining through the skylights was subdued by the dark walls of luggage surrounding her. Despite this, she could make out the shapes of two people on the floor. She strained her eyes and caught sight of a man tucking in his white shirt and pulling his braces over his shoulders.

"SS-Unterscharführer Mann!" Rachael exclaimed before quickly adding, "Sir."

The SS officer was on his knees, his hands fumbling frantically at his shirt, his trousers, and his braces seemingly at the same time.

Rachael withdrew from the wall of suitcases. Her initial sense of acute embarrassment at this comical scene was supplanted by one of fear. Under no circumstances were members of the SS permitted to fraternize with the women prisoners, especially Jewesses. This could cost Mann his job, and it could cost Rachael her job, or her life. She had seen it happen all too often in Birkenau; the cowering Jew on the ground, the bullet in the back of the neck delivered by an SS officer, and the problem went away. No trial, no discussions.

Rachael contemplated running out but was sure Mann had recognized her voice, German delivered with a Dutch accent.

She remained standing in the clearing, head bowed. She heard his boots as he approached. He walked past her without breaking his stride, leaving a pungent whiff of men's cologne in the air. When the shed door slammed shut, she raised her head.

"Rachael?" the woman asked. "Are you all right?"

"I'm, I'm not sure," the Dutch woman replied. Fear was in her voice.

"It's okay," the voice continued. "He's infatuated with me. You and I are safe." The voice sounded youthful and remarkably calm.

"Zuzana?" Rachael asked, recognizing the voice of Zuzana Kováčová who worked in Shed 3, another clothing shed. She was a pretty Czech girl with curly dark hair, who, when smiling, displayed straight white teeth and prominent, round cheekbones. Rachael understood how Mann might be attracted to Zuzana, but she was a young woman and could not imagine the risks she was taking. She might incur the wrath of her fellow prisoners as well as their SS oppressors. Those who had relationships with SS officials were regarded as traitors by the prisoners.

Rachael saw no benefit in a relationship between an SS officer and a prisoner, except for the two individuals involved. She was worried by Zuzana's apparent devil-may-care attitude because, if the authorities found out, Mann's support might not save her. He might even turn on her.

In Kanada, the rules in place elsewhere in the camp were not enforced strictly. Once indoors, the women were permitted to remove their headscarves and to exchange damaged and dirty clothes for better ones. When Zuzana appeared, her hair was hanging loosely over her shoulders. She looked like a regular young Czech woman during peacetime.

Zuzana's smile slipped when she saw the stern look on Rachael's face, and she quickened her pace as she departed. Rachael waited. She did not want them to be seen leaving at the same time. She picked up some cases and threw them around until both of the clearings had been covered.

As Rachael closed the shed door behind her, she wished she had never found it open.

CHAPTER FIFTEEN

March 1944

During the following weeks, Rachael and Ludwig met with increasing frequency until the point where, unless there were exceptional circumstances, they met daily. They could not avoid discussing camp matters. Birkenau was all-consuming, but they sought to take their minds off the daily horrors they continually faced by sharing their life stories.

Their early lives had been quite different, with neither a country of birth nor a social background in common. Rachael had enjoyed a middle-class upbringing in a respectable part of Amsterdam. Her father was a university professor, and she had followed him into academia before qualifying as a schoolteacher. Having been born on a farm, Ludwig's upbringing had been very different. He enjoyed the outdoors and found the classroom environment claustrophobic. His parents encouraged him to develop the basic skills of mathematics and language but were content when he expressed a preference for working on the farm—a decision none of them ever regretted.

Their lives converged when the Nazis appeared in their respective homelands. The Nazis may well have adopted different methodologies in the Netherlands compared to Poland, but the systematic and increasing persecution of the Jewish population was common to both.

From listening to Ludwig, it was apparent to Rachael that the Poles knew the true intentions of the Nazis much earlier than the Dutch. In Amsterdam, the populace had been duped by lies and propaganda, which the Jewish Council had believed and unwittingly supported. The cattle cars leaving Camp Westerbork destined for Auschwitz were full of people expecting a hard labor camp and without the slightest inkling of its real purpose. She had believed the Nazis were cruel but never guessed the extent of their barbarity and inhumanity. She shuddered at the thought of it, but Germany lay between the Netherlands and Poland, and the Nazis were able to dispel the rumors about Auschwitz before they arrived in her country. Auschwitz was actually in Poland, where the rumors were never fully suppressed. Unlike the Dutch, many Poles traveled in their cattle cars fully aware of the fate awaiting them.

Ludwig could not help but admire Rachael for her participation in Dutch resistance activities. Not only was she tremendously brave, but the tasks she had undertaken would have been completely alien to any man or woman from an academic background, but she did them anyway. The stories of her courage and persistence made him feel stronger and more confident in himself.

"Do you think you can get hold of a pencil and some paper?" Ludwig asked Rachael part way through one of their conversations.

"We find plenty," Rachael replied. "They're low down on the SS's list of valuable items, but they're high on their forbidden list because they're terrified of any written record of this place surviving the war. Paper's also in high demand among the prisoners."

"Why would the prisoners need writing paper?" he asked.

"You know!" she answered, raising her eyebrows. "Toilet paper!"

"Of course!" he replied. "There's never toilet paper so the prisoners will use anything as a substitute. Pages from books or magazines or newspapers. Last week, I saw a prisoner using a banknote! Somebody somewhere has saved that money, and now it's only use is to wipe backsides. How could that happen?"

Neither of them spoke.

"I know it's a risk for you," Ludwig said finally, "but I'd be thankful if you could try to find paper and pencils.

"And a thermos," he added suddenly. "Preferably two or three."

"Thermos?" she asked.

"There are a few of us in the SK who want the pencils and paper to write our testimonies about life in the Birkenau SK," he replied. "When we've finished, we're going to bury them in the grounds of the crematoria.

It's not worth trying to smuggle them out of the camp with potential escapees because they invariably get caught and killed, so the notes would go nowhere. We'll bury them here and pray somebody chances upon them after the war. If we've got three thermos flasks to keep our testimonies dry, hopefully at least one will survive."

Rachael thought for a moment. Shed 10 contained a wide variety of effects, including children's toys. Most of the women shied away from working there. The sight of discarded toys and contemplating the fate of their owners were simply too much to bear. Rachael would never send young mothers to Shed 10, choosing those without children instead. Even in the absence of bodies, death was an ever-present specter in Kanada.

Parents would often bring paper, pens, and crayons for their children to play with, and these usually ended up in Shed 10. Rachael felt sure she could get hold of the items, but that shed lay at the end of Storage Road 1, which was the busiest part of Kanada so would carry some risk for her.

"Okay," she replied. "Leave it with me."

Ludwig was impressed by the confidence in her voice.

"It's essential we provide eyewitness testimonies," Rachael said.

"I must. I must," he said. His voice trembled and a single tear rolled down his cheek.

"Do you want to talk about it?" she asked.

Ludwig took a step forward. Rachael worried he might be seen by the distant watchtower. He was unsteady on his feet, so he sat down. She reciprocated. They were a few feet from each other, separated by the fence.

Rachael and Ludwig had never struggled for topics of conversation, but an awkward silence fell between them. She would wait as long as it needed for him to speak.

The constant throbbing of the electric current coursing through the barbed wire was the only sound. It was mesmeric, like a soft whisper, "Touch me, touch me," it seemed to plead. Having seen prisoners dying gruesomely against the wire, Rachael still felt a strange attraction, an impulse to reach out. Just the merest caress and it would be over. The torment would end, but not for Rachael. She was looking for her brother.

Finally, Ludwig spoke. "This will be a terrible story about working in C4. It'll give you nightmares. The same nightmares I've been getting."

"I'm happy to share your nightmares," Rachael replied. "In Birkenau, one nightmare simply replaces another."

"Okay." Ludwig took a deep breath. "You know that, from the beginning, my work has involved dealing with dead people. Taking bodies out of the chamber after they've been gassed. Dragging them into the incinerator room. Loading them three at a time onto metal trolleys and feeding them into the ovens. Then shoveling the ash into pits. If the pits are full, we spade the ashes onto the back of a truck. The SS force us to sit in the back of the truck among the ashes until we pull over, get out, and dump them in the River Vistula. Thousands and thousands of people become a sprinkling of dust carried away by the current, but they're dead, and their suffering has ceased. I've become numb and emotionless in the face of death, and the work in C4 is somehow endurable.

"A few weeks ago, not long before we first met, they were short-staffed in the undressing room. Of course, it had to be a member of the SK who filled in. An SS guard pointed at me, and Toszka had to send me straight away. I had no time to think."

"You've kept this pent up inside for weeks?" Rachael interrupted.

"Yes," he murmured. "I didn't want to upset you.

"It was calm when I entered the undressing room," he continued. "SS guards and kapos were milling around, giving instructions. They were almost polite to the prisoners—'hang your clothes on the hooks,' 'remember your hook number for collection of your belongings later,' 'remove all jewelry, it will get soaked in the shower,' 'mothers, please help your children undress quickly,' 'everybody must take a disinfecting shower to prevent diseases spreading in the camp,' 'you'll feel much better after a good shower, and there'll be a cup of soup waiting for you afterward,' 'after a good night's sleep, you'll be ready for labor in the morning,' 'anybody feeling unwell after the shower, we'll take them to the Red Cross van for treatment,'—an SS guard drives a white van with a red cross on its side and parks outside the entrance to the undressing room before the prisoners arrive.

"I watched all this, knowing what was actually going to happen."

Blinking back tears, Ludwig saw Rachael watching him intensely.

"People were nervous, of course! But most...most of them had no idea what was about to happen. They just walked into the gas chamber. They took up places under the metal showerheads. Some were talking with their neighbors. Mothers were placating their children.

"Suddenly, the atmosphere changed. The SS guards moved closer and, brandishing their rifles, shouted for the remaining people to hurry inside. The SK men began pulling the clothes off those they thought were dawdling and, instead of cajoling, harshly shoved the remaining prisoners toward the chamber door.

"'You!' an SS officer shouted. 'They're loitering around the doorway. Go inside and get them moving!' His rifle was pointed at me.

"I followed an SK man inside. Without speaking, he manhandled the occupants farther into the shower room.

"I couldn't bear to look the prisoners in the eye. I kept my head down and swung my arms to encourage them to move. If they wouldn't budge, I'd brush my arm against them. Luckily, this was enough. They seemed to realize resistance was futile and moved farther inside.

"'Undressing team, exit shower!' the SS guard shouted. 'If you don't get out, you'll be locked in!'

"I was confused and couldn't move. I didn't want to move. At that moment, I thought it would be better to die there and then with my fellow Jews. How could I reconcile leaving them to their fate and walking out to survive? These defenseless, naked people. Men, women, and children. Minutes away from death. And me, a bystander at best. An accomplice, at worst.

"'You must get out of here!' I heard the voice of a young woman. I lifted my head and felt shame at seeing her naked body.

"The woman looked about twenty years old with short, light-brown hair and a pretty, but serious, face.

"'I know we're going to die,' she whispered, her breath close enough to warm my skin.

"'It's just a shower,' I said in my head, but no words escaped my lips.

"'I can stay,' I stammered. 'With you. We'll all be together.'

"'No! You must go!' she insisted. 'You've got the chance to stay alive and be a witness.

"'I know staying alive seems to be more difficult than dying,' the young woman added. 'But it serves a much greater cause. Do you understand?'

"I nodded. I felt shame.

"'So do you promise me you'll stay alive as long as you can and be my witness? A witness for us all?' she asked.

"I nodded.

"'You must go now,' she urged, turning her back on me.

"I was the last person to leave the shower room. The rubber seals squeaked as the door was shut tightly and bolted.

"I tried to run away from the undressing room, but Toszka held me back. Otherwise, I would've been shot on the spot. 'Stay alive,' the woman had pleaded, and already I was dicing with death.

"The Red Cross van drove up to the side of the building. Instead of medics, two SS guards got out, and having opened the rear door, another four clambered out. They put on gas masks and thick gloves before three of them each carried a metal container with a yellow label to the outside wall of C4. From where I was standing, they looked like ordinary tins of paint.

"The remaining soldiers climbed back into the van and were driven to the other side of the building, where we could no longer see them. A few minutes later, the van returned but with only one soldier inside.

"Positioned on the outside wall of C4 were three ventilation ducts protected by a wire mesh cage. A soldier approached the building, removed a cage, then opened a vent in the brickwork. He kneeled down by the metal tin, grabbed a mallet suspended from his belt, and struck the top of the tin several times, firmly, but not violently, before removing a circular piece of metal from the container lid. The other two guards followed suit.

"'Ready?' a guard shouted, raising his head.

"After a few moments, a reply came from the other side of the building. 'Ready!'

"Carefully, each soldier stood up, holding his tin in both hands and placing the lip of the tin beside the vent aperture.

"'Start the shower!' the guard shouted, carefully pouring the contents of the tin into the vent. Once emptied, he closed the vent and replaced the wire cage. The other two guards carried out the same process.

"Almost immediately, there was muffled thudding coming from the shower room, which grew louder and louder as the crystals vaporized and the gas spread. Screaming added to the thudding—the desperate pitch of women and children screaming for air. I'm sure I heard their fingernails frantically scratching the concrete walls, but my mind might've been playing cruel tricks on me.

"The thudding drummed for only a few minutes before it started receding. After five minutes, it was barely audible. After ten, it had stopped. And after fifteen, the gas chamber door was opened. By then, the rest of the C4 SK team had arrived to remove the corpses. This was one of my normal daily duties, dealing with the dead, not the living, and I joined them in their work.

"And that, Rachael, is my reason to live, to be a witness," he concluded. "It's so dreadful, I didn't even want to tell you. I'm sorry."

"There's no need to apologize," she said. "It's good you've shared it. It must be a horrific burden to carry."

Ludwig was short of breath. He was no dispassionate narrator. He could not tell his story without being transported to that time and place.

When he looked up, Rachael's arm was outstretched, her fingers poised between two horizontal wires of fencing. Tentatively, he moved his hand to meet hers, scared that his clumsy fingers would push hers onto the wire. His fingers edged forward.

Ludwig almost leaped backward, convinced he had felt an electric shock from the fence, but it was not the fence, it was their fingertips touching. Their touch remained unbroken. A few centimeters above their fingers was death. A few centimeters below was death. And yet they experienced a sense of comfort and security.

Ludwig could not remember the last time he had touched a woman. He felt the soft skin of her fingertip as if the warmth of her flesh was passing into his hand and spreading through his body. And he trembled at the thought of the stiff female corpses he had to touch each day.

"If you're going to be a witness," Rachael said, "I'd better go find you a pencil and paper." She withdrew her hand carefully, stood up, and was gone.

Ludwig stayed several minutes longer, his outstretched hand still holding its position between the wires. Finally, he returned to Crematorium 4's incinerator room.

CHAPTER SIXTEEN

March 1944

Elke took the paperwork off Rachael and examined it absentmindedly. "Last night, I went for a quick nap behind the clothes bales in Shed 3."

"And?" Rachael asked.

A small annex had been erected to the rear of Shed 3, able to hold a dining table with eight chairs and a long, lockable sideboard to store liquor, but little else. Access was not possible from inside the shed; the only door opened outdoors.

The annex was secluded, and the SS had adopted it as a private relaxation area. Well away from the main camp and with a plentiful supply of alcohol and food from the Kanada stores, it attracted members of the SS from across the camp. Before long, the lower-ranking soldiers were excluded, leaving the annex for the exclusive enjoyment of SS officers. It became so popular SS-Unterscharführer Mann had to introduce a booking system. Prisoners were not allowed in the room unless they were delivering supplies or serving at SS parties.

The workers paid little attention to the annex until a cooperative and well-bribed kapo allowed sick or excessively fatigued workers to sleep for a while behind the bales of clothes at the end of Shed 3. The women, once rested, would be back in time for the end of their shift.

The sounds of merriment emanating from the annex, which were muffled to those working at the tables, were clearly audible from behind the bales. The SS men and women were mostly too drunk to be coherent.

An officer had gotten hold of a gramophone, and the annex rang to the sounds of German folk songs.

From time to time, a conversation of significance would arise, the noise would abate, and the prisoner on the other side of the party wall would listen.

"I didn't catch everything," Elke replied. "They were talking quietly, but Mann was shouting his mouth off again. He can't help himself, and the more he drinks, the more his self-importance grows, and he gets loud and indiscreet."

"Go on," Rachael said, taking the papers back.

"Well, there's good and bad news," Elke said. "They were talking about going home. Apparently, the Red Army has broken through in the east and is decimating the retreating German army. They say the war's lost for Germany. It's only a matter of time."

"And the bad news?" Rachael asked.

"The Nazis have persecuted and murdered enormous numbers of Jews from many countries across Europe," Elke replied. "But there's still one left untouched."

"Where?" the Dutch woman asked.

"Hungary."

Rachael was confused and a little embarrassed. "I'm sorry. I don't know much about the Jews of Hungary."

"Well, there's a lot of them," Elke said, pausing. "They say there's over half a million Hungarian Jews to transport."

Rachael raised her eyebrows. "Transport?" she said. "Surely, they're not transporting Jews if they've lost the war? What's the point? And even if they tried, how on earth could they move so many people? That's five times as many as the Netherlands! And which camps are they destined for?" She shook her head.

"Mann said it was madness. But madness isn't a stranger in Birkenau," Elke replied. "It's already been planned and needs to be done before the Soviets take control of Hungary." She looked her friend in the eye. "And they're not sending them to different camps. They're sending them *all* here."

"That can't be possible!" Rachael said. "With a hundred people in each cattle car, that's..." she paused "...five thousand cattle cars."

"Are you sure you don't mean five hundred?" Elke asked.

"No, I've checked it in my head. It's five thousand."
"Well, that *does* explain something else."
"Explain what?" Rachael asked.
"Mann said they're going to build another railway platform."
"Where?"
"Right into the center of Birkenau. They're going to extend the railway track from the old ramp to a new platform on Lagerstrasse. The trains will stop one hundred meters from C2 and C3."

"I need to tell Ludwig," Rachael said. "This is going to affect the SK workers."

Since her arrival, Rachael had grown close to Elke and had confided in her about her meetings with Ludwig, but she had not told another soul.

"One more thing," Elke interrupted. "Mann said there won't be many European Jews left to transport once the Hungarians are *treated*. With the Soviets approaching, the SS will want to kill the Hungarian Jews, close Birkenau down, and get out of here as soon as they can."

"I need to tell Ludwig," Rachael repeated.

CHAPTER SEVENTEEN

March 1944

The subject of finding Hannes bothered Ludwig. It had been exceedingly difficult to obtain information about his whereabouts. Rachael had informed him that over 100,000 Dutch Jews had been transported to Auschwitz and Sobibor. He had expected to find pockets of Dutchmen across the camp, but he had heard nothing, and as more and more trains arrived in Birkenau, his contacts informed him the accuracy of the prisoner registers in many barracks could no longer be relied upon. The imminent arrival of the Hungarians would make matters worse.

However hard he tried to resist, Ludwig's mind drifted inexorably to the crematoria, and it seemed inevitable enormous numbers of the Dutch had been driven straight into the gas chambers.

When members of the SK team bribed their way into other parts of the camp, it was to meet friends or family or prostitutes, not to help Ludwig find a boy he did not know.

Not only did the SK men not display any interest in finding the young boy, but they also questioned Ludwig's motives. He could understand their reaction. He refused to divulge Rachael's involvement, and the story he created of Hannes being a distant cousin was unconvincing because he was a poor liar.

Without the help of his SK colleagues, Ludwig was left to locate Hannes on his own. No sooner had he made inquiries about one barracks than half of its prisoners would be selected or transferred, and new occupants would arrive. There was also a steady flow of prisoners between Auschwitz, Birkenau, and the sub-camps. There were over fifty sub-camps. Ludwig made three trips beyond Barracks 13, none of which yielded any leads. In a camp of over 100,000 souls, it seemed an impossible task.

Ludwig was weighed down with guilt for bribing kapos and SS guards with valuables that could otherwise support the planned SK action. As an SK member, who was supposed to be isolated, the cost of bribes was higher than for other prisoners.

The cruelty he witnessed every day made him certain this young Dutch boy from a pleasant middle-class background could not survive on his own, but how could he tell Rachael that? He couldn't, so he had to find out if her brother was dead or alive, definitively.

A kapo in Barracks 4 who hailed from the same Polish village as Ludwig offered him advice, which gave him a glimmer of hope. Still fraught with danger, this idea would determine whether Hannes was alive or dead.

The kapo explained that when a prisoner was selected and tattooed, their details were transferred to a central register held in the Administration Office housed in Auschwitz I. This register was kept in tattoo number order. At the end of every roll call, the list of prisoners for each barracks was sent to the Administration Office to amend the register for arrivals, deaths, and transfers.

Rachael would have been tattooed at more or less the same time as Hannes. Finding Rachael's number on the register would mean Hannes's was not far away. They would surely locate his details quickly and learn his fate.

Ludwig could have kicked himself. It was such a simple idea. Why hadn't he thought of it? Sure, the Administration Office was well guarded, but many people worked there, both members of the SS and prisoners. Finding just a couple of people with access to the relevant information might be enough to locate Hannes.

"Look, I'll tell you what," the kapo said. "I'll see if I can get hold of the names of kapos or SS guards who might help. Come back in a week with the most valuable bribes you can lay your hands on, and we'll work from there."

*

"That sounds positive!" Rachael said, smiling and squeezing Ludwig's hand.

The couple had taken to placing their hands on the ground. With just the one electric wire above, the sense of jeopardy when holding hands was reduced. Ludwig would insist she lay her hand down flat, facing upward, and his hand would cover it, lending her complete protection.

Behind her words, Ludwig sensed she was unsure of her own optimism. At such a formative stage, his camp registry plan did not warrant that level of enthusiasm. She had not seen her brother for months, and the Pole had not found any clues. Despite her smile, he saw a look of disappointment etched on her face. He loved her smile, but that look made his stomach churn.

"You shouldn't really touch me," Rachael warned. "Barracks 13's in crisis. Half the prisoners have fallen ill, almost overnight. You'll catch an infection."

"It's a risk I'll take," he responded, gently pressing his hand down on hers. "You've got the Kanada washrooms to keep you clean. I'm sure that helps."

"I've still got to sleep and eat in the barracks!" she said. "The bunks are more crowded than ever. With building the new railway platform, they've put men into B1 barracks, and the evicted women have been redistributed. There's now five or six to a bunk. It seems like there's more women than lice."

"It's okay," he said. "As each day passes, the Soviets and liberation come closer. Remember, we both have to survive!"

"You're right. I need to survive for Hannes until I know for sure that he's..." Her voice tailed off, and her head dropped.

"Alive," he said emphatically. "Perhaps there's another reason to survive... For each other?" he ventured.

"Perhaps." She raised her head.

"I'm a farmer who's never been to the big city," Ludwig said, changing the subject. "I'd like to see Amsterdam. Perhaps you could show me around one day?"

"It's a beautiful city," she answered. "The canals, the parks, and the flowers. Sitting outside coffee shops in the sunshine, watching the boats and cyclists passing by." For a moment, she remembered happiness.

"What about SS-Unterscharführer Mann?" Ludwig asked suddenly.

"Sorry, what do you mean?"

"He's an SS officer of rank and takes the gold ingots up to Auschwitz I every day. If we can persuade Mann to cooperate, the entire plan to find Hannes becomes much easier."

"And we have two ways to persuade Mann to help," she said. "Bribes... and Zuzana Kováčová." Ludwig was pleased to see a genuine smile on Rachael's face.

Although Rachael acknowledged Zuzana's youthful immaturity, she was uncomfortable with the Czech woman's behavior since being caught with her lover in Shed 28. Zuzana flaunted her relationship with the SS officer and showed no contrition for her actions. Rachael interpreted the continual references to her influence over him as taunts directed at the other Kanada workers.

The thought of having to plead for Zuzana's help irritated Rachael, but the commitment to find her brother ranked above all other considerations.

"I'll speak to Zuzana in the morning," she said, praying the Czech's sway over Mann was as strong as she suggested.

CHAPTER EIGHTEEN

April 1944

Reichsführer-SS Heinrich Himmler wanted the Hungarian Jews to be exterminated with the utmost speed. SS-Obersturmbannführer Adolph Eichmann, who was in charge of the deportation of European Jews, confirmed the Nazis' transport infrastructure could deliver half a million Hungarians to Auschwitz-Birkenau in three months, an average of almost 6,000 human beings every single day, even more if there were peaks and troughs in supply.

Former Camp Commandant SS-Obersturmbannführer Rudolph Höss and the Auschwitz hierarchy discussed the plan at length. They were aware of Himmler's enthusiasm for transporting the Hungarian Jews but did not think he was truly aware of the limits of the Birkenau extermination facilities. The camp population might surge above 150,000, and with the Red Army advancing, there was a risk the Soviets would find the camp full of prisoners.

*

There was silence among the SK workers who were gathered in the courtyard of Barracks 13.

"It's serious," Smizer said. "I thought the rail-track extension and the Hungarian transports were bad enough, but bringing Höss back and giving Moll responsibility for the four crematoria is a different scenario altogether." The block manager paused before adding, "And they'll both be here in a matter of days."

"They're evil bastards," another man said.

"Höss is a skillful administrator. He knows how to kill people en masse," Smizer continued. "Those are his orders, and he carries them out exceptionally well, and now he's been asked to kill nigh on half a million Hungarian Jews, he'll probably find a way.

"Moll's evil streak's way beyond anybody else in the SS. His hatred of Jews runs through every fiber of his body, and no torture's beyond him. Including women, children, and babies."

There was a murmur of agreement among the men.

"Until now, the SS has given protection to the Sonderkommando and granted us additional privileges," Smizer said. "Moll will stop that. He'll watch our every move like a hawk."

Ludwig could not help but think about his time spent with Rachael by the Crematorium 4 fence, and what the consequences would be for Rachael and himself if Moll found out. The SK man would gladly accept the risks involved, but he would not compromise Rachael's safety.

"Our hopes of survival have just plummeted," Filip Toszka said. "So perhaps we should consider other options."

"Do you mean escape?" Ludwig asked.

"Maybe," Toszka replied. "But escape's futile. I've been in Birkenau for over two years, and every escape attempt ends in failure. Even those who make it beyond the perimeter fence invariably get caught and executed, and as a deterrent, the SS mete out reprisals upon their friends and relatives."

"Wetzler and Rosenberg made it out," Ludwig said.

"True, and they've never been heard of since," Toszka replied. "So they might be dead or alive. And anyway, look..." He spread his arms wide. "If they made their way safely to London or America or somewhere else and told the world about Birkenau, I don't see many allied planes or tanks coming to our rescue. Do you?"

Toszka lowered his head and scanned the surrounding faces. "Come closer," he whispered. "I was considering a revolt which might save thousands of lives." He took a deep breath. "If we destroy the crematoria, Höss won't be able to fulfill his murderous objectives. Germany has lost the war on the Eastern Front, the Red Army's approaching, it's only a matter of time. Even if our revolt's only partially successful, it will cause a delay and *will* save lives."

"But we'll be killed," one of the group said. "Either killed during the revolt or executed afterward."

"You're probably right, Wojciech." Toszka shrugged. "But Moll will probably kill us anyway. When he was in Sachsenhausen, he shot Jews for looking at him. We've got nothing to lose."

"Carry on," another man said.

"The ovens in C4 and C5 are in a poor state of repair," Toszka continued. "It's not going to take much to put them out of action permanently. A small quantity of explosives placed strategically will suffice."

"And how do we get hold of explosives?" Wojciech scoffed. "You make it sound so easy!"

"I'm coming to the explosives," Toszka replied patiently.

"Yes, but what about the gas chambers?" Wojciech asked.

"It's true we'll need explosives to blow up the gas chambers as well, but we'd still be severely disrupting the SS extermination process if we destroyed the ovens but not the gas chambers. The ovens are crucial because they're a bottleneck."

"So we destroy the crematoria and wait around for the SS to gun us down?" Wojciech asked.

"No," Toszka responded. "I know it's a long shot, but we'll try to escape afterward. The perimeter fence is close to C3, and there's only one watchtower there.

"I've been in contact with some like-minded prisoners in camp. They see what we see, and we've discussed a general camp revolt, carried out at exactly the same time as ours. The whole of Birkenau will be in chaos, giving us the opportunity to destroy the crematoria and make our escape.

"Some of us SK men might want no involvement in this plan. Some might want to help with the destruction of the crematoria but not escape. We're forcing nobody. With the Red Army on its way, some may want to try to last it out."

"And where will weapons and explosives come from?" Wojciech asked.

"With weapons, we'll need to be innovative," Toszka replied. "Knives, axes, spades, I'm sure we can lay hands on from the repair shops, but when the revolt starts, it's vital we capture a few SS guards and take their weapons.

"There are several Soviet POWs with military backgrounds in the C5 team who've got experience making rudimentary explosive devices. We know where there are explosive materials, but getting hold of them is going to be extremely dangerous." Toszka paused a moment.

"There are explosives in the Union factory," the kapo continued.

The Union factory was the camp name for the Weischel Union Metallwerke factory, which had been built in 1943. Situated approximately halfway between the Auschwitz I and Birkenau camps, every morning 2,000 young Jewish women were marched by their kapos to the factory, where they would manufacture ammunition for the Germany army. The Weischel corporation benefited from the outstanding output of its workforce, all provided free of charge. Their daily quotas were routinely achieved, and the factory managers, the only paid employees on site, would warn the kapos against harming the women, as this would directly affect the German war effort. The kapos were still given license to deal with those whose performance lagged, but good workers had to be preserved.

The Union factory management selected a workforce of young women because they produced small caliber ammunition, which was well suited to their dexterous fingers. Several of the machines operating in the facility were also better handled by younger people with sharper reactions. Men were speedy but prone to make errors. Men had lost fingers or even hands in the machinery when they had made errors. A worker who seemed indispensable suddenly became a liability and would lose his job, or even his life. The women were more methodical.

The factory was full of dangerous explosive materials which, in the wrong hands, could cause major problems. While the men might succumb to temptation, the management was convinced the women were less inclined to smuggle goods out. The kapos' daily searches of the women did not reveal any breaches of the rules and seemed to justify the managers' conclusions.

"Are you joking?" Wojciech exclaimed. "Stealing explosives from the Union factory!"

"I know it's a risk," Toszka replied. "But it *actually* makes sense. There's never been a case of smuggling from the Union factory. A woman won't ever be suspected."

"You know what'll happen if she gets caught?" Wojciech asked.

"Like any other prisoner in Birkenau who's caught stealing or smuggling, the SS will execute her," Toszka replied matter-of-factly.

"If a woman knows the risks and accepts them, she's as brave as any man," Ludwig interjected.

"Correct," Toszka said. "We've spoken to four women who work there and are willing to play their part."

"What's the rush?" Wojciech asked, concerned.

"There's no rush," Toszka answered. "We've got to do this properly or we'll certainly die for nothing, but we *do* need to act quickly. Once the Hungarians are processed, we don't believe there'll be many more transports to come, and the SS won't need six hundred SK workers. We've got firsthand experience of the most dreadful part of the Nazi regime, and the SS won't want a single one of us surviving the war to tell the tale. It's the choice between revolting now or waiting for Moll to kill us later."

"Some of us must survive as witnesses," Ludwig said. "The notes we've buried...who knows if they'll survive the rain, snow, and baking heat?"

Rachael had provided Ludwig with paper smuggled from Shed 10, some clean and white, some crumpled and dirty, then located two thermos flasks that could accommodate rolled-up sheets of paper. He was impressed when she offered him the choice between pencils or a fountain pen. They agreed ink would have a greater chance of surviving intact.

Ludwig gave the thermos flasks to the others and buried his testimony in an empty wine bottle and cork, which Rachael had retrieved from the SS annex in Kanada.

Ludwig buried the bottle at the edge of the trees near to where he met Rachael, hoping this would be far enough away from the crematorium building to not be found by the SS but near enough to be discovered in the future. The surrounding area was flat, and the earth was soft but not wet. It was too risky to take a shovel from the incineration room, so he had to use his metal eating spoon, spending time each day digging until Rachael arrived.

He pondered how deep the hole should be. Too deep and the message might never be discovered. Too shallow and the SS might find it, or it would be spoiled by the weather. In the end, he dug a hole that left fifteen centimeters of soil above the cork, tamping the earth down with his foot and covering it with a few clumps of grass.

Toszka, Smizer, and other SK workers buried messages as well. Messages representing hundreds of thousands of people.

All they could do was hope.

CHAPTER NINETEEN

April 1944

Rachael acknowledged Zuzana had only been a teenager when she arrived in Auschwitz in 1942. A short time earlier, she and her friends would have been happy-go-lucky teenagers, chatting on street corners, flirting with boys, or studying at college.

Now they had been surrounded by death for well over a year. It must have been an extraordinary shock for them. Rachael's involvement with the Dutch Resistance had at least given her experience of the cruelty of the Nazis, and the danger, and the death. She could not imagine being a teenager in Birkenau.

However, Rachael could not warm to the young Czech woman. She could hardly blame her for taking advantage of Mann's infatuation, but it rankled that Zuzana made it so obvious to the women around her. Kováčová was one of few workers in Kanada who regularly smiled, and she acted as if her relationship with Mann offered her a protective shield. Which, of course, it did. She displayed little respect for her fellow prisoners and behaved like a spoiled child. She would stop work and show off gifts that Mann had presented to her, knowing full well she would never be challenged.

Behind his back, Zuzana expressed her indifference toward Mann but played along when in his company, the rewards of which were clear to see.

Mann himself was only a couple of years older than Zuzana, having joined the SS aged eighteen. Prior to being appointed SS-

Unterscharführer, he had been the leader of an SK team, taking part in the platform selections and escorting prisoners to the gas chambers. In this role, he displayed the same brutality as the other SS soldiers and kapos, although the prisoners noticed a softening in his attitude after his affair with Zuzana started.

Rachael entered Zuzana's shed, where metal objects such as pots and pans were stored. This is where she had found the thermos flasks for Ludwig. Even for items as basic as these, she had taken them when the other women were outside during lunchtime to be sure she was not spotted. Ludwig had told her to trust absolutely no one. To do so might jeopardize all their lives.

In this shed, the metal goods were washed in clean water, dried off, and packed in cardboard boxes to be sent to Germany. It was a straightforward job, albeit noisy. Mann had asked Rachael to move Kováčová into Shed 1. The Czech had refused point blank, not wishing to be bothered by him all day long. Rachael had lied to Mann, reporting that she thought their working so closely might attract the suspicions of the SS and be dangerous. He accepted this logic and remained unaware of the true reason.

Zuzana was wiping the inside of a metal cup with a peremptory brush of her drying cloth when she saw Rachael entering. Without asking permission, and ignoring the kapos nearby, she stood up and walked around the table to meet her superior.

Kováčová was wearing a blue-striped work dress, but it was clean, and the stripes were a vivid blue, unlike the dreary, faded stripes worn by the others. Her long, curly hair hung down her back.

The Czech woman had lost none of her body shape. Most of the other women were half-starved, their skin hanging limply from their bodies, their mouths hanging open in a desperate wait for food. Zuzana had youthful round cheeks, and her figure curved around her chest, waist, and hips. Rachael wondered if she had found some makeup to put on. The young woman would have not lasted a day in Barracks 19, she thought. Physically, she was a match for Grese's beauty, something the SS monster would never have allowed. Grese would have killed or disfigured her, depending on her mood that day.

"Do you want me to ask Franz to get you something?" Kováčová asked.

Rachael was surprised and embarrassed Zuzana had guessed her motives so easily, but on reflection, the Kanada women steered clear of Zuzana and only approached her when they required a favor. The Dutch woman suspected that, without Mann, Kováčová was quite lonely.

"Any news of your sister?" Rachael answered, evading the question. The young Czech woman was looking for her own sister, and Rachael hoped this would make her understand the loss of Hannes.

"Not yet," the Czech woman replied, her head dipping. "She's not in this camp."

"I'm trying to find my brother," Rachael said. "Unlike your sister, he *is* in the camp. I just don't know where. We were separated inside the Disinfection Facility on our first day. His tattoo number must be very similar to mine." She held out her forearm and pulled up her sleeve but regretted it immediately. It was a clumsy gesture. Of course Zuzana knew about tattoos. She had her own. "I don't need anything stealing. I just need someone to find his details in the prisoner register in the Administration Office."

"Gosh, that's so dangerous!" Kováčová answered. She spoke slowly, with an unusually serious voice, stretching out every syllable. Zuzana's tone was inauthentic, Rachael thought.

"Let me know what sort of recompense SS-Unterscharführer Mann will require," Rachael said.

"Diamonds," Kováčová answered without hesitating.

"Don't you want to ask him?"

"No! For something so dangerous, it's got to be diamonds!" the Czech responded. "I can't guarantee anything, of course, but I'll try next time I speak with Franz." A thin smile formed on her lips.

By using her lover's first name, Zuzana intended to impress the other women, but in reality, they hated and feared her for it. Consorting with the enemy was regarded as an act of betrayal.

Rachael was conflicted. Helping her find her brother was an act of support, whatever its motivation.

"I'd be ever so grateful," Rachael replied. "He's barely more than a child."

"Birkenau's a dangerous place for children," Zuzana said. The smile slid from her face. Rachael was unsure if the Czech's expression was one of empathy or indifference.

CHAPTER TWENTY

May 1944

Ludwig pulled up some tufts of grass and placed them in a little pile, which was accumulating by his side.

Since the moment they had sat down by the fence, something had been preying on his mind. He had another request to make of Rachael, which, given the associated risks, he half hoped she would decline but was certain she would accept. He wondered if he should ask at all. Deep down, he knew he had to.

"Is there anything wrong?" Rachael asked him. "Do you need me to get more valuables for you?"

He did not reply. He wondered how she seemed to possess a sort of telepathy that enabled her to read his thoughts. She hardly knew him, and only from the other side of the fence.

Ludwig knew that by involving Rachael in the plans for the SK revolt, she would become a party to a plot that included killing SS soldiers, destroying parts of the crematoria, and helping prisoners to escape.

Those who sought to escape from Auschwitz and were caught were hanged or shot. They had heard stories about Block 11 in Auschwitz I, a punishment block, which was surrounded by a tall brick wall and was the epicenter of SS torture and execution. As a general rule, prisoners who were sent there did not return. Killing an SS soldier would elicit unimaginable torture before the relief of death.

The prospect of Rachael becoming embroiled in the revolt plan was excruciating for Ludwig. The Crematorium 4 SK team discussed the issue at length, but the kapos and SS guards would require significant bribes, and the Kanada sheds were the best source of valuable items.

"We need some tins, please," Ludwig blurted out.

"Tins of what?" Rachael asked.

"Nothing," he replied. "Just empty tins."

"Okay," she said. "Empty tins are easier to get hold of."

"And nails," he added.

"Nails," Rachael said. "That'll depend on how many you want and how big. Can I ask you what they're for?"

"We're going to make grenades," he said. "The tins will be filled with an explosive, with nails for shrapnel. Any sharp metal object will do the job."

"I can't get explosives!" Rachael exclaimed. "I've never seen any come through Kanada."

"That's no problem," he replied calmly. "We've got a source for the explosives. As long as you can find the tins and shrapnel, we'll have all the materials we need." The Pole paused, and Rachael felt his fingers twitch. "But we'll need someone in Kanada to receive the explosives and pass them to the SK revolt team. It's risky, I know…"

"Well, we don't want to divulge the plans for the revolt to too many prisoners," she replied pragmatically. "So the obvious solution's for me to accept the explosives and pass them to you."

"It is," he replied, nodding and marveling at her apparent calmness when all he could see was danger in every direction.

*

When Rachael had arrived in Birkenau late in 1943, there had been 500 workers in Kanada. Since the first transport from Hungary had arrived in the middle of the month, the number of Kanada workers had risen sharply to 800 and was still climbing. Plans to keep the belongings indoors were shelved as the trucks dumped their loads against the outside walls of the sheds before returning to the new platform.

The extended railway track that passed through the arched entrance to Birkenau split into three halfway along Lagerstrasse, one of which continued to the end of the sector, halting just short of Crematoria 2 and

3. On regular occasions, two transports arrived at the same time. As soon as one train had been selected, the cattle cars of the second were opened by the SS, and the next selection would begin. The SK men and the trucks had twice as much work to do.

As it transpired, both May and June were warm and dry, so the SS could tolerate the belongings being stored outdoors. However, the work for the women was debilitating, and gave Rachael an opportunity to gauge her relationship with SS-Unterscharführer Mann by requesting a fifteen-minute break for the workers every three hours. She could see from his expression he was not enthusiastic, so she made the request again, adding, "It'll be the best for all parties concerned." The redhead let the silence hang in the air and never took her eyes off the SS officer.

After a few moments, he shook his head.

"Sir?" Rachael asked.

"No way," Mann replied. "I can't spare a single minute, never mind fifteen. You'll just have to work through. The Hungarian operation should be over in a few months." Rachael hoped Zuzana Kováčová would be more persuasive with her request of the SS officer.

CHAPTER TWENTY-ONE

May 1944

Rachael found it difficult to read Zuzana's expression as the young Czech entered Shed 1 and approached. Her confident smile was absent, which was not a positive sign. The Dutch woman was reticent about talking to her under the watchful eye of SS-Unterscharführer Mann, who was sitting in his office a matter of meters away.

When Zuzana drew near, she reached inside the collar of her blouse and retrieved a gold necklace. Rachael noticed its links were more substantial than most chains they discovered in Kanada, and the single diamond that hung from it and was cradled in the young woman's palm was shaped in a rare princess cut.

"Let me show you this necklace!" Kováčová said, bending forward so their heads were almost touching before whispering, "I've got some news about your brother."

Rachael jerked back in surprise, but Zuzana grabbed the lapel of her blouse and pulled her closer.

"It's not been easy," the Czech woman continued. "There's been so many Hungarians arriving, the administration departments haven't had enough workers to keep up. So the search for a Dutch boy's not on anybody's priority list."

"And...?" Rachael urged.

"Well, there's good news and bad news," Zuzana said.

The Czech's serious expression filled Rachael with trepidation.

"The good news is, I think he's alive," Kováčová said.

"*Think* he's alive?" Rachael said. "What does that mean?"

"We've found Hannes's registration card and tattoo number. We gave your number to one of the prisoners working for the camp registry in the Administration Office. They waited until they received notification of the death of someone with a similar number to yours and, when they retrieved that card, they scanned the filing cabinet and found yours and Hannes's. That's the good news. Those who are sent straight to the gas chambers don't receive a tattoo and aren't registered. It was as if they never existed. Having a registration card means your brother entered the camp alive."

Keeping close to Rachael while retrieving a sheet of paper from her coat pocket and reading from it, the Czech continued. "Johannes Franck Kisch, born in Amsterdam, date of birth May sixteenth, 1929. Tattoo number 58021."

Rachael smiled. Her brother had remembered, or been told by a friendly stranger, to lie about his date of birth and make himself old enough to qualify for hard labor. Fourteen years old must have convinced the SS to accept him, but she knew his birthday had been earlier that month, and he was only eleven.

"So why did you say you *think* he's alive?" the Dutch woman asked.

"That's the bad news," the Czech replied. "His registration documents aren't all there, which means he's gone somewhere else."

"Somewhere else?" Rachael replied, her sense of elation ebbing away.

Zuzana saw the expression of distress on Rachael's face and tried to assuage her fears. "There's no record of his death, so he's probably not dead, but after selection, he was sent to the men's camp in B2, and he's not there now."

"So where could he be?" Rachael asked, becoming increasingly agitated, her voice rising above a whisper, making a worker nearby look up.

"Franz says this might be an administrative error," Kováčová continued. "So Hannes could be in another part of the camp. Or possibly sent to a completely different camp like Gross Rosen, but that's unlikely. It could be a simple misfiling of his documents."

"So he might be dead already, and they've misfiled his death records?"

Zuzana thought for a few moments before slowly nodding. "Yes, he might."

"There's no good news. It's just bad news," Rachael groaned. "I already knew he was alive when we were in the Disinfection Facility together. All I've got is uncertainty."

"Look, we've made progress," Kováčová countered. "We've got his tattoo number, which will follow him wherever he goes. That's good news! If he's in Auschwitz or Birkenau or another camp altogether, his number will be on a list somewhere."

"Just not on a list in the Administration Office," Rachael said.

"That's one list," the Czech replied. "They've got several other lists. He might be on one of those."

"What can we do now?" Rachael asked. "I'm not giving up."

"We can keep looking, but we'll need the continued cooperation of people in the SS. That's not easy, and not cheap."

"What happened to the jewelry I gave you?" Rachael asked impatiently.

"Well, Franz has taken a substantial risk," Zuzana said. "And he's had to use up all the bribes you gave him."

Rachael could not help but think of the gold chain and diamond around the Czech woman's neck, and wondered how much cooperation they could have bought, but at least the young woman had uncovered the first tangible clue of Hannes's whereabouts, which was more than she and Ludwig had accomplished.

The Dutch woman smiled thinly before speaking. "Thank you, Zuzana. Please tell SS-Unterscharführer Mann I'll find more bribes by the end of the week. Let me know if he has any special requests."

The women's heads stayed close together during their conversation. Rachael picked the diamond off the Czech's palm and looked at it admiringly.

"Beautiful," she said before lifting her head and walking away.

Rachael was torn. The princess-cut diamond was the same shape as her mother's engagement ring. She tried to dispel the sadness and anger stirring in her, but Zuzana had found a record of Hannes and had promised to pursue the search for him.

Rachael decided the concentration required to melt gold would occupy her mind and subdue her racing thoughts, so she approached the furnace and lit the coal.

CHAPTER TWENTY-TWO

May 1944

The first transport arrived from Hungary on May 15, 1944. It was not exceptionally large, with 1,800 prisoners on board. The twenty cattle cars were unloaded on the old platform outside the camp.

Within two weeks, the new platform was ready. The single track from the old platform wound its way into the Birkenau camp before splitting into three separate tracks on Lagerstrasse.

Reichsführer-SS Heinrich Himmler had insisted the Hungarian Jews were to be dealt with speedily. SS-Obersturmbannführer Adolph Eichmann, who was in charge of the transportation of European Jews, confirmed the Nazis rail infrastructure could deliver half a million Hungarians to Birkenau in three months, an average of 6,000 people every single day.

Camp Commandant SS-Obersturmbannführer Rudolph Höss and the Auschwitz hierarchy discussed the plan at length. They were aware of Himmler's enthusiasm for transporting the Hungarian Jews but did not think he was truly aware of the limits of the Birkenau extermination facilities. The camp population might surge above 150,000. With the Red Army advancing, it was inconceivable to allow the Soviets to find the camp full.

*

Ludwig was working in the Crematorium 4 incineration room when Moll arrived that morning.

SS-Hauptscharführer Otto Moll had the appearance of a textbook Aryan Nazi with slicked-back blond hair. His thin, tight lips naturally formed a permanent, cruel smile on his face, but he never knowingly smiled. His sole preoccupation was to follow orders and fulfill his sadistic whims, and there were plenty of opportunities in Birkenau.

Behind his back, the prisoners nicknamed him *Cyclops* because he had a glass eye. They joked it was difficult to determine which of his cold, emotionless eyes was the real one.

Moll had worked in several camps prior to Auschwitz, and in each was renowned for his brutality, becoming known as the most savage SS officer. Even fellow members of the SS grew apprehensive on hearing the growling engine of his motorbike, which he drove erratically and at such high speeds he seemed to appear from nowhere. Although Crematoria 4 and 5 were several hundred meters from Crematoria 2 and 3, Moll seemed to be present in all the compounds all the time, watching the SK men with studied malevolence.

Ludwig's original job of hauling bodies had been simple but strenuous work. Not long after the Hungarian transports started, the SS had been forced to use the outdoor yards in both Crematoria 4 and 5 as emergency undressing areas because the SK team could not move the bodies quickly enough from the gas chambers to the incineration room and keep the indoor undressing room clean. It was significantly more difficult to persuade the prisoners to calmly undress in the open air, and more physical force was required.

Ludwig's gruesome new role, as an oven stoker, was more demanding psychologically. In the center of the incineration room, there were two furnaces, located back-to-back, each with four incineration ovens. Each oven was designed to accommodate three bodies at any one time. The Pole was assigned to Oven 6 where he was targeted to burn as many bodies as possible with as little costly coke as possible. If the oven was too hot, its brick lining could be damaged, and they had to turn it off. If it was not hot enough, the bodies would not burn, and he had to watch them slowly melt while he stoked the oven. And after this, he had to meet his shift target for incinerating bodies. Three bodies every thirty minutes for eleven hours, followed by one hour for cleaning down. Oven 6's daily target was sixty-five bodies per shift. If Ludwig and his assistant missed the target, they would both be beaten.

The SS management had given instructions for the optimum loading for each oven: one well-nourished body, one emaciated, and one child or small adult. The fat generated from these would generate enough heat to turn the three into ashes without the need for extra coke to be added.

Moll would beat any stoker he saw breaking the rules for feeding bodies into the ovens.

The nameless corpses were dehumanized, part of a calculation, the subject of efficiency targets, weighed and balanced like commodities. In half an hour, converted into a few handfuls of ashes. Once, when cleaning out the oven grate, Ludwig lingered to look at the ashes on his shovel. A kapo caught sight of him and gave him a severe beating. Ludwig had become almost numb to a *normal* beating, but this one left his arm and shoulder aching.

When the kapo finally relented, he leaned over Ludwig and spoke. "Just do your job, don't think about it...it's not worth it. Work, don't think!"

Ludwig told himself he was an undertaker, dealing with dead people. Remember, they're already dead, and you're alive! You're a witness.

Every time Ludwig looked over his shoulder, the piles of bodies grew larger. It was the same story for the other stokers. Eight ovens simply could not keep up with the gas chamber. The poor souls entering the gas chamber were crammed in with no room to sit or lie. Hundreds could be killed in one quarter of an hour by simply pouring Zyklon B crystals into a vent. The ovens were forever in need of maintenance.

The incineration room was as hot as hell, and the stink of burning coal and flesh hung in the air as a permanent reminder. The SS guards stayed in their rooms or stood outside, leaving the kapos to supervise indoors and to come out to give their reports.

One day, Moll strode into the incineration room with the SS supervisor stumbling behind him.

"From now on," Moll barked at the supervisor, "there must be at least one SS soldier on duty *inside* the hall. At all times! Don't trust those fucking kapos, whether Jews or not. You watch them with your own eyes. Understood?"

The SS supervisor nodded meekly, but Moll had moved away. He methodically circled the ovens, like a beast stalking its prey, stopping by each of the eight ovens before returning.

"Come here!" Moll insisted, leading the supervisor to Oven 7, next to Ludwig at 6.

The Oven 7 stoker looked weary but was concentrating on the task at hand. He was taken aback when the two SS soldiers appeared. Every stoker had an assistant. Between them, they selected the appropriate three corpses from the piles, hauled them onto a steel feeding bed, pushed the bed into the oven, then the assistant would withdraw the bed while the stoker used a two-meter steel poker to hold the corpses in position. The steel oven door could then be closed.

The stoker was a Pole called Nowak who, prior to the war, had been a coal miner. His diminutive stature and a permanent stoop concealed a surprising strength and aptitude, but having reached sixty years of age, that strength was diminishing. Toszka paired him with Szymański, another Pole who was the strongest man in Crematorium 4. Between them, Nowak and Szymański regularly achieved the highest outputs across Crematoria 4 and 5.

"What's this old Jew doing here?" Moll demanded.

"He's one of our best stokers," the SS supervisor stuttered.

"Best stoker!" Moll scoffed. "I bet he couldn't lift his own puny body, never mind somebody else's!"

Moll closed in on Nowak until he was directly in the stoker's eyeline.

"Keep going!" he shouted. "I didn't tell you to stop!"

Nowak was visibly shaking. Szymański grabbed the handle of the steel bed to push it into the oven flames. The miner took hold of his poker, but its curved end became trapped under the lip of the oven base. He shook it, but it would not come free.

"This man's not fit for the job!" Moll said.

"But…" the SS supervisor replied.

"Don't *but* me!" Moll shouted. "Do you want me to do your fucking job for you?"

Nowak lowered his poker, gave it a tug, and it slipped free. He was about to turn around to show the SS men when a bullet from Moll's pistol passed through the back of his neck, just below his skull line.

"Don't just stand there!" Moll addressed the assistant stoker. "Get him into the oven!" He turned on his heels and departed, cursing as he went.

Ludwig wanted to feel pity for Nowak, but his overriding emotion was one of relief. The ends of the pokers included two barbs that regularly snagged on the upturned rim of the oven base. It happened to all the stokers. It could have been him that day, he thought. But it wasn't, and he had no choice other than to continue his work.

CHAPTER TWENTY-THREE

June 1944

"You, come here!" Moll shouted at Ludwig, who came running. "Go stand outside!"

Ludwig was terrified what he might find in the yard outside Crematorium 4. His emotions were heightened when he was faced with three SS guards carrying guns and marshaling nine of the other Crematorium 4 SK team. There was a truck, its engine idling, on the road running between the crematoria. When Moll left the incinerator room, he led the group to the truck. Energetically jumping on the back of the truck, the SS-Oberscharführer threw various items off: spades, shovels, wood saws.

An area of open grassland lay in the far corner of the Crematorium 5 compound, bordered on three sides by two barbed wire fences and a group of trees. The entrance to the crematorium gas chamber provided the fourth side. Moll led the men between the building and the trees.

Moll took a tape measure, some nails, and a ball of string from his trouser pocket. Ludwig thought the nails would be ideal for the grenades they were making. He would need to be exceptionally careful with Moll around, but if they were left with just the SS guards, he felt confident of snatching a handful.

The SS officer anchored one end of the string in the earth with a nail, hammering it forcefully. He laid the end of the tape measure on the ground and walked on. After several paces, he stopped, checked the tape measure, and moved on again. He did this once more before inserting another nail into the ground, pulling the string taut and wrapping it around the nail. He continued until there was a patch of grass marked out in a rectangle of string. Then he repeated the process, and there were two rectangles next to each other, a few meters apart. Ludwig was accustomed to measuring out paddocks on the family farm and estimated that each rectangle was forty meters by eight.

"Right! Get digging, you lazy Jewish bastards!" Moll roared. "Dig exactly along the lines, not a centimeter over, not a centimeter short. To a depth of three meters." With that, he rode away on his motorbike, its roaring engine disappearing into the distance.

"Come on, come on!" one of the SS guards shouted, shoving the butt of his rifle into the back of the nearest SK worker. With Moll in charge, the guards seemed to adopt his excessive brutality, even when he was not physically in attendance.

The SK men split themselves up evenly across the two rectangles. The sun was bright and warm, and the ground was hard on the surface, with a dense, cloying soil not far beneath. One worker removed his blue-striped jacket from his sweating torso.

"What the hell are you doing?" a guard shouted. "It's not a beach trip! You're here to work, not enjoy the sunshine! Put it back on!" He waved his rifle menacingly until the shirt was replaced. The guard returned to his colleagues, who were standing in the shade among the trees.

Ludwig kept his eyes open for any mislaid nails, but Moll had been careful, using nails only when the string was not taut enough to maintain the straight line. Ludwig counted eighteen nails in each rectangle. He would have to wait. Perhaps when the outline of the pits had been dug out, nails might be lost in the soil and find their way into his pocket.

Hardly any time had seemed to pass before they heard Moll's motorbike approaching, loud and menacing. The SS guards abandoned the shade of the trees and stood up straight in anticipation, and the workers redoubled their efforts.

"What the fuck?" Moll's face was red with anger. "You look like you've hardly started! And you," he turned to the guards, "you're supposed to be supervising! Have you been sleeping in the woods?"

"The ground's very difficult, sir," an SK worker ventured. "We need more workers."

Ludwig winced as soon as he heard these words.

"How dare you speak to me like that!" Moll replied. Dipping his hand to his holster, he withdrew his revolver and shot the worker in the head. The guards shouted at the remaining workers, brandishing their batons and pointing their rifles in a threatening manner.

The prisoners were accustomed to dealing with the dead, and without being asked, two of them made to move the body.

"Stop!" Moll shouted. "Leave it there! It'll serve as a warning to any other lazy Jews who don't pull their weight." He stepped over the string and into the first pit, which was dug a few centimeters deep. He tested the ground with the heel of his boot, having to kick down firmly to make an impression.

"Do you know how many trains we've got tomorrow?" Moll asked the guards. They did not answer. "Five. Five trains. That's fifteen thousand stinking, fucking Hungarian Jews in one day. And SS-Obersturmbannführer Höss and I are responsible for giving them special treatment."

The remaining workers carried on digging.

Moll addressed the guards once more. "Go fetch another ten workers. There's no fucking point having two pits half finished. Put all the workers in one pit. Make it two meters deep. That should suffice. Thirty centimeters an hour's the target. Measure them every hour, and if they don't reach the target, shoot one of them and get a replacement from C4 or C5." The SS officer threw his measuring tape at the guards. "I'll be back in six hours, and if at least one pit isn't finished, I'll shoot one of you bastards as well."

Ludwig had never heard an SS officer speak to fellow SS soldiers in this manner, but there was a maniacal urgency in Moll, making him completely oblivious to obstacles in his path. Two of the guards rushed off to commandeer extra workers. Moll stayed to watch. Ludwig felt as if every dip of his spade was being scrutinized. The heat and hard work, without break, were intolerable but were nowhere near as worrying as this monster, observing them with that cruel sneer.

The SK workers were on tenterhooks until Moll departed. Then Ludwig could collect his thoughts calmly. Fifteen thousand Hungarian Jews in one day was an incomprehensible figure. Five Trains. Three thousand passengers per train of thirty cattle cars, each containing one hundred men, women, and children. The SK would usually expect two thousand passengers in twenty cars.

Rachael was right about the inevitable effect on the Kanada stores. Ludwig contemplated the impact on other aspects of Birkenau; the platform selections, the number of prisoners held in barracks; the gas chambers; the incineration of bodies; the sharing of what little food and drink there was available.

The gas chambers could cope. All four chambers were in good working order, but the ovens would be under extreme pressure. The incineration room in Crematorium 4 was out of operation yet again, with more damage to its internal brickwork. The SS did not understand that burning more bodies with less maintenance time led inevitably to more breakdowns.

The other three incineration rooms could burn a maximum of 7,000 bodies in twenty-four hours. Moll had insisted on burning five bodies at a time, instead of three. The SS guards knew this would be counterproductive, resulting in more damage to the ovens and a surge in coke usage, but they followed his orders.

There would be no choice other than to send the surplus prisoners into the barracks until there was incineration capacity available. That would make living conditions in the camp even more intolerable, if that were possible, but Birkenau had redefined the word *intolerable*. The SS had added layer upon layer of persecution, deprivation, and misery onto the prisoners, and when it seemed it could not get any worse, the SS made it worse. When death was so near, a human being could withstand anything to stay alive.

Something did not quite make sense to Ludwig. Why were they digging more ash pits? And there was always the Vistula when the pits were full. Thousands upon thousands of human beings ended up as a pile of ashes on the back of a truck before being scattered on the river and carried away by the current. Gone.

Ludwig placed his foot on the shoulder of his spade and forced it into the ground. And stopped. Of course! They were not digging ash pits, but cremation pyres. He had heard that, in the past, the SS had burned bodies in open cremation pyres. It was inefficient and so unpleasant many SS guards refused to take part. Himmler understood their situation and issued an order stating no SS soldier would be disciplined for refusing to supervise a cremation pyre. Of course, Moll would not give a second thought to the sensibilities of the guards if he needed to incinerate bodies outdoors. It was a simple solution. The bodies would be dragged out of the gas chambers and taken either left to the incineration room or right to the cremation pyres.

What the SS guards were permitted to ignore, the SK teams were forced to witness. In the furnaces, they would load the bodies onto the steel feeding bed, slide them into the ovens as swiftly as possible, and slam the metal door shut. The men were partly divorced from the process that turned prisoners into ash. Open pyres would involve them watching their fellow Jews being consumed by flames before their eyes. God help us all, Ludwig thought.

CHAPTER TWENTY-FOUR

June 1944

Although Ludwig wanted to shield Rachael from the gruesome work he was undertaking, he succumbed to her calming, supportive words and told her about the pits they were digging. Each time she squeezed his fingers, his torment receded a little. He knew it would return, but for a while, he suffered less. He hoped his nightmares would not take root in Rachael's mind. She was mentally stronger than him, he acknowledged. Her determination was palpable, and she rarely wavered, whereas he always needed the solace of her company.

"Three trucks arrived in the C5 compound this morning," Ludwig said. "Moll was there, as usual. Two were full to brimming with thin tree branches and wooden posts." He paused. "The other truck confirmed what we had feared. It contained materials for the pyres—chlorinated lime, railway sleepers, methanol and petrol, two-meter-long steel pokers, and a contraption with two rollers, which we learned was a bone pulverizer."

"And the tree branches?" Rachael asked.

"They were to build a wattle fence," the Pole answered.

"I'm sorry, what's a wattle fence?"

"You take thin strips of wood, lay them out in vertical and horizontal rows and weave them together. The wood must be strong, but flexible."

"Why do the SS want a wattle fence as well as barbed wire?"

"It's a screen to obscure the crematoria buildings. It's not tall enough to conceal the chimneys."

"I don't understand," she said. "Prisoners and new arrivals, we've all seen C5 in operation. It's a bit late to hide it now."

"Let's wait and see," he said. "Moll wants it erected by tomorrow night."

Rachael looked thoughtful. "Is this fence just for C5?" she asked.

"No, C4 and C5," he answered. "I've heard they're doing the same for C2 and C3."

"Will it screen the barbed wire...here, where we meet?"

"It's intended to go all the way round the C4 compound, but don't worry. I'll make sure we can still meet. I told Moll I used to build wattle fences on the farm, so he's selected me for the fence-building team."

"And did you build wattle fences?" she asked.

"Sure," he said. "We had kilometers of fences back home. Wattle fencing's cheap, simple to erect, and strong enough to hold sheep. On the farm, I used to sit on a stone wall, weaving a hazel wattle and marveling at the valley stretching into the distance. I would stay there for hours. I wish I was there now, with you, instead of in this hell on earth. Anyway, I'm sure you're not interested in farming and fencing."

"I am," she insisted. "I'm a city girl and ignorant about farms and the countryside. Help me learn more. Please."

"Okay."

For the next few stolen minutes, Rachael listened while Ludwig stared into the distance and described life on the farm. Watching the crops thriving in the June sun, eagerly awaiting harvest time. Walking through the orchards blanketed with thousands of apples on the brink of ripening. As he spoke, the agitation in his voice abated, and the tenseness in his fingers eased.

CHAPTER TWENTY-FIVE

June 1944

The day before, when the pits had been dug out exactly to his dimensions, Moll instructed the workers to dig a channel along the center of each one, six centimeters wide and fifteen centimeters deep. He insisted the channel ran downhill from one end to the other. When the first one was finished, he poured a jug of water into it. With parched lips, the prisoners watched the water flow. It dribbled past the halfway point, then stopped and became a pool.

"Who dug this fucking section?" Moll screamed.

The men knew not to delay, it would only lead to more cruelty.

Lewandowski stepped forward, head bowed. A tall, thin man, he was the fastest among the C4 and C5 workers. He was holding his spade, ready to re-dig his section.

"I'm going to give you a chance." The SS-Hauptscharführer smirked. "I'll let you go to the wire. That's a nice, quick death, but it's too easy because the fence is only a hundred meters away. We require more of a test for a desperate, fucking Jew," he mused. "Okay. So, you can race against the dogs." The SS guards were holding two German shepherd dogs on leashes.

"If you get caught before you reach the wire," Moll continued, "I'll haul you back, and it'll be your blood and boiling fat flowing down that channel."

Lewandowski did not move.

"What are you fucking waiting for?" Moll shouted.

Lewandowski set off like a hunted animal. He looked vaguely comical, limbs flailing in a blue-striped uniform that was far too small for him, but for a starving man, he was surprisingly swift.

Lewandowski's speed took the SS soldiers by surprise, and they delayed in releasing the dogs, who were sniffing around curiously.

"Let the dogs go!" Moll shouted.

The dogs sprinted off in frenzied, salivating pursuit.

But Lewandowski was almost at the fence, arms outstretched. A few strides and one last desperate leap and his body would plow into the barbed wire, and it would be over.

There was a loud clap, like thunder. Lewandowski lurched forward and fell to the ground, his arms still outstretched.

"Fast for a fucking Jew!" Moll said. "I couldn't give a Jew the satisfaction of reaching the fence."

Ludwig looked at Moll, who was replacing his pistol in its holster.

When Lewandowski's body was dragged away by two of the SK team, there was an expanding patch of red on the back of his jacket. Moll's aim had been good, and Lewandowski would have died before the dogs set upon him. Moll looked disappointed that he had missed the opportunity to control the last moments of the prisoner's life on the edge of the pit.

"Throw him in," Moll said, walking away. "Make sure the drainage channels are functioning properly before you return to barracks."

The SK men re-dug the channels with more severe slopes to make sure the liquid would flow. The additional time taken meant they were late finishing their shift. Escorted by Moll and his motorbike, they had jogged back to Barracks 13 after thirteen hours of work.

"I've got a different job for you tomorrow." The SS-Hauptscharführer grinned.

*

"If any of you fucking scumbags utters a single word about your work in the crematoria, I'll kill you all. I kill a lot of Jews, but in your cases, I'll make sure your deaths are drawn out and you suffer indescribable pain."

The words of Moll echoed in their heads as the ten members of the Crematorium 4 team made along the path between Crematoria 2 and 3,

The Heroine of Auschwitz

which were, apart from their smoking chimneys, obscured from view by the three-meters-high wattle fence.

Wherever they were going, they were glad to be away from Moll. Ludwig had never felt so much at risk of being murdered for no good reason. Moll was killing more and more Jews and still devising ever more gruesome ways of doing so.

As they walked, Lagerstrasse stretched out before them, flanked by camps B1 and B2. Ludwig had never seen Birkenau from this vantage point. The road ran in a straight line from where they were standing to the entrance and guardhouse, almost a kilometer away.

The arched entrance was barely visible: a yellow summer haze shimmered in front of it, and the dense smoke from the two billowing chimneys threw dust storms of black specks into the air, blurring the landscape like swarms of insects.

Three railway tracks and a ramp ran along the left side of Lagerstrasse. Two trains stood there, separated by the width of the ramp, but the gated entrance to the camp was open, and another train was waiting to enter. Piles of belongings were strewn across the third railway track and graveled road.

The cattle cars stretched into the distance like gigantic black snakes. Passengers were being disgorged from the belly of one, while SS men stood guard by the closed doors of the other.

So this was why Moll had sent them, Ludwig thought. Three transports in quick succession would amount to some 9,000 poor Jews, and the SS needed more SK men to work on the ramp.

SS-Obersturmbannführer Höss, who was responsible for the success or failure of the Hungarian Jews' plan, demanded all staff be made available, irrespective of seniority. It was understood that he had pulled rank on Mengele and insisted he attended all selections. When it came to the selection process, Mengele was the quickest and the best. The doctor had argued that the spike in arrival numbers would lead to more opportunities for meaningful experimentation, and he would have less time for the selections. Höss prevailed, and Mengele was ordered to attend.

As the SK men approached, Ludwig spotted an SS soldier standing on the roof of a cattle car, carrying a camera and apparently taking photographs of the selection process below. Why on earth does the SS want to record this? Ludwig thought. The prisoners, exhausted after their journeys and being forced into lines, were oblivious to the photographer. Perhaps Höss's ego had taken over, and wishing to be seen as the returning hero called back to Birkenau as commandant to sort out the Hungarian Jews, he was recording his achievements for posterity.

The SS usually insisted on leaving no traces of their nefarious activities. With the Red Army rampaging through the German forces and certain to liberate the camp during the coming months, Ludwig felt sure there would be no benefit to Höss if a photographic record of the Birkenau operation fell into the wrong hands.

It was noon on a hot summer's day, and most of the passengers on the first train were in lines. The dust on the newly concreted ramp was being whipped up by thousands of shuffling feet. It looked like a desert sandstorm. Ludwig had arrived in Birkenau in winter, starving and dehydrated. How these people fared, traveling in cattle cars in high summer was unthinkable. He had heard about the Jews of Corfu who arrived during the previous week. Their journey took thirteen days, nine of which were in cattle cars. Rumors abounded that half the occupants died in transit.

SK teams in blue stripes were already on the new platform, building piles of belongings. The SS, with their dogs and batons and guns, were in charge, but there were too many people on the ramp and maintaining order was difficult. Intermittent gunshots rang out.

The kapo led the men to heaps of belongings that were well away from the ramp. There were several handcarts standing to the side.

"Will there be no truck?" one man asked.

"No spare trucks," the kapo replied, shrugging. "All being used."

This SK kapo was attached to the Kanada stores. His work group would convey the stolen belongings by truck or handcart from the platform to the stores, where they would be unloaded. Contact with the Kanada women was forbidden, and almost impossible given how busy everybody was.

The kapo lived in Barracks 13, but the Crematorium 4 team had only brief contact with him. He was not allowed into the crematoria sectors and knew not to ask questions.

Introducing himself as Dieter Richter, he was a man in his forties with fair hair and blue eyes, who was sweating profusely and continuously removing his gray cap to wipe his brow. He wore the familiar kapo armband. Ludwig was relieved to see there was a plain yellow star marked *Jude* on his jacket, without the inverted green triangle, which was the symbol of a criminal and often a guarantee of cruel treatment.

Silently, Richter watched them loading the carts, never raising his wooden stick. When the five carts were full, five pairs of men pulled them to Kanada where they were emptied among the enormous piles of belongings lying outside every shed. Rachael had told Ludwig the sheds were unmanageable, but he had not imagined these scenes. Piles of clothes had been dumped against the side of one shed, so high they toppled onto the tarpaper roof. There must have been forty women working on that section alone, clambering over the clothes like dogs scavenging on a rubbish tip. Each time they fingered an item of clothing that was potentially harboring valuables, the women dashed to the tables indoors. The kapos harried them to work faster, giving no quarter to the females, their sticks whirring through the air. The SS guard looked on, his eyes hungry for the sight of a jewel in a Jewess's palm that he might pounce upon and pocket on his way to the tables.

Whenever Richter spotted an SS soldier, he would raise his club angrily, strike the wooden side of a cart, and shout loud obscenities. His pretense would cease when the guard had passed.

At lunchtime, more carts arrived in Kanada, carrying sacks of bread and tureens of soup. The soup was the everyday thin gruel, sparsely populated with vegetable lumps. The bread was brittle and dry, and each worker received two lumps. No sooner had the women received the food, than the kapos harassed them to recommence their work. Eating, drinking, and running, the women left a trail of puddles and crumbs in their wake. Ludwig and the rest of Richter's team took their rations.

Richter led his team away from Kanada to the water treatment plant, which lay halfway to Crematorium 3. It was a quiet place between the chaos of the storage sheds and crematoria, and the workers ate their food in the shade of the trees whose branches blocked out the chimneys.

Richter was from the Netherlands. Without expectation or notification, he had been made a kapo during the previous week. Having been in Birkenau for over a year, he knew the SS did not like Jews to be kapos, preferring criminals, political prisoners, Jehovah's Witnesses, or any other category of prisoner to be appointed. Only if there was no alternative would a German Jew be selected, or if all else failed, a Jew of a different nationality. The SS intended for the kapos and prisoners to hate each other for reasons of nationality or religion, preferably both.

Over recent weeks, there had been a shortage of kapos, and Richter had been selected as a kapo working on the railway platform for the Sonderkommando.

Relieved to be talking to a kapo who was both Dutch and not a monster, Ludwig asked, "Where in the Netherlands do you come from?"

"Rotterdam," Richter replied.

Ludwig's heart sank as his hope the kapo might know the Kisch family vanished.

"Where are the Dutch living here?" the Pole ventured.

"The men are mostly in B2d and B1b. The women, what's left of them, are in B1a." He paused before adding, "I can't remember when I last saw a Dutch child."

"Do you have family here?"

"Not anymore." Richter shook his head. "Not anymore."

Ludwig felt awkward asking these heart-wrenching questions, and a part of him hoped the Dutchman would fly into a rage and refuse, but the Pole had made a promise.

"How...how many Dutch are left?" the Pole asked. "Does anybody know?"

"Until the end of 'forty-three, there must've been one transport arriving every week," Richter replied. "But this year's been more like one a month, and each one's getting smaller. The Nazis are emptying the Jews out of the Netherlands like a sponge, being squeezed tighter and tighter until *there's not a drop left*." Richter spoke his last words slowly, looking at the ground as if he were indeed watching the last drops falling on the hot, dry earth and fizzling away. "I can only guess that tens of thousands arrived and only a few thousand are left."

"Does anybody know more accurately?" Ludwig persisted.

"There's a Dutch block manager in B1b," Richter replied. "He's your best bet. Perhaps he'll know. Why's a Pole interested in the Dutch?"

"It's for a Dutch friend. She's in the women's camp. She's looking for her eleven-year-old brother."

Richter glared at him. "You shouldn't take advantage of somebody in that way by giving her false hope! The Dutch Jews, we've been obliterated!

The women and children went straight away, and most of the men have followed. An eleven-year-old child won't have made it past the first selection. God rest his soul."

"But the boy *did* survive selection, and he made it to the Disinfection Facility before his sister lost him," Ludwig replied. "And there were a lot of Dutch people there…so he might've gone into the main camp with the men?"

"Being a member of a crematorium SK team's the worst job imaginable," Richter said. "But I guess you've never lived in the main camp, have you?"

Ludwig shook his head. "But Rachael, the boy's sister, lives in B1a, and she's told me some things about life there."

"The SK's got to deal with the outcome of mass murder," the Dutchman continued. "It's horrific, but the prisoners are already dead, and you can do nothing for them.

"When you live in the barracks, the prisoners are alive. You work and sleep with fellow Jews, watching them starve and waste away. A friend steals a piece of stale bread for a sick friend, and the kapos beat him to death before your eyes. Within a minute, somebody's taken the bread.

"You go to sleep and wake to find the man sleeping by your side is dead." Richter took a breath. "You march out of camp in your work group. The man beside you is weak and collapses. The kapo insists you complete his quota, as well as your own, and carry him back, barely alive. And an SS guard shoots him dead when you reach the roll call yard.

"I try not to remember the faces of the living, so I don't recognize them dead. Birkenau has numbed our feelings and compassion, so the face of an unknown dead man means nothing anymore. Why get to know somebody when you're going to have to see them dead?"

Ludwig pondered Richter's words.

"Unfortunately," Richter continued. "You've got to assume the poor boy's gone to the flames."

"I *do* assume he's gone to the flames," Ludwig said. "But until it's proven, and while there's still the slightest chance he's alive, I'll keep looking. It's a promise I've made and won't give up."

"I suggest you get hold of a pass to meet the block manager in B1b," Richter said.

Ludwig asked himself whether he was trying to save a Jewish boy or Rachael's brother. Of course, he was saving her brother, but it had changed. At first, he had regarded the attempt to find her brother as an honorable favor for a fellow Jew. As time passed, his commitment to finding Hannes had increased as his feelings for Rachael had grown, and now, he possessed a determination to locate the boy without fear or regard for the consequences.

Richter might have wanted to avoid looking at people, but every time Ludwig was with Rachael, he couldn't take his eyes off her.

CHAPTER TWENTY-SIX

July 1944

Each morning, tens of thousands of prisoners formed into their work groups like lines of ants, trailing from the barracks to the roll call yards and then onto Lagerstrasse. It took over an hour for them to exit the camp.

The continuous streaks of black smoke across the skyline were never-ending torture for Rachael. The hope she held in her heart was buried a little deeper each day, and the pain of Hannes's absence grew. She consoled herself that at least she had the comfort of uncertain hope, whereas most of the prisoners experienced the agony of knowing the fate of their loved ones.

As the summer wore on, conditions in the camp deteriorated further. The lack of food, the absence of clean water, the rampant sickness, and the unremitting cruelty of the guards and kapos made survival an almost insurmountable mountain to climb. Rachael focused on making sure she woke up the next day, on staying alive to find Hannes, and on meeting Ludwig, who regularly appeared in her thoughts.

Occasionally, she snatched a few moments to stand outside Barracks 19 and look toward the men's camp, separated by the width of Lagerstrasse and two sets of electrified fencing. She attempted to dispel thoughts of Birkenau, but every time she imagined pleasant events from her past in the Netherlands, they were promptly consumed by the reality of camp life.

*

In some ways, it was the easiest time to smuggle gunpowder from the Union factory to the SK revolters. The transportation of the Hungarian Jews was at its peak, and the SS guards were spread thinly across the camp. Every one of the camps in B1 and B2 was forced to accept surplus Jews who could not be sent straight from the new platform to the gas chambers. When not working, prisoners would avoid the stench of the overcrowded barracks by standing outside in droves, making it impossible for the SS guards to apply their normal vigilant supervision, and when the brutality of the guards subsided, the kapos typically followed suit.

Rachael leaned against the rear wall of Barracks 19 where there were fewer prisoners and kapos milling around, and where she was out of the sights of the watchtowers dotted along the fence between the women's camp and Lagerstrasse. Apart from wearing a coat that was too thick for a summer's day, Rachael's appearance was unremarkable.

The women smuggling the explosives alternated their trips to Barracks 19 to avoid raising the suspicions of the guards. That afternoon, it was the turn of Roza Robota. Robota was a Polish Jew from the town of Ciechanów. In her early twenties, she was slight of build, almost delicate, but this disguised her determined character. Quiet and unassuming, she was the ideal resistance worker.

Robota approached Rachael, who withdrew a cigarette from her pocket and offered it to the Polish woman. From a distance, it looked as if Robota passed a bank note to Rachael in exchange for the cigarette. In fact, it was a scrap of paper, folded several times and containing precious granules of gunpowder, which Rachael placed in the same pocket. After a few minutes of conversation, Robota turned and walked quietly away, and Rachael went back into Barracks 19. She would hand the explosives to Ludwig at their next meeting.

*

"I'm sorry to keep asking favors," Ludwig said, "but we need a camera."

Ludwig and Rachael were sitting in their usual places. The recently erected wattle fence screened the Crematorium 4 compound from Kanada. The incineration pyres were burning, and prisoners who had been selected were being forced to undress among the trees where they could see neither crematorium, save for the black smoking chimneys.

Although Moll would never praise a Jew, he had been impressed by Ludwig's fence-building skills. He tested the tightness of the wattle by attempting to penetrate it with his fingers, but without success. So Moll had made Ludwig team leader for the fence erection, supervised by a ginger-haired guard, SS-Schütze Klein. As a result, Ludwig could leave a loose section in the wattle, about a yard wide on the far side of the Crematorium 4 compound, next to the solitary birch tree. He pulled it back when meeting Rachael, replacing it when she left.

"A camera?" Rachael replied. "Pen and paper are relatively easy to smuggle. They're small and plentiful. Getting hold of a camera's more difficult, and it's much bigger to keep hidden. I assume you'll need film with it?"

Ludwig nodded.

"From time to time, we come across a camera in a suitcase. Suitcases are being emptied in Sheds 12 and 18, but there's so many new prisoners, we've fallen far behind," Rachael said. After a few moments, she continued. "I was going to use an extra shed, but if we stay in Sheds 12 and 18, they'll become chaotic. I don't like disorganization, but it could work in our favor. If we create a little mayhem, it'll be trickier for the kapos and guards to monitor us, and easier for us to smuggle a camera out.

"With all these extra suitcases, I'm sure we'll find a camera and film. We'll just need to keep our fingers crossed that we're not spotted."

Ludwig squeezed her hand.

"I can't believe how brave you are," he said. "I think you're a heroine. You're the most effective member of the resistance! The Camp Resistance talks a lot about taking action but always makes excuses for doing nothing. You're *doing* things!"

"I know, but if a resistance worker gets caught, they get killed," she replied. "And the SS takes reprisals, and it invariably leads to ten innocent people being murdered. So we're taking risks, which *could* have repercussions for the other prisoners."

"Let's make sure we don't get caught before the Soviets arrive," Ludwig said. "What's happening behind the wattle fences is inhumanity beyond description. We're trying to get photographic evidence, not just written or verbal testimonies."

"The incineration pyres are horrific. The ovens in Crematoria 4 and 5 have been overloaded and overworked and are breaking down all the time. They're nowhere near keeping up with the gas chambers. When we empty the chambers, we turn left for the ovens, right for the pits. We're going right more often than we go left now.

"In the incineration room, we slide the bodies into the ovens and slam the retort doors shut. Then we turn away for thirty minutes and there's nothing but ashes left, but the pits are wide open, so we see the bodies in every stage of burning. Bodies we've laid out ourselves. Moll has bought railway sleepers, which are layered in the pits to improve the airflow and burn the bodies more quickly. Yet again, the Nazis strive to improve efficiency.

"Moll's proving himself to be the devil incarnate, and the pyres are the hell where he reigns. He loves making people suffer before killing them. He'll stand women and children by the edge of the pyres and shoot them. If a few prisoners are left over when the gas chamber is sealed, he'll shoot them as well. He doesn't need the SS guards. He's happy to pull the trigger. Genuinely happy. Even women cradling their babies! Yesterday, he tried killing a mother and baby with one single bullet. It's unspeakable.

"There was a boy," Ludwig continued. "Must've been nine or ten. The SS found a few trinkets on him, a ring or two. He must've picked them up off the floor. Moll had him thrown alive onto the pyre. I've never heard screaming like it.

"I thought emptying the gas chambers was horrific, but watching people burn is beyond words, and if an SK worker underperforms in Moll's eyes, he's thrown in the pit as well. Alive! So what choice is there but to carry on? Moll behaves in the most barbaric way possible."

"I'll find you a camera, but who'll take a photograph knowing what will happen if Moll discovers them?" Rachael asked. "It's an enormous risk!"

"The camera must be hidden and nearby," Ludwig answered. "And the photographer will have just a few seconds to take the shots when there are no kapos or guards in the vicinity. So he'll need a couple of lookouts to tell him when the coast is clear. I don't think he'll be able to raise the camera to his eye and aim. It's too risky. Maybe he'll hide it in his coat and shoot from around his midriff. Without aiming, he might take photos of the sky or the ground, rather than the pyres. Let's hope not."

"And who'll be taking these risks?" she repeated.

"There are six of us in this action group," Ludwig answered. "So it will be three of the six."

That evening, with the promise of increased rations from SS-Unterscharführer Mann, Rachael and Elke worked extra hours to help clear the backlog of belongings in Kanada. They went to Shed 12, collecting four other trustworthy women workers on the way. There, they tore the suitcases open with only one aim in mind: to find a camera and film.

CHAPTER TWENTY-SEVEN

July 1944

It felt like hell to Rachael. It was midday, and the summer sun was searing. Whether inside the sheds or outside among the piles of belongings, it was unbearably hot. The slightest movement was tiring for the women, but the Hungarian prisoners' possessions kept coming, from the continuous stream of trucks running from the new platform and the gas chambers, and the heavily laden handcarts pushed by the exhausted men.

Operating the Kanada gold-melting furnace only added to her discomfort, but she thought of Ludwig and the other SK workers manning their ovens and realized it was they who were living in the flames of hell. She was merely working in extreme heat.

SS-Unterscharführer Mann brought her a cup of water while she was stoking the coal. She thanked him profusely but wondered whether it was human compassion or the greed for gold that motivated him.

Rachael passed the gold ingots to Mann, which he weighed and left the shed to carry to the main Auschwitz camp. Even in this scorching heat, he would not delegate this task to anybody else.

The shed door had scarcely shut when Zuzana arrived. Rachael could tell the Czech woman had information by the way she walked straight toward her, never losing eye contact. Unable to wait, the Dutch woman moved forward to greet her.

"What is it?" she asked urgently. "Have you got news? What's happened to Hannes?" The questions tumbled uncontrollably from her mouth.

Zuzana's demeanor, which was neither positive nor negative, made Rachael wary. The Czech's expression was normally open and obvious. Perhaps her emotions had been ground down by life in Birkenau as well, Rachael thought.

"I do," Zuzana replied.

"What is it? What is it?" Rachael begged.

Zuzana paused, and Rachael's spirits sank. All she wanted to hear were the simple words "he's alive," no more, no less. That would have sufficed, but the few moments' pause told her that would not happen. There were no happy endings in this place.

"He's in Dachau," Zuzana replied.

"What?" Rachael spoke so loudly several of the women working at the tables looked up. This was a response she had not anticipated.

"Hannes was sent to Dachau in June," Zuzana explained. "That's why some of his paperwork was missing. With all the Hungarian transports arriving, his transfer form was stuck on some administrator's desk being processed. When it finally was processed, it was returned to the camp registry. Luckily, we'd given Franz the extra bribes, and when his SS contact returned to the Administration Office, a prisoner went back to Hannes's file, and the transfer form was there.

"It's good news," she continued. "Hannes was definitely alive last month."

"But why was he sent to Dachau?" Rachael asked.

"Apparently, the Red Army's smashing the German army and is advancing through Eastern Europe. Birkenau's as full as it's ever been, and the SS are worried the Soviets will liberate the camp with tens of thousands of dying prisoners still here. So they've been sending transports *out* of Birkenau, destined for camps farther west, well out of the way, but there are so many transports coming in, the capacity of the railway lines has only permitted a few out."

"So this is the same news as last time," Rachael said with resignation. "Hannes may be alive but may be dead." Since the day of their separation, Rachael had been preparing for tragic or exhilarating news about her brother. This news stranded her in a kind of limbo and in a persistent state of anxiety.

"And I'll say the same as I did last time," Zuzana responded. "Most people know their family members are dead. Your position's much better. And anyway, Dachau's a concentration camp and Birkenau's an extermination camp, so that's much better for Hannes."

"You're right," Rachael conceded. "Thank you, Zuzana." She found herself admiring the Czech woman for her mature and comforting words.

The two women exited Shed 1 to tackle the chaotic mounds of belongings and the blazing rays of the sun.

CHAPTER TWENTY-EIGHT

August 1944

"This is the largest roll call I've ever seen," Rachael gasped.

"It could last for hours," Elke added, standing directly behind her friend.

Women prisoners were thronging in front of the kitchen barracks in such numbers they were spilling into the gaps between the accommodation barracks opposite. The block managers were running around frantically, trying to herd their prisoners into lines, but the new arrivals from Hungary had never attended roll call and, not understanding the German language, were walking around aimlessly and unwittingly, causing more chaos.

"It's going to be a selection roll call," Rachael said.

"How do you know?" Elke asked.

"Mann told me both C3 and C5 broke down yesterday, so all the Hungarians were sent into the barracks," Rachael answered before adding, "Usually, the SS is in a rush to finish roll call and get us sent out to work. Today, they're taking their time. They know it's going to be a long one."

"The situation in the Kanada sheds is bad enough without its workers being stuck here," Elke said.

Block leader Kaminski stepped forward to address the women. "You must be extremely tired. If any of you don't wish to be standing around for hours, by all means, sit down and take the weight off your feet."

"Nobody sit down!" Elke urged those around her. "It's a trick! Those who sit down are volunteering themselves for selection. Pass the message on."

Voices spoke up among the women, and some of the new arrivals who had sat down stood back up, but the message did not gain widespread understanding, and many others sat on the ground and, when prompted by an SS guard or kapo, willingly moved and joined the new group of sitting prisoners. The Hungarians simply did not understand what was happening.

"No, no!" Elke moaned as the group steadily grew, like a pool of blood spreading across the ground.

If one of the sitting group tried to move back to the main roll call, a kapo would beat them until they sat down again. The women, many of whom had only arrived the previous day, looked terrified.

Kaminski had found a Hungarian woman who spoke German, and together they walked among the crowd, repeating the offer to sit down. A steady stream of women accepted and took their places without showing signs of distress.

After an hour, the roll call lines were still not organized and there were hundreds of women in the sitting group.

The rising sun cast its first rays onto the roll call yard. On Lagerstrasse, the orchestra started playing a familiar marching tune, and the block managers of the women's camp continued to scurry around like frightened mice, desperately searching for the women on their barracks lists. The bodies of those who had died during the night had been placed in rows in front of the block leaders but because of the increasingly diminished space were piled four high.

The women, whether standing or sitting, were feeling uncomfortable from the summer heat on their skin and not having moved for so long. Rachael felt a cramp in her leg, but had to let it recede of its own accord. She was near the front of her row, and the kapos were targeting those who were not standing up straight.

Once a kapo latched on to a prisoner, it could become a death sentence. For not standing up straight, the kapo might administer a beating so severe it was impossible for the victim to stand erect afterward. Although the prisoners' clothing was shabby and filthy, a kapo might resort to violence over a missing button or upturned lapel.

"My God!" Elke exclaimed. "Both Mengele and Grese are here!"

Rachael looked up to see SS-Hauptsturmführer Mengele and SS-Oberaufseherin Grese walking through the gate of B1a. They joined the SS roll call officer and engaged in conversation. The Dutch woman was too far away from the SS soldiers to hear their words but watched them closely. Mengele was agitated, his hand directed to various parts of the roll call yard before he finally pointed at the officer himself.

The roll call officer, a small man with a complexion as pale as any of the starving prisoners, stepped toward the group of sitting prisoners and coughed before speaking.

"Attention!" he shouted. "It can't be comfortable sitting on the hard ground. You'll be escorted to a barracks that will shield you from the bright sunlight." He turned to face the rest of the prisoners. "If you're tired, this is your last chance to join this group. Go now, if you wish." The German-speaking Hungarian continued to translate his words.

Despite the warnings of the experienced prisoners, scores of women made their way to the sitting group. With the orchestra playing loudly in the background, the SS soldiers and kapos screaming at the prisoners, and the discontented murmuring of a crowd of thousands upon thousands, the confused Hungarians did not know what they were doing.

"No!" Elke moaned. "It's a trick!"

"Try not to worry," Rachael said. "Somebody has to be selected. It's better for it to be them rather than us."

"I know," Elke replied desperately. "Why not just tell them the truth, rather than give them false hope? The SS are so cruel! Killing people is barbaric, but the deception is insane."

"You know we can't do that," Rachael replied, placing her hand on her friend's shoulder.

"I know!" Elke repeated.

"We must concentrate now Mengele and Grese are here," Rachael said. "Otherwise, we'll be selected, even though we work in Kanada."

The pale SS officer addressed Kaminski. "The dead bodies are getting in the way. I want your block manager to get them removed. Tell him to liaise with the other managers so their registers are correct. If they don't tally with my sheets, we'll be here all day. I'm holding your manager responsible if they don't."

Kaminski approached Lisowski. Rachael watched and saw the block manager's shoulders slump when he received his orders. The block elder addressed him sternly, and the manager strode off to search for the other block managers. Within a few minutes, he had gathered twenty of the thirty block managers employed elsewhere in the women's camp and led them to the bodies. After two hours of roll call, the pile of corpses had grown.

Lisowski surveyed his paperwork and addressed his fellow managers.

"We've got to remove these bodies," he said. "I'll call out the tattoo numbers, and you shout out if they're on your list."

"Mine don't have tattoos," a manager with sharp features and brown hair replied.

"What do you mean?" Lisowski asked. "All new prisoners are tattooed."

"Not anymore," the manager said. "There were so many arrivals yesterday, they had to give up tattooing to keep the prisoners moving."

"If there's too many arrivals, then they go to—" Lisowski was interrupted before he could complete his sentence.

"There was no capacity for that either," the brown-haired functionary said. "So loads of them were sent into camp without tattoos."

"All my arrivals have tattoos," Lisowski said.

"Then you're a lucky bastard, Lisowski," the manager said. "None of the new arrivals in my barracks have tattoos. I must have a hundred names without numbers. How do I identify the body of someone I don't know without a tattoo?"

Lisowski rubbed his chin nervously, racking his brains for a solution to satisfy Kaminski.

"Look, who cares about a dead body with no number?" he said eventually. "We'll go through the pile, pull out the bodies with numbers, delete them from our registers, and dispose of them right away. Exactly as we normally do." He drew a deep breath before continuing. "The remaining dead women are anonymous, so when we dispose of a body, we just delete a name with no number off the register. Whether it's a Schmidt or a Müller or a Bauer, who cares as long as one body's carted away and one name's taken off the register?"

The block managers gave their assent with varying degrees of enthusiasm, and Lisowski kneeled among the corpses and started reading out numbers. He ordered four nearby blue stripes to carry the bodies away.

*

The mid-morning sun was blazing, the sky to the south azure. To the north, four dirty black clouds hung above the tree line and blotted the sky.

The SS roll call officer insisted the women stand to attention throughout, staying bolt upright with headwear removed. When women, overcome with the heat, replaced their headscarves to provide shade for their boiling shaven heads, the kapos and blue stripes descended upon them like hyenas on a carcass.

Rachael wanted to put her headscarf back on. Although as a Kanada worker she could grow her hair, and it sheltered her head and neck from the sun, she was frightened. Her striking red hair stood out, even when it had been clumsily shaven. Standing out to the SS guards and kapos who only needed the slightest incitement to pluck a woman from the line, and most of all, standing out to Grese, who had been following Doctor Mengele during his selections, it was only a matter of time before she was spotted. The doctor had started his selection at the far side of the roll call yard but was moving inexorably toward her.

SS-Hauptsturmführer Mengele was making slow progress with his selection. It was the hottest day of summer, and he had stayed in the shade of his office until well after the start of roll call, correctly surmising that there would be chaos after the recent transports of Hungarian Jews. The ground itself seemed to radiate heat. He dragged his feet, even when SS-Oberaufseherin Grese joined him with her growling dog straining at its leash.

Doctor Mengele ordered the women to strip naked prior to his examination. This would slow the process down further, but enabled him to make considered, methodical decisions. Like everybody else, he knew the Red Army was on the march, and he was keen to make sure his last weeks or months of experimentation were as fruitful as possible. He needed patients with the greatest likelihood of withstanding thorough testing over a short period. The last thing he needed was patients dying of typhus part way through an experiment.

The naked women fascinated Mengele. He had studied anthropology and medicine at the University of Bonn and subsequently developed a fanatical interest in the human body and how it could serve the Aryan race and philosophy. Having access to innumerable numbers of Jewish and Roma prisoners, both dead and alive, permitted him to enhance his studies with physical experimentation.

The physical procedures and operations were not to Mengele's taste, so he used Jewish and Roma doctors to perform these. An increased daily food allowance and the hope of avoiding the gas chamber was ordinarily enough to make most prisoner doctors comply. Scientific research was his passion, and he was proud to share his results with medical institutions in Germany and Austria.

Doctor Mengele's selection routine was more in-depth, as it included an additional step. As well as extermination and hard labor, he selected women for experimentation. The naked women whom Mengele deemed to be beyond their reproductive years were selected for the gas chamber. Pregnant women or sets of twins of any age would be chosen for experimentation, unless they were sick. The rest were subjected to a physical examination, carried out with the pointed end of his wooden baton. The Nazi prodded their flesh and coaxed their mouths open with its tip. He walked around them as if he were evaluating a statue in a museum.

Rachael wondered what the Hungarian arrivals made of the sight of Grese's beautiful face peering over the doctor's shoulder, smirking and leering at the women's bodies. The SS-SS-Oberaufseherin might watch twenty women being selected for death and then, without warning, pounce on the next woman and hand out a severe beating.

*

The midday sun was scalding. The selection had been in progress for six hours, and the ash clouds were filling the sky like ink on blotting paper.

During those hours, Rachael attempted to estimate the size of the roll call. Usually, the women would line up in rows of five between the kitchen block and the B1b fence, then overflow into the narrow spaces between the living barracks. Lisowski told them such a roll call would comprise 1,000 women in front of the kitchen and 4,000 between the barracks, stretching halfway along B1a.

But the arrival of the Hungarians changed everything. Inside the barracks, the ground-floor berths were full, and there was no deference shown to the higher bunks where five or six women now slept. The hospital barracks contained more prisoners than patients, and the SS came in daily to select the sickest for transfer to Block 25.

Outside, the women were lined up seven in a row with barely enough space for a kapo or SS guard to pass between the prisoners and the barracks walls. The lines reached the farthest boundary of the camp.

Rachael had no accurate way of calculating the number of women present for this roll call, but based upon the information from Lisowski, she thought it must have been at least double his figure.

More than ten thousand in one roll call, shoehorned into B1a of the women's camp.

It seemed incredible. On the other side of the barbed wire fence, the crowd in B1b was of a similar size, and on the other side of Birkenau, prisoners from B2 were spilling onto Lagerstrasse when camps had overflowed.

Birkenau's throngs of people looked chaotic and out of control. The SS would not tolerate a lack of order. Rachael knew there would be an extremely high number of selections that day.

The roll call seemed far from a conclusion. The block managers continued to run around with their registers flapping in the air, but they had slowed down noticeably. Even they were feeling the heat, and the fear of a beating could not speed them up.

Lisowski's plan for the registration of bodies had partially succeeded. The correct number of names had been deleted from the registers, but the managers had guessed which barracks each body belonged to. As a result, some barracks registers had accounted for every single inmate, but women from those barracks were still standing, uncounted. The managers sought to shuffle names between registers, but every time Lisowski approached the roll call leader to sign off a count sheet, there was a discrepancy.

Every time there was a discrepancy, Lisowski was summoned by Kaminski, then chastised, then beaten. The pain he was suffering was visible as he hobbled between the lines.

*

After eight hours, women were succumbing to the heat every minute. Earlier, they would have been held up by their neighbors, but now, if they collapsed, it was their neighbors who hauled them away. The roll call yard was still crammed with women overflowing into the spaces between the barracks and the fences, so those selected were immediately carried or dragged to Barracks 25 of the women's camp, where prisoners were held prior to being sent to the gas chambers. The carriers themselves were frequently so exhausted they did not return.

This was the cruelest selection Rachael had experienced. Usually, the Kanada workers were released early. But not today. The women had to keep standing to cling on to life while watching the SS and senior kapos drinking water and eating their food. The block managers could not take a break until their respective registers balanced. And none of them balanced.

By this time, SS-Hauptsturmführer Mengele had selected a hundred inmates for experimentation, who had been escorted by the kapos to a barracks adjoining his office in B2e. The hundreds chosen for extermination were taken to wait in Barracks 25. With his job done, Mengele returned to his office.

With Mengele gone, SS-Oberaufseherin Grese took a more active role in the remaining selections. She unleashed her dog, which, despite the debilitating heat, matched the vigor of its owner and pounced at the women, who shrank back in absolute terror. A long, insistent moan swelled from the rear of the lines as the women squeezed together, and those at the back were crushed against the brick kitchen block. When the congestion eased, many had died, and the block managers had to have the bodies removed so they could take their roll call counts again.

Grese continued selection, leaving the dog nuzzling at the bodies on the ground.

Rachael watched as the SS woman drew closer, row by row, until she was a few meters away.

Suddenly, Grese looked toward her. Rachael tried to look away, but too late, and their eyes met.

"It's my pretty redhead!" Grese said. "I see you're still alive. You know you've got the nicest hair in the women's camp? Though that's not saying much, looking at these Jewish hags."

Rachael nervously fidgeted, hoping the SS officer would not approach. But without looking, she sensed her looming presence.

"I thought I might never find you again," the SS woman continued. "But your hair stands out like a flame in this glorious sunshine, whether it's long or short or just been butchered by those clumsy barbers. I suppose this is one time when your hair hasn't helped you. Sorry, I'm being insensitive talking about flames in front of you Jews, aren't I?" Grese laughed.

"Look at me!" the SS woman demanded.

As she always did, Rachael held her head bowed. Suddenly, she felt a searing pain as her ragged hair was tugged so violently, she was dragged out of the Barracks 19 lines and found herself standing, head up and facing the SS-Oberaufseherin.

Grese looked at the strands of Rachael's hair, which were nestled in her fingers, before throwing them to the ground and wiping her hands against each other as if removing stubborn and unpleasant dirt.

"I'm so sorry," Grese said, smiling. "Your hair just came off in my hand!"

A patch of Rachael's scalp was stinging, but she remained impassive. As a Kanada worker and assistant to Mann, she was usually safe from the SS monster, but this roll call was so large and chaotic, she could assume nothing. This was confirmed when Grese next spoke.

"I think you need to be examined!" she said. "Take your clothes off!"

Rachael was incredulous and did not move.

"Take your clothes off!" Grese demanded, rapping her baton insistently against her palm.

Although she had been asked to do the same thing as hundreds of women had done that day, Rachael felt exceedingly vulnerable standing in front of Grese. Despite the piercing heat of the sun, she shivered as if an icy breeze were brushing her skin. Being there, in the open, among thousands of women and, beyond the fences, thousands of men, was more humiliating than her experience in the Disinfection Facility on her first day in Birkenau. Somewhere out there was Ludwig. How she longed to be sitting by the fence with him at that moment. Or better still, sipping a coffee with her friends in Dam Square in Amsterdam.

Grese was standing with her arms crossed, smirking at the Dutch woman, whose discomfort amused her. After a couple of minutes, she raised her baton and poked Rachael in the chest. Rachael felt it probing her soft flesh before meeting the solid resistance of her ribcage. Grese withdrew the weapon, and Rachael looked down to see a small red indentation in her breast, but her skin remained unbroken.

The SS soldier stepped forward and put her mouth to Rachael's ear.

"If you're *very* nice to me, I could be *very* nice to you," she whispered

The words were spoken in a lascivious tone, which sickened Rachael, but she remained impassive.

The SS-Oberaufseherin observed Rachael for several more excruciating minutes.

"Okay. Get dressed and get back in line," she said emphatically before returning to her selection duties.

Rachael put her clothes back on. Over recent months, she had shared all her experiences in Birkenau with Ludwig, but she would never speak of this episode with him. With anyone.

BOOK THREE

WINTER 1944/45

REVOLT AND LIBERATION

CHAPTER TWENTY-NINE

September 1944

"They've murdered them all!" Ludwig said.

"Murdered who?" Rachael asked.

"The extra two hundred SK men who were used to dispose of the Hungarians."

"But you told me they'd been transferred to a different work camp!"

"The SS lied. We should've known. They'll never let the SKs work anywhere else in case they tell people what goes on in the crematoria." His fingers squeezed her hand uncomfortably firmly, but she made no protest.

"How do you know they've been murdered?" she asked.

Ludwig shook his head. "Last night, the C3 SK workers were sent back to the barracks early. That's never happened before. The SS told them some bodies of German soldiers who'd died in combat against the Red Army had been sent here and were to be given the dignity of being cremated by Germans, not *filthy* Jews. So the SS would carry out the incineration."

"Take your time, my love," Rachael said, sensing his rising anger.

"For once, the SS haven't been so smart," Ludwig continued. "The C3 stokers have incinerated thousands of Jews, and they've become highly proficient workers. The SS guards watch from a distance and don't truly understand how the job's done.

"In each oven, there are nooks and crannies that are unseen and difficult to access. The SS men didn't clean down properly after their work was done. The next morning, one of the stokers opened the retort and looked inside. He found a fragment of blue-striped cloth, for goodness' sake!

"The other stokers found some familiar objects among the ashes—a half-melted ring bearing the remnants of an inscription, which an SK man recognized. Even a glass eye, which must have fallen out of its socket. How we prayed it was Moll's!" Ludwig said. "But of course, it wasn't. It was Kucharczyk's, a distinctive pale blue."

"So what happens next?" Rachael asked.

"Well," he replied. "The murder of these two hundred SK men means the extermination of the Hungarians is finished, and there are barely any European Jews left to transport. There are no trains arriving today, and with the Red Army advancing, there'll be no Soviet prisoners arriving either. So it's only a matter of time before Moll kills the next two hundred. And so on." Ludwig paused before adding, "Of course, it's completely different in Kanada! You've got months of work piled up in the sheds."

"Okay. So what happens next?" she repeated.

"We can't wait any longer!" Ludwig answered. "We can't wait for the SS to kill us. We must revolt now! We could have revolted weeks ago but allowed people like Wojciech to delay us. We should have acted and not debated..." His voice tailed off for a moment.

"The four women in the Union factory have been risking their lives for months, smuggling tiny amounts of gunpowder from every shift they work. Yesterday, we finished our twentieth grenade. We can't let their efforts be wasted." He paused. "We can't let *your* efforts be wasted. After all, you're the one who's been collecting the explosives from the four women and passing them to me.

"We've rehearsed our plan. At the shift changeover, we attack and kill the SS guards in C4 and C5 and steal their weapons. Then, the Camp Resistance starts disturbances inside the men's camp, where we'll join them later. Together, we work our way through each of the camps, building our numbers and gathering weapons and ammunition as we go. When we've got enough, we open the main camp gate, and those who wish to make a run for it can do so. We'll return to destroy the crematoria buildings, overcome the watchtower guards near C5, and then make our escape."

Rachael leaned forward until she could feel the vibration of the electric current brushing her face. She placed both her hands on his hand and wrapped it tightly in her fingers.

"But you must survive, my love," she pleaded, staring at him. "You've promised you'll stay alive. Not just to be a witness. The Red Army will be here soon. Why take the risk?"

He replied without raising his head. "Moll will take the next two hundred soon. Perhaps next week. Then he'll shut down C2 and C3 or C4 and C5, and that's another hundred of us gone. And when he incinerates the last body and destroys the last crematorium, he'll murder the rest of us. And if the Soviets get here first, the surviving SK workers will be killed the day before they step foot into the camp. The SS wants no witnesses."

He placed his other hand on hers. Together, their hands formed a pyramid shape on the ground, barely five centimeters under the lowest length of wire.

"Before, I needed to survive, but you've made me want to stay alive," Ludwig said. "And I'll do my very best, but death's not far away from the SK men."

Usually, Rachael left their meetings first, but today, it was Ludwig who departed when he heard the growl of Moll's approaching motorbike, leaving Rachael to spend a few moments contemplating her position.

She had given up trying to keep the prisoners' belongings indoors. The arrival of the Hungarians had stretched operations in every area of Auschwitz, and none could cope. Not even the renowned organizational skills of the Nazis could bring order.

She had managed the gold and valuables closely, and Mann was especially pleased when the number of ingots increased significantly. But the Dutch woman was thankful the most senior SS officers never visited Kanada because, in her efforts to find and melt gold and valuables, the other sheds had been neglected. Prosthetic limbs, spectacles, and hair were thrown together in the far corner of the compound, sometimes bagged up but often left strewn across the ground. Empty cases, shoes, and clothes that had been examined for valuables were piled up everywhere, against the outside walls of the sheds or in mounds on the grass where the women used to spend their spare time. But SS-Obersturmbannführer Höss's only concern was the gold and his plans to destroy the Auschwitz camp network, not the condition of the Kanada stores.

Mann earned a great deal of kudos from the camp hierarchy. Rachael would note the smile on the SS-Unterscharführer's face when he returned from Auschwitz I each evening. This was the best time of day to ask favors of him, and he rarely turned her down.

Although wearing a headscarf was not a requirement in Kanada, Rachael wore one when her hair had grown, only removing it during her time with Ludwig. With his endearing reticence, he had expressed his liking of her red locks, and as she tucked her hair in, she thought of this Pole whom she had chanced upon weeks ago, and the way they had squeezed each other's hands.

It was as if Rachael's heart was enclosed in barbed wire. She was permanently aware of its presence, not touching her but close by and threatening. If she controlled herself, her heart would remain intact, but whenever it raced and expanded, the barbs pierced her. The more it raced, the more it hurt. She dearly wished it would stay calm, but every time she met Ludwig, she could not prevent it pounding. A shriveled heart would feel no barbs, but she could not stop it, no matter how much it hurt.

The redhead tucked the last wisps of hair underneath her headscarf and stood up to make her way back to the sheds.

CHAPTER THIRTY

September 1944

Rachael was already waiting for Ludwig as he approached the fence. Her head was bowed, and her upturned hand lay on the ground beneath the wire.

He took her hand and looked at her face. Their meetings had been oases of contentment, but today, his pleasure at their meeting was not reciprocated. Her face was drawn. It was only a day since he had last seen her, but she had aged, looking tired and emotionless.

"What's wrong?" he inquired. "What's wrong?" he repeated, gripping her hand tightly.

Rachael drew herself up and took a deep breath

"It was today's roll call," Rachael stammered, fighting back tears.

Typhus reigned in Barracks 19 of the women's camp. The whole of B1a had succumbed to a severe outbreak of the disease. Although the intention was to exterminate the Hungarian Jews, there was simply not enough killing capacity available, so a substantial number of the 400,000 arrivals were sent into the camp, meaning most barracks, already overflowing with prisoners, had to accommodate several hundred more.

The disease took hold, spreading like the plague as infected lice proliferated among the women sleeping ten to a roost. Advanced symptoms caused coughing, vomiting, and diarrhea, which only led to further deteriorations in their filthy and unhygienic living conditions. The night air was haunted by the moaning of the afflicted.

"This morning, there were fifteen women who'd died during the night," Rachael continued. "Baumann insisted on an inspection and selection roll call. He said the SS had to identify those unfit for work. They're trying to reduce the overcrowding."

"But the Kanada workers are okay?" Ludwig worried. "You stay clean by having your own latrines and washrooms."

"But the lice get everywhere," she replied. "Kaminski asked Baumann if we could go straight to the sheds, but before he could answer, Grese told him she'd spotted some weaklings among the Kanada workers who needed weeding out, so he refused."

Ludwig's heart sank when he heard Grese's name.

"So he made everybody stay for the duration," Rachel continued. "It was yet another massive roll call. Usually, there're fewer than ten names selected. But not today. Baumann and Grese, plus both kapos, physically inspected every woman.

"Those selected could scarcely walk. They had to be helped to Barracks 25. Of course, Grese ordered me to escort them."

"Barracks 25?" Ludwig asked.

"They put the women who've been selected in Barracks 25," Rachael answered. "It's like a holding area. Only when the SS have enough to fill the gas chamber will they send them off."

"So they're selected to be gassed and then forced to wait?" Ludwig asked with incredulity. "That's beyond cruelty."

"We all know the gas chamber lies in wait for us," she replied. "But we go to sleep each night, holding a fragile hope. The souls in Barracks 25 go to sleep without hope, knowing they're going to be gassed soon but not knowing when. That must be agonizing."

Ludwig squeezed her hand. "You were telling me about roll call?"

"There must've been over fifty women taken to Barracks 25. All sick with typhus.

"As ever, Grese was dressed immaculately and wearing makeup, which highlighted those cheekbones and blood-red lips. She kept using her gloved hands to wipe specks of dust from those shiny black jackboots. She inspected the prisoners, using her baton to examine their hair and prod their bodies. Has there ever been a greater contrast? Between a woman looking like a curvaceous movie star and prisoners as thin as twigs, with every trace of their femininity buried beneath layers of filth and starvation.

"Grese may be beautiful on the outside, but on the inside, she's dirtier and uglier than any woman in the whole of Auschwitz."

"I wonder what'll become of those who survive this place," Ludwig remarked. "Will they ever know love, happiness, and forgiveness again?"

"Love's hibernating in Auschwitz," Rachael said. "For the survivors, it'll bloom once more." She smiled thinly at him, her face framed by the barbed wire. Then her expression became stern.

"Anyway, Elke's had a cough," Rachael continued. "It's not typhus, it's just a cough, but Grese heard her, and I swear she was looking at me as well as Elke when she spoke.

"'Not feeling so well? Typhus making you feel tired and feverish?' Grese asked. Elke shook her head vigorously but couldn't stop herself from coughing.

"'It's just a cough,' I said. I know I should have kept quiet, but I couldn't stop myself.

"'I wasn't talking to you,' the monster said. 'I was talking to your friend here, who's contracted typhus, which is deadly.' She was taunting me, so I said nothing, but it was too late. Grese had already pushed Elke with a firm prod of her baton.

"I was at the front of the line, facing the kapos and Baumann. Grese was behind me, guiding Elke toward the group of women destined for Barracks 25.

"'She works as a supervisor in Kanada!' I pleaded with her. A few months ago, the block management might have listened, but they ignored me. They had a selection target to hit.

"Watching Elke being taken away and seeing her for the last time was unbearable. She'd been the one who stood beside me as a friend from my first day in Birkenau and who taught me how to survive the daily horrors of the camp.

"Elke raised her head, turning it slowly in my direction. She clasped her hands together against her chest as if in prayer. I gave up praying long ago. I mouthed the words 'thank you' and smiled. I think she smiled back, but I can't be certain. It was so fleeting."

Ludwig looked at Rachael, her head remaining bowed. "Remember what we promised," he said. "We must survive. No matter what horrors are put in our path, we must overcome them. Every time somebody dies, it's a tragedy, but we must be thankful it isn't us. Grieve now, then let the grief pass and carry on living. It's the only way."

The pair sat in silence until Ludwig heard a cough coming from Crematorium 4. SS-Schütze Klein was standing outside the building. Ludwig could not afford to fall out of favor with the guard, whom he bribed into letting him meet Rachael. He squeezed her hand, let go and, as he stood up, spoke.

"I love you."

The words appeared from nowhere, as if he had not intended to say them out loud. He was frozen with embarrassment. He was standing and she was sitting, so their eyes did not meet. They gazed in opposite directions.

The silence was broken by another cough from Klein, and Ludwig walked away.

"And I love you, too," Rachael whispered after he was gone. Love was a difficult word in Auschwitz. Amid the death and degradation, the threat of immeasurable pain and suffering was only ever a heartbeat away. It was best not to nurture love; it could not survive there.

She rose to her feet and made her way back to Shed 1.

CHAPTER THIRTY-ONE

October 5, 1944

"We need two hundred more Sonderkommando workers," Moll bellowed. "They're required for special projects in a labor camp in Germany."

Does he think we're idiots? Ludwig thought. This pretense is worse than telling the truth and shooting us dead on the spot.

"Of course, the SS could select the names," Moll continued. "But we'll give you the opportunity to do so. The work in Germany is important and urgent, so you must decide promptly. I expect the two hundred names to be in my hands by the morning of October seventh. You've got two days."

Moll turned on his heels and walked out of the Barracks 13 yard, the camp functionaries scuttling after him.

The SK men dispersed from their roll call rows, some making their way into the building, others remaining outside, gathering in small groups. Ludwig joined the revolt group, a circle of men in the far corner of the yard.

All the members of the group were speaking at once, but the message was clear. They had to act quickly.

"Moll's likely to arrange a transport or murder the two hundred during the night," Ludwig said. "Either way, we must act on the evening of the October seventh at the latest."

"We won't be able to get the Camp Resistance on board in that time," Wojciech complained.

"Their stance has been to say a lot, but do nothing," Smizer replied. "I propose we carry out our action with or without the participation of the Camp Resistance."

There was a murmur of consent from the other members of the group.

"So we'll revolt on the evening of October seventh, when the night shift relieves the day shift," Smizer added. "Each of us knows his role. We've rehearsed them often enough. During the morning, I'll move the grenades from their hiding place in C3 and put them in the agreed places in each crematorium. Stealing SS weapons is critical to our success, so we're relying on Zieliński and his C3 team to overcome a few of their guards. The sound of gunfire will be the cue for the other three crems to start."

"Tell the rest of the men," Toszka said. "Remember! This is the critical time. Not a single word out of place. Tomorrow must be an absolutely normal day so we can have a thoroughly abnormal day on the seventh."

Birnbaum did not display any interest in selecting the two hundred SK workers, so was easily persuaded when Smizer and Toszka volunteered to carry out the task that evening.

The block manager and kapo sat at Smizer's desk with the Barracks 13 prisoner register, together with several blank registration sheets. They ticked the names of those who had volunteered to take part in the revolt, as they were critical to the action's success and were not to be selected. This exercise eliminated 240 names, leaving 420 workers remaining.

"More or less one in every two workers needs to be selected," Smizer said despondently. "Fifty men from each crematorium. Agreed?" Smizer asked.

"Agreed," Toszka replied. "But which ones?"

Faced with lists of names, both men felt the magnitude of the decisions they were about to make. They knew the members of the revolt team, but many of the rest were unknown to them.

"One in two workers needs to be selected," Smizer repeated. "Let's choose every other name."

"Are you being serious?" Toszka asked.

"It's as good as any other way," the block manager replied. "Odd numbers are selected, even numbers are saved," he added, passing a small pencil stub to his companion.

In total silence, the two men made their way down the registers, transferring those workers with an odd number onto the blank sheets, omitting the rest.

Toszka tried to concentrate by counting through the names, one, two, three, four, but he realized the significance of the numbers. Odd, even, odd, even, odd, even. His heart grew intolerably heavy, and each name became harder to inscribe as he repeated in his head: dies, lives, dies, lives, dies, lives, dies, lives.

When the two-hundredth name was entered on the final sheet, neither of the men had spoken since the start. Toszka stood up and left the block manager's office, dragging several gulps of air into his lungs before taking his place on his bunk. Smizer remained sitting to complete the sheets for presentation to Birnbaum.

*

October 7, 1944

The day of October 6 passed without incident. Three crematoria were operating while Crematorium 4 remained idle because of damaged brickwork in its flues and chimneys. Ludwig was working on the maintenance team in Crematorium 4, ferrying bricks back and forth, brushing the ovens free of every speck of ash so they could be repaired.

Although no one was sure whether the Crematorium 4 ovens would ever be relit, Moll would still return later to inspect the work, so the SK team treated each brick as if it were made of fine China pottery.

That morning, Birnbaum had taken the selection list from Smizer without bothering to look at it, apart from making sure it contained 200 names. Moll did the same and rode straight to the main camp.

Ludwig cursed Wojciech. The men had agreed the planned revolt and their respective tasks, but Wojciech had continued to ask needless questions, which had angered some members of the group and increased their nervousness and uncertainty.

Early in the afternoon, Moll arrived and ordered the SK workers to gather in the concrete yard outside Crematorium 4. The men walked out to be faced by Moll, two SS soldiers carrying rifles, and three kapos.

Ludwig was unaware what awaited them.

Moll stepped forward. "When I call your name, line up there," he shouted, pointing at the ground between the crematorium building and the wattle fence.

"Petrov!"

Petrov, a Soviet prisoner of war, stepped forward and walked to one side.

"Ivanov...Smirnov..."

Ludwig was stunned. These men were on the selection list. None of these three Russians wished to take part in the revolt, so had been put on the list. The SK team had been dumb, calculating Moll would wait until evening. They should have planned for such an eventuality. A risky action just became much riskier.

Moll continued to read out the names.

The rest of the SK men realized what was going on. Ludwig turned to Smizer, who was standing a few meters to his left. The two men stared at each other. Smizer made a discreet, calming gesture with his hands.

Ludwig thought hard. The revolt was only a few hours away. Surely, these men would be sent to barracks and nothing would happen to them in the meantime? If the revolt were a success, the SK men would break into the main camp and release them.

"Wojciech!" Moll shouted.

Ludwig was aghast. Wojciech wasn't on the list at all. How did he get on it? Wojciech was on the revolt team. He shouldn't be on the list.

"Wojciech!" the soldier repeated.

Wojciech was on the far side of the yard, shaking his head and glaring at Smizer, his face red with anger. Smizer was staring at his feet. Smizer had written up the final list. Had he added Wojciech's name at the last moment?

"Wojciech!" Moll yelled.

Wojciech stepped forward diffidently, still staring at Smizer and feverishly clenching and unclenching his fists behind his back.

Moll watched Wojciech with curiosity, his head cocked on one side.

Wojciech's hands stopped clenching and moved up to the waistband of his blue-striped trousers. In a second, he was running toward the nearest SS soldier with a small knife in his hand. The soldier's rifle was slung over his shoulder, and he could not retrieve it in time. Using his hands as shields, he fended the Pole off but could not prevent the prisoner from gashing the side of his cheek with the rusty blade.

"No, no!" Smizer moaned. "Not yet!"

Moll was the first to react, shooting Wojciech in the head as he drew the knife back to attack again. The shot rang out and threw the yard into chaos.

The terrified prisoners were in a state of panic. The SS soldiers and kapos were not in formation and were standing behind Moll. It took several moments for them to gather themselves and take up clear shooting positions. When they did, they were presented with the sight of prisoners running in all directions and Moll enthusiastically discharging his pistol. The soldiers joined in.

Some prisoners headed toward the compound gate. Since the erection of the fence, this had become a narrow space, and a few prisoners attempted scaling the wattle rather than be caught in the melee and become sitting ducks for the SS guns. Two SS men hastily set up a machine gun and pointed it at the gate. Running to the gate was an act of suicide, Ludwig thought, so he ran toward the place he knew best, the Crematorium 4 building itself.

The gas chambers and undressing areas were sparsely furnished and provided no hiding places, so the Pole rushed into the incineration room where he knew the equipment exceptionally well. Each of the eight incineration chambers possessed a flue that led to one of the two chimneys. A base plate was clipped to each chamber, which enabled access for cleaning. Ludwig removed one of these and slid inside. It was too low for him to sit up, so he lay down. And waited.

Ludwig was not in complete darkness. A couple of ventilation plates allowed weak daylight in. A thin layer of ash remained within the oven, and he tried to lift his reclining head to prevent tiny shards of bone piercing his scalp. Thousands of people had been killed in Crematorium 4, and even after a sustained period of inactivity, the stench of burning remained and a familiar bitter tinge filled his nostrils.

The camp siren sounded as the shooting outside continued. The rebels' plan had been to start the revolt in Crematorium 3, not 4, to overcome some SS guards and steal their weapons, but that had clearly not happened, and for a half hour, Ludwig listened to the ceaseless *rat-tat-tat* of the SS machine gun outside.

The rebels who made it through the Crematorium 4 gate came face-to-face with the Crematorium 5 entrance. Some of them ran toward the nearby trees, while others dashed through the gate. Some evaded the guards; some did not.

The light escaping through the chamber grate had almost disappeared by the time the gunfire ceased and silence reigned. Ludwig's limbs were aching, and the longer he remained inside the chamber, the more desperate he became to rid himself of the bitter taste in his mouth and the odor of burned ash.

Alone in this dark place, Ludwig's mind wandered. Every speck of ash he was lying on had once been part of a human being, and he had incinerated many of them himself. He had loaded them on the trolley and shoved them inside, like animal meat. Moll's words echoed in his head, *"Remember! One man, one woman, and one child's the ideal combination for an effective burn using a minimal amount of coke. Self-basting!"* The monster had laughed.

The coarse ash grazed his fingers, and he felt revulsion. He had pushed scores of wheelbarrows full of ash and poured them into the River Vistula without giving them a second thought. Perhaps he felt vindicated or excused because he was surrounded by his fellow prisoners and armed guards. What else could he have done? Here in the gloom, he was alone, surrounded by the ghosts of those murdered on that very spot. *Why did you kill us?* they were asking. *You've done nothing to save us.* Ludwig wondered how the SK workers could justify what they had done. What would have happened if all six hundred of them had simply refused to work? Would they have been shot?

For a moment, he wished he had gone to the fence and been done with it all, but he remembered the young woman with the serious face in the gas chamber.

"You must survive. You're a witness." Ludwig heard Rachael's voice in his head, scattering his dreadful, guilt-ridden thoughts and providing him with some renewed purpose.

On his own in the dark flue, Ludwig was unsure how many hours he had been hiding when he tentatively crawled out of the chamber and carefully brushed the ash off his clothes. Looking through the incineration room windows, he saw distant searchlights panning across the camp. There were so few places to hide, he presumed he was the only prisoner left alive in the whole C4 compound. Those hiding in the surrounding woodland would soon be discovered. Inside the wattle fence, C5 would be frenetic, with prisoners arriving from the woods and bodies being hauled out of the gas chambers to the ovens or the pyres so a C4 worker could blend in with the others. Ludwig's name was not on Moll's selection list, so he would not be recorded as missing.

Ludwig resolved to move. With the C4 compound empty, he would wait until he heard and knew that prisoners were being transferred from the woods, then would mingle unnoticed with the SK workers herding them into the C5 compound.

The door from the incineration room into the undressing area was open. The door to the courtyard was also ajar. Ludwig dropped to the floor, laid himself flat, and slithered out like a snake, staying tight against the wall of the building. It was dark. Even the smoke billowing from the Crematorium 5 chimneys was not visible against the black curtain of clouds. The smell of the smoke and the intermittent bursts of flame were the only signs of activity.

Ludwig crawled slowly onward, still hugging the wall. When he rounded the corner of the building, the wattle fence lining the approach to the crematoria came into view. The fence he had built was so tightly packed, he could see nothing, but he knew a crowd of people was behind it because of the discontented murmuring, punctuated by crying and wailing, and countered by the shouts and orders of their captors. He recognized the shuffling of hundreds of feet on the gravel as they approached and squeezed through the gateway. This was usually the point when other SK workers would leave their stations to assist with the corralling of the prisoners into the undressing room.

This was Ludwig's chance. He crawled to the next corner of the building so he could plan his escape through the compound gate and into the melee. If the gate was locked, he would await his moment, climb over, and dive straight into the crowd. He would cover his face, so even if the guards saw him, he would be lost in the crowd so quickly they would have no chance of catching him.

The Pole was expecting to see guards, but guards who were outside Crematorium 5 managing the arriving prisoners, and two guards were actually standing in front of the gate, inside the compound, facing not the new arrivals but Crematorium 4 itself. That bastard Moll, he thought. Why post guards there? What's the point? His heart sank.

Ludwig waited a few minutes to gather himself, in the forlorn hope the guards might depart, but they continued to stand there, the burning tips of their cigarettes glowing like distant beacons.

Dejected, he crawled back, hugging the crematorium wall until he was indoors once more. He returned to the incineration room, not sure whether the guards would be doing their rounds during the night, so he resigned himself to more hours spent hidden inside the flue, in the company of ghosts. His mouth felt like it was full of bone-dry ash, and no matter how hard he tried, he could not produce one drop of saliva to ease his discomfort. Thoughts of the day pounded in his head like incessant rain. Uncomfortable in mind and body, sleep evaded him until exhaustion took over and he lost consciousness.

*

In Birkenau, prisoners who slept for too long were usually awoken by a firm fist into the ribs, but Ludwig was stirred by the sound of voices, not knowing how long he had slept. He had learned to switch rapidly from a state of drowsiness to one of alertness.

The Pole heard the metallic echoes of nearby voices. Terrified of making a noise, he warily shuffled his body closer to the vent. His nostrils welcomed the smell of cool, fresh air. From here, he heard the voices clearly.

"You two empty the gas chambers. You four collect the bodies lying around the compound. Toszka and I will take care of the incineration room. The SS are on the gate, but they'll not come near, so we can take it nice and slow." Ludwig recognized Smizer's voice.

When he heard the other men leaving, Ludwig raised his lips to the vent.

"Smizer!" he whispered.

The block manager continued talking to Toszka.

"Smizer!" Ludwig repeated, louder, and this time, the conversation stopped.

"Smizer! I'm here. In Oven 3."

Ludwig heard footsteps approaching. He looked through the vent and saw Smizer's face peering down at him.

"Ludwig Albin! I wondered where you were," the block manager said. "Nobody had seen you. Once the SS had taken back control yesterday, they went berserk, shooting and killing at will. We were afraid the SS had thrown you into an oven and burned you alive. A few have suffered that fate.

"But here you are! In an oven, but very much alive," Smizer concluded.

"I tried to escape from C4 last night, but there were guards on duty," Ludwig said, clambering out of the oven and stretching his limbs. "What exactly happened?"

"Well, when the SK men in C2 and C3 heard the noise from C4, they assumed we'd started the revolt early. Seeing that some SS guards had been ordered to go to C4 as reinforcements, they grabbed their opportunity and started their revolt.

"The Soviet prisoners threw one of the kapos into an oven alive and launched their grenades," Smizer continued. "They made straight for the perimeter fence with weapons taken off three soldiers they'd killed. Who knows where they are? We'll find out soon enough.

"So how do we get this man out of the C4 compound?" Smizer asked, looking at Toszka.

"I don't think the guards were paying much attention when we walked in," Toszka said. "We're just a gang of men with a couple of handcarts."

"I think you're right," Smizer agreed. "Ludwig, are you okay with this? Nice and simple. You just walk out pushing a cart with us."

"It seems simple, but nerve-wracking," Ludwig replied. "But it can't be done if there are new arrivals around. It would cause pandemonium if they saw dead Jews riddled with bullets."

"That's a good point!" Smizer remarked. "We must act fast! There's a transport arriving today, and with C2, C3, and C4 being repaired, all the prisoners will be sent to C5."

The group of SK workers silently gathered the bodies that were strewn across the compound. It was a traumatic experience because the dead were members of the SK whom they knew. The corpses of the SK men had no jewelry, but Moll had ordered them to be stripped naked to humiliate the dead and the living.

"Hurry!" Toszka said, as the familiar screeching of train brakes could be heard in the far distance. Within the hour, the first selected prisoners would be there, waiting among the trees, unaware of what lay behind the wattle fence.

The road that separated Crematoria 4 and 5 ran in a straight line to the sector entrance. This path was not hidden by the wattle. The SK men knew they had less than sixty minutes to move the bodies from Crematorium 4 to 5.

"Ludwig," Smizer said. "Take one of the cart handles. Bend down low to conceal your height, and keep your head down. We'll overload this cart and push it with the three of us instead of two. I'll stand right beside you to obscure the guards' view, and Toszka will do the same. Once inside C5, we'll unload the bodies where we're told to. Then we'll return to C4 to fetch the rest of the bodies, but without you. You tag on to a work group as soon as you can.

"Apologies in advance if I have to hit you. In front of the guards, I'll need to be convincing playing the role of a strict kapo. Good luck."

The men loaded the corpses onto the cart. Ludwig and Toszka worked together. The bodies were bloodied by the barrage of shots rained down by the SS machine gun. Ludwig thought their deaths were heroic, but as he lifted their bodies and felt their lifeless limbs in his hands, he realized they were the same as the rest of the dead. Birkenau was an extermination camp, designed and built to dehumanize and kill Jews, and they were all victims. The Nazis achieved their objectives in the end.

Smizer raised his wooden stick and smashed it against the cart handle millimeters from Ludwig's hand. Ludwig screamed in fake agony and cowered behind the kapo.

"Put your back into it, you lazy bastard!" Smizer shouted as they approached the Crematorium 4 gate. They shuffled up to the two guards manning the gate.

"Orders from SS-Hauptscharführer Moll to dispose of SK rebels' bodies," Smizer said, removing his blue-striped hat and noting the guards had changed since their arrival. One of them had a long, thin face and drooping eyelids, which made him appear to be half asleep. The other was more inquisitive and leaned over to look inside the cart. The overpowering smell of alcohol stung Smizer's nostrils. Since the pyres had been burning, many SS guards had taken to drinking while on duty. To numb the pain. Their SS supervisors did not punish them; in fact, many joined them. Standing on the edge of a burning pyre was acknowledged as being traumatic for all but the most committed members of the SS.

"Go through!" the guard said. "And hurry up!"

The SK men pushed the cart across the path toward the Crematorium 5 entrance, where the gate was opened. Whereas the Crematorium 4 compound had been quiet, Crematorium 5 was fully operational.

SK workers were scurrying back and forth to a nearby truck, ferrying wheelbarrows full of coke to the incineration room.

The impending arrival of a transport was always a frenetic period, but with Moll in charge, it was worse for the SS and SK alike. The sheer volume of human traffic meant the guards could not check every prisoner movement, so Ludwig and the others slipped unchallenged into the Crematorium 5 compound.

"Smizer!" A shout stopped them in their tracks. There had been up to a thousand men working in the Sonderkommando, and it was rare for anybody to use or even know another prisoner's name.

Smizer turned around and saw the kapo armband before he saw Birnbaum's face. The block elders did not ordinarily leave their barracks, but in recent weeks, it had become necessary as prisoner numbers had soared.

"Yes, sir?" Smizer whined.

"Stand up straight, you fool!" Birnbaum said. Ludwig recognized the emotionless and calculating tone of his voice.

"I need two of your men," the block elder said. "There's a load of Jews on their way from B2, and after yesterday, we don't have enough SK men to supervise them. I need them immediately."

Before Smizer could answer, Birnbaum spoke.

"I'll take him," he said, pointing at Ludwig. "I know him. He's big and strong."

Ludwig let go of the cart and stepped forward. Toszka did the same. Birnbaum signaled for both men to approach.

Smizer coughed, barely audibly. The block elder looked up and saw the block manager pointing at the cart laden with corpses.

"Perhaps they can help me unload this cart before they go?" Smizer inquired.

"Fuck off, Smizer," Birnbaum spat back. "It'll do you no harm to carry out some manual labor for a change. You always were a lazy bastard."

Smizer nodded and bowed and recalled the number of times the block elder had made an unreasonable request of him, day or night.

"What are you waiting for?" the block elder asked. "Are you expecting me to say please and thank you?" He laughed. "Letting you live is generosity itself. You should be thanking me. In fact, do that! Thank me for keeping you alive."

Surrounded by his fellow prisoners, Smizer was about to face further humiliation. Birnbaum's tone left no doubt a reply was expected.

"Thank you for keeping me alive," Smizer mumbled.

"Louder, I can't hear you!" Birnbaum shouted.

"Thank you for keeping me alive," Smizer repeated.

"It's a pleasure." The elder smirked. "Now piss off and do your work!"

Smizer grabbed the cart handles and trudged slowly off, while Ludwig and Toszka followed Birnbaum out of the Crematorium 5 compound.

*

Birkenau was under curfew during the platform selections, so there was hardly a soul to be seen around the barracks that night. Newly arrived prisoners looked like worker ants in lines stretching from the railway platforms in the distance to Crematoria 2 and 3, or along the perimeter of B2 toward 4 and 5.

The gateway to the Crematoria 4 and 5 sector was wide open and the Jewish prisoners were streaming through, then gathering among the trees as Birnbaum and the two SK workers approached.

The Hungarians represented a wide range of humanity: men, women, and children; old and young; dark and fair; tall and short. Families clung together, and individuals stood still. Some were sitting serenely on the cold, hard ground while others paced about, nervously posing questions to anybody within earshot.

"This is an enormous transport, fifty cattle cars, and C5 isn't ready yet," Birnbaum told Ludwig and Toszka. "Keep the prisoners calm and spread out among the trees on both sides of the path so they can't gather in larger groups. Listen out for words of dissent. Moll will be here soon."

Neither Ludwig nor Toszka wished to find themselves in the immediate vicinity of SS-Hauptscharführer Moll. Ludwig wandered among the trees, not speaking to the prisoners and putting his finger to his lips whenever they tried to address him. If any Jews strayed beyond the tree line toward the wattle fences, he guided them back. The slightest physical contact distressed him, so he refrained from touching them, as if to do so would be a physical contribution to their impending deaths. He used his outstretched arms to cajole them, and only in the event of stiff resistance did he use his hands to guide them.

A group of Hungarians was sitting among the trees, gathered in a small circle. There were no adult men present, solely women, children, and babies. The adult women were mostly dressed in black or dark colors, and each wore a plain headscarf tied over her hair. The boys looked like young men, sporting flat caps and dark jackets. It was the young girls who brought color to the scene. Despite the fall weather, they wore dresses of vibrant hues. Green, yellow, and red were visible underneath their winter coats. Their yellow star badges seemed lost against the blaze of color.

A vivid-pink child's coat caught Ludwig's eye. It belonged to a little girl whose back was turned toward him. From her size and her soft, downy hair, he guessed she was three or four. She had blond hair, just long enough to kiss her shoulders, and a bow, which matched the color of her coat, was tied on the crown of her head.

Ludwig watched her playing, trailing her fingers through the grass, tearing off clumps to throw into the air. The blades floated haphazardly to the ground. Although he could not see her face, he sensed her excitement as she waved her arms around, and her head darted from side to side.

The child leaned forward, tugged at the ground, and a yellow dandelion appeared in her hand. She held it up as if to show it off. The winter sun brushed its petals, and the flower shone like gold. For a fleeting moment, the rest of the world seemed to be cast in shadow, and the sun's undiluted light and energy were concentrated in that one flower held in the child's fingers.

The flower looked so beautiful. Ludwig yearned to touch it, and to grow his own. To grow a field of yellow flowers and to lie among them.

The moment was broken by the growling engine of an approaching motorbike, and Ludwig wondered how many more sunrises he would experience and if he would see Rachael again.

Moll dismounted and climbed onto a nearby tree stump.

"Ladies and gentlemen! Boys and girls! Welcome to Birkenau!" the SS-Hauptscharführer said, his voice loud enough to carry into the trees where Ludwig was standing.

"You're about to enter the disinfection facility," Moll continued. "It's a chilly day, and I'm sure you'll enjoy a hot, cleansing shower, followed by some hearty, steaming soup. We'll soon warm you up! You'll be roasting!"

Every member of the SK team knew this routine. Moll had repeated it many times with the conviction of a talented actor. Ludwig never understood how the Nazi fulfilled this task with enthusiasm and relish. To allay the fears of the waiting prisoners was cruel but was a logical approach to making the extermination process run smoothly, but to extend the barbarity beyond that purely for personal gratification made Ludwig more frightened of Moll than anybody else in the entire camp complex. No level of physical or mental torture was beyond him.

"We've got a slight problem," Moll added. "There's been some repair work required in the undressing room, so you're going to have to undress here and walk a short way. It's just over there, behind the fencing we've put up to protect your modesty. It might be best to run to keep the chill off."

The women were agitated. Some of them muttered indecipherable words at Moll, whose expression, for a moment, flashed with contempt.

An SS guard who had made his way from Crematorium 5 approached Moll, saluted, and whispered in his ear. Moll nodded and, still on the tree stump, addressed the prisoners.

"Okay everybody!" His tone had hardened. "There's to be absolutely no fucking delay! Start undressing at once. My men will escort you to the showers. There's a lot of you, so the shower room will be full. If you don't hurry, you'll miss your shower." Moll paused before adding, "And you don't want to miss your shower."

The first few prisoners to undress made their way along the path, accompanied by a guard, but nobody followed. Moll sprang off the tree stump, removed his wooden baton, which had been tucked inside his belt, and waved it menacingly above his head.

The nearby women cowered and threw their arms around their children.

"Hurry!" Moll shouted. "Leave your clothes here!" He omitted his usual lie of telling the prisoners they would collect them later.

He waved his baton again, but this time struck an elderly woman across the back. She had not yet removed her coat, which cushioned the blow. She winced.

"Don't be shy, fucking Jews!" he continued. "Keeping your clothes on will be much worse than taking them off."

The remaining prisoners hurriedly obeyed. Most of the SK workers and SS guards were standing by, watching as Moll raged through the trees like a cowboy corralling his cattle, his venomous blows becoming more and more forceful until the prisoners were running onto the pathway only partially undressed.

"Faster, faster!" Moll shrieked, sprinting up and down and swinging his baton at the SS guards and kapos to encourage them to do the same.

Ludwig remembered the relative calmness of his own selection months ago, and even those prior to the Hungarian project, and scarcely believed the chaos he was witnessing. The sight of hundreds and hundreds of Jews, in various stages of undress, being driven like animals toward the dense wattle fence that concealed the means of their certain deaths, appalled him.

Toszka had told him that to survive in the SK, he had to detach himself from the events unfolding around him. Endure the physical pain and banish thoughts from his mind. Doing, not thinking. Thinking would drive him to the fence.

And here he was, walking among the trees, watching events unfolding, bombarded by thoughts.

The Pole stepped forward to help an old woman who had collapsed. Blood trickled down her knees, grazed by the gravel path. He instinctively averted his gaze from her naked body. He abandoned his "no contact" rule, by lifting the fallen to their feet and supporting those who were lagging. Anything to prevent the monster from beating or killing them, although he knew they would soon die whatever he did.

And as he did these things, his tormented thoughts became vaguer until they slipped out of his mind completely.

As he walked onward with the prisoners, Ludwig noticed a yellow dandelion growing on the edge of the path. He stooped down, plucked it from the soil, and slipped it into his coat pocket. He would give it to Rachael when they met next. Whenever that might be.

*

Ludwig walked through the gateway in the wattle fence and entered the Crematorium 5 compound. He guided the naked prisoners toward the building that stood before them.

The fence on the left ran around the compound until meeting the southern edge of the building. The cremation pyres that lay beyond were concealed, save for the enormous plumes of smoke that rose into the sky. The prisoners would have detected something unpleasant in the air as soon as they disembarked from the cattle cars. The foul smell would have grown with every step they took until, when standing meters from the nearest pit, the stench was overpowering. Charred wood, burning oil, and human flesh combined, forming a nauseating, acrid odor so thick it felt like fingers were clawing at the insides of the prisoners' throats.

And to the right, the two chimneys spewed out their own toxic fumes, tinged with coke rather than wood.

Ludwig noticed how eerie the compound had become. The wattle fence shrouded the pits beyond, and the SS ceased distressing activities during the prisoner arrivals. It was still, almost calm. The naked Jews, amid the smoke and flames, walked silently into the gas chamber in quiet resignation. The only noise was the sporadic exhortations of Moll. "Hurry! Hot soup after a hot shower!"

Those people who had been selected and sent straight to the gas chambers were never counted, nor tattooed. Every spot of the chamber floor was occupied. The blue stripes pushed as many people in as they could until the SS guards took over and, by brandishing their guns, forced a few more inside. With most of the prisoners coaxed into the gas chamber, Moll could dispense with his charade. He took the leash of an SS dog and allowed it to snarl and bite within millimeters of the human flesh in the doorway. A space was created for another person to be crammed in. The monster fired his pistol into the air, and another space appeared, and when he shot a waiting woman from point-blank range, another two prisoners were squeezed in.

When the door was finally bolted shut and the rubber seals checked, there were about twenty prisoners remaining. Moll turned to them and raised his eyebrows.

"I did warn you not to be the last in line," the SS-Hauptscharführer said.

The remaining prisoners were the oldest and frailest, together with a couple of mothers holding young children in their arms.

"Take them to pit three," Moll said, no emotion in his voice. "I'll be along shortly."

Following that order, a kapo pulled back a portable section of the wattle fence, revealing two incineration pits where SK workers were throwing bodies into the flames.

*

"The camera's here," Toszka whispered to Ludwig.

"What?" Ludwig replied, taken aback. "Moll's on duty. We agreed there'd be no attempt to take photos while he's around, and we've just had a revolt! It's far too dangerous."

"I know, but Georgis can't wait. He thinks the SS will stop using the pyres any time now, and our chance will be gone. He's already taken a couple of photos of prisoners on the way from the woods."

Georgis was a Greek Jew, transported from Thessaloniki late in 1943. During his twelve months in Birkenau, his jet-black hair had turned gray, and his olive skin tone had lost its luster, but he was lucky. Most of the Greek Jews died in transit or shortly after arrival.

Ludwig's stomach lurched. Before the SK revolt, there were ten SS guards supervising Crematoria 4 and 5, and it would have been easier to plan and take photographs without being detected. Now Moll had increased the SS presence, and the SK men were on tenterhooks. The Pole wished they had sought the camera earlier.

"We need more lookouts and diversions," Toszka continued. "But that's not possible because much of the revolt team's been wiped out. There're fewer than two hundred SK workers left—"

"What?" Ludwig interrupted. "That can't be right. There were six hundred before the revolt!"

"You might not think it, but you've been lucky, Ludwig," Toszka replied. "While you were concealed inside the oven, just about everybody in C4 was killed in the revolt or executed afterward. The SS found an unexploded grenade and recognized the military expertise required to make it. So they rounded up the Soviet prisoners of war and shot them. Shot the lot of them whether they were involved in the revolt or not." Toszka sighed. "And then they did the same in C2 and C3. I only survived by making it to C5 and mingling with the other workers.

"Worst thing is..." Toszka paused. "The SS know from the grenade that the explosives came from the Union factory."

Ludwig's breath caught in his throat. When the four Union women smuggled the explosives, it was Rachael who had received them. She had hidden them behind a cabinet in SS-Unterscharführer Mann's office before passing them to Ludwig under the barbed wire. He was certainly safe, because Rachael would never reveal his identity, but with horror, he realized it would only take one of the four women to succumb to SS torture and Rachael's cover would be blown. He had to inform her.

"So we lost more men than if we'd just given up the two hundred workers the SS asked for in the first place?" Ludwig asked. "What was the benefit?"

"Well, C4's finished," Toszka replied. "It was forever being repaired, and it was badly damaged yesterday, so it's been closed permanently."

"But if C4's closed, I won't be able to see Rachael." Ludwig groaned. "I won't be able to tell her she's in danger."

"Not for the moment," Toszka replied. "But the Russians have taken Warsaw from the Germans. They're only two hundred kilometers away. The SS are planning to empty their offices, burn all their papers, and abandon the camp. Keep close to Moll, if that's possible. He's preparing a team to dismantle C4, brick by brick."

A wave of relief spread through Ludwig.

"Come on!" Toszka said. "Focus on the matter in hand or you'll be dead by the time the Red Army gets here."

"We can't afford to bring more people into our confidence at this stage. It's too risky. So it's down to those remaining in the revolt team to muck in."

"Go on," Ludwig said. "Tell me what I must do."

"All four pits are burning today," Toszka said. "Moll's standing between the two larger pits where he can watch more deaths. Georgis believes he can take photos of pit 3 from the entrance to the gas chamber, and from there, he can't be seen from the larger pits."

Ludwig nodded.

"When the chamber has been emptied," Toszka continued, "the pits and the incineration room will become the centers of attention. You and I will join those on cleaning duty in the gas chamber. We must empty it as quickly as possible so everybody, including the SS and Moll, will be preoccupied with dealing with the bodies. We'll remain cleaning the chamber, keeping watch and giving Georgis the signal to take the photos."

As Toszka finished speaking, a gray van painted with a red cross drove away. The gassing of the Hungarians was over.

CHAPTER THIRTY-TWO

October 1944

The SK workers descended on the gas chamber like vultures. Moll had never seen them working so keenly. Even Smizer, the block leader, was hauling bodies out. The SS guards supposed the men were working harder without the usual threats and beatings because of the killings during the SK revolt, which had terrified them.

"Move away. You're getting in the way!" Smizer shouted at an SK dentist, who was holding a large pair of pliers and a metal dish.

The dentist moved to one side and stood by a wall.

"What the hell are you doing, scumbag?" a guard cried. "You're supposed to be removing gold teeth, not standing up against a wall like a Jewish whore!"

The dentist fell to his knees, grabbed the nearest corpse, and plunged his pliers into its mouth. A few seconds later, he withdrew the tool with a gold tooth wedged between its prongs, covered in blood and flesh. The tooth made a wet clinking noise as it struck the dish.

"Finished!" the dentist called, and a pair of SK workers arrived to carry the body away. The dentist moved on to the next body.

Inside the gas chamber, Ludwig lifted a third body and held it under his right armpit. The others were draped over his shoulder and held under his other arm. They were so emaciated, he barely felt their weight. Normally, he would use a crook or hold the bodies by the wrist, which meant he had little or no physical contact with them, but this way, he could carry three, and that was quicker. Their cooling flesh made his skin crawl. The hip of one dug into his ribs, so sharp he feared it might pierce the paper-thin, translucent skin that loosely covered it.

The bodies had fallen into piles. Like the Roman victims of Mount Vesuvius, they were frozen like statues, performing the last act of their lives. Families embracing each other tightly; some clasping their hands in prayer; some, despite everything, desperately clinging to life by clawing at the walls, leaving scratches or thin trails of blood behind, the anguish of death showing in their wide eyes and gaping mouths. Even those who appeared calm and had accepted their fate when entering the chamber could not prevent a desperate last gasp for clean air.

For an instant, Ludwig yearned so badly to touch Rachael's warm, living hand that he almost cried out. He closed his eyes and clenched his fists.

"Come on, Ludwig," Toszka said, squeezing his friend's shoulder. "There's work to be done."

*

There was a narrow strip of land between Crematorium 5 and the camp's perimeter fence. Half of the area was taken up by log piles as high as a man, which ran up to the edge of the pyres. The pre-cut lengths were burned if the SS ran out of sleepers for the pits. Moll gave specific instructions to the SK workers for the optimum positioning of the bodies in the pits and the correct amounts of wood, burning oil, and lime.

The other half of the area was for the bodies, hundreds of which were laid out on the rough ground between the pits and the entrance to the incineration room. There was no space for vehicles, so a continuous stream of handcarts passed in both directions, filled with ashes or bodies. Smoke seared their eyes, and their nostrils were flooded with the smell of burning flesh.

It had taken less than an hour for the SK workers to empty the gas chamber. Ludwig was on his knees, scrubbing urine and excrement off the floor with Toszka and Georgis, the three of them waiting for a gap in the human traffic outside.

"How long will you need?" Ludwig asked Georgis.

"Not long," the Greek replied. "I've only got three or four shots left on the film."

"What?" Ludwig asked. "You've only got three or four shots left?"

"The camera already had film loaded," Georgis replied tetchily. "The counter only had seven frames left when I received it. It's better than nothing. One focused and well-directed image is enough to tell a story."

Toszka nodded.

"I hope Georgis has a good aim," Ludwig whispered to Toszka. "It'll be a catastrophe if we smuggle out images of nothing."

"We've got to give him an unimpaired view of the pyres. If anybody walks across his line of sight at the wrong moment, the shot will be wasted. We've got no second chances."

Georgis came up close on all fours, with a scrubbing brush in his hand. Rubbing it lazily across the concrete floor, he looked through the doorway.

"This is the best angle," Georgis said. "It's to one side, so I'm out of the direct light coming in. I can't stand in the doorway. I'd be spotted straight away, and if I stay a meter or so inside, I'll still have a view of pit 3." He paused. "Do you think you can keep that clear for me?"

Ludwig looked down at the scrubbing brush in his hand. It was shaking. He wondered how Georgis would ever be capable of holding the camera steady.

"The ovens are full!" came a shout from outside, followed by, "All bodies now to the pits!"

"Get the camera!" Toszka urged.

"It's here," Georgis replied, pointing to a bulge in his blue-striped jacket.

Ludwig swallowed hard. There was no doubt about the amount of danger they were in. Three unsupervised men in a gas chamber with a camera. Being discovered would mean a bullet in the head, or Moll might have them thrown alive into the flames.

After the ovens announcement, the number of handcarts passing reduced. The SS guards and SK workers moved to the pits, leaving the area in front of the gas chamber doorway empty. The SS offices were beyond the ovens, but if an officer did appear, it would take him several seconds to reach the gas chamber.

Ludwig and Toszka were kneeling in the shadows on either side of the doorframe, each position offering a partial view of the yard. If a fuller view was required, Ludwig was to pretend to scrub the door threshold to steal a look outside. Georgis was standing with his back to the wall, out of sight, fiddling with his camera.

"Get ready!" Ludwig said.

Two SK men struggled past, pushing a handcart crammed with bodies whose limbs were contorted in every direction. Ludwig scrubbed an imaginary stain off the floor and glanced up.

A space opened up before Ludwig, and he saw the operation with total clarity, a picture etched in his mind. Mounds of corpses lay along the perimeter of Pit 3. Every few meters, a pair of SK workers was picking up the dead and tossing them into the flames. Without chimneys to carry it away, the smoke spread across the ground like industrial smog, only intermittently allowing an unobstructed view of the pit. The SS guards walked circumspectly around, staying well away from the edge of the burning pyre. In the background, Moll was shouting, but he was out of sight.

Ludwig ducked back into the shadows.

"Now, now, now!" he said.

There was a movement behind him, and Ludwig heard the click of the camera. In the nervous stillness of the gas chamber, it sounded like cannon fire. Georgis winding the film to the next shot sounded like a grandfather clock being wound in an echoing hall. Another click followed. Ludwig was convinced they must have been heard outside.

Ludwig could wait no longer, so he shuffled into the doorway. He glanced up to see nobody was looking in their direction, and there was nothing in the line of sight to pit 3. His body sagged with relief.

In the background, Georgis was already opening the door that led to the stairs to the attic where the Crematorium 5 SK men were quartered. The plan was for Georgis to hide the camera and give the spent film to Smizer, who would arrange for it to be smuggled out of camp.

After waiting a few minutes, the two Poles stood up, deposited their cleaning materials by the doorway, and walked out into the Crematorium 5 yard, where they joined the team ferrying logs to the pits.

CHAPTER THIRTY-THREE

November 1944

Several months earlier, Moll had ordered some SK workers to be quartered in the attics of the crematoria buildings. This left them within easy reach of their work when large numbers of Hungarian transports arrived. It also constantly left them meters away from the sounds and smells of death. Once the Hungarians action was finished, a few workers remained in the attics.

Crematorium 5 was in operation twenty-four hours a day. The men could not sleep above the heat of the ovens, nor above the screams from the gas chamber, so they occupied the space above the undressing room, which was much smaller than Barracks 13.

Ludwig was sitting on the floor. The bunk he shared with four others was occupied by snoring men. He would join them soon as fatigue spread, cell by cell, through his body.

He contemplated the events of the past few days. Georgis, who was sleeping nearby, had thrown the camera into an oven and passed the film to Smizer, and there was no sign the SS had the slightest idea of its existence. The action had succeeded. So far.

Ludwig sensed the tide was turning and the bleak darkness of Birkenau was receding. The Russians were coming, and the Nazis were covering their tracks. Filing cabinets were being emptied and their contents burned. Most importantly, Ludwig had persuaded Smizer to put him on the team designated to destroy Crematorium 4.

Ludwig took a deep breath and closed his eyes. An image formed in his mind, of Rachael's open hand lying on the ground, palm upward in anticipation. He yearned to reach out and touch it. One touch would be enough to tell each other they were alive.

He envisaged himself walking across the empty Crematorium 4 compound, glimpsing her face through the gap in the fence, returning her smile and pulling the wattle branches apart.

Stop, he told himself. No complacency. On a whim, Moll could destroy his plans with one squeeze of a trigger, but Ludwig's determination was reinforced by the proximity of the Russians. The SK men were receiving daily updates as town after town fell to the Red Army. Temporarily delayed by the Nazis in Warsaw, it was only a matter of time before they liberated the camp.

Ludwig climbed up to his bunk, pulled the blanket over his shoulders and, for the first time in months, he fell asleep and his mind was not drowned in pictures of death and destruction.

*

For once, Moll had helped Ludwig, albeit inadvertently. The SS-Hauptscharführer had intended to bring in a bulldozer to destroy Crematorium 4, but when he had seen the SK men tackling the brickwork with rubber mallets and chisels, he resolved to let them suffer the back-breaking work without help. It would also save the cost of obtaining the machine.

As yet another act of cruelty, Moll insisted the individual bricks be preserved intact. Each broken brick would lead to a lash of his whip.

The situation was ideal for Ludwig, who set to work on the southeast corner of the crematorium building, which had been used as the coke store. Not a single piece of coke remained inside; just a thick layer of black dust covered the concrete floor.

From this vantage point, the Pole could work and watch the gap in the wattle fence that he had opened earlier. With his considerable strength, he could do both and still remove more bricks than any of his fellow workers. Preserving the condition of the bricks slowed progress for the entire team, and Ludwig thought he might be working on Crematorium 4 for some time. He was hopeful of seeing Rachael.

There was no sign of Rachael during his first shift.

During the second day, Ludwig continued to work dismantling the incineration room while keeping the fence in sight. It was in the afternoon when he saw a movement in the opening in the wattle. He stopped working to look more closely, then went to find Klein.

Ludwig could not make his mind up about SS-Schütze Klein. He was approachable, almost kind when on his own, but brutal when others were present. To be safe, Ludwig had made a point of steering clear of the SS guard, but the situation changed when Klein was ordered to supervise the demolition of Crematorium 4. Ludwig realized he could not hope to meet Rachael without the cooperation of this man. Before the revolt, it had been easier to disappear for a few minutes. Not now.

Initially, Ludwig had not wished to take part in the theft of prisoners' belongings but had done so when needing bribes to find Rachael's brother.

According to Reichsführer-SS Heinrich Himmler, becoming a member of the SS demanded the highest levels of professionalism and discipline, and he abhorred those men who demeaned themselves by stealing. Even theft from Jews could be severely punished by demotion or imprisonment, but the readily available loot, some with significant value, was too much of a temptation for many SS soldiers. And a soldier succumbing to this temptation would accept an item of value from a prisoner in return for a favor. The risk for the prisoner was markedly greater since theft could lead to a severe beating or death.

The Hungarian action had placed a significant extra strain on the crematoria operations. With new prisoners being held among the trees and required to undress there, and with the general chaos caused by using both the pyres and the furnaces to incinerate bodies, Ludwig and the other SK workers took valuables and hid them in the deserted attics of the crematoria buildings. This lessened the risk of being caught.

Provided they were allowed their share of the spoils, the SS guards more or less gave up searching prisoners. The exception was when Moll was nearby, when theft ceased for both the SS and the SK workers.

Once the wattle fence went up, Ludwig guessed he might encounter difficulties in meeting Rachael, so he built a personal hoard of items of varying sizes and values to be used as bribes for SS guards or kapos.

This hoard included a gold pocket watch, passed to him by an elderly man who was undressing in the woods and had said to Ludwig, "Look after this for me."

Ludwig was overcome by a feeling of nausea, which made him dizzy. He longed to tell the man the truth, that he would never be reunited with his beautiful watch, but he was lost for words. Remarkably, the old man showed him an empathetic smile before walking away. Ludwig wiped his eyes before any tears could escape and run down his cheeks.

The gold watch became the bribe that persuaded Klein to allow Ludwig to make his way to the fence, should Rachael appear. On handing him the watch, Ludwig had wanted to punch Klein, who was examining the once-precious timepiece like a piece of secondhand junk.

Klein had simply said, "If you want to see your girlfriend, that's fine with me. But if another member of the SS catches you, I'll shoot you both."

Both Ludwig and Klein were standing outside the incineration room. Ludwig nodded at the SS guard, who dipped his head in return and made his way around the corner of the building, out of sight. The SK worker almost broke into a run as he rushed to the wattle fence, forcing himself not to shout her name out loud. He collapsed to the floor and grasped her waiting hand.

"Rachael! Rachael!" were the only words he could breathlessly muster.

He looked up and saw his joy reciprocated. Rachael's mouth was drawn into a smile. It had only been a short while since they had last seen each other, but it was like seeing her again for the very first time. The prisoners were forever working, forever exhausted, and the concept of the passing of time was lost to them.

A wave of affection, excitement, and relief coursed through Ludwig's body. Like adolescent children, they held hands, smiled and talked without a break for several minutes, until the specter of life in Birkenau inevitably crept up on them.

"So what'll happen next in Kanada?" Ludwig asked.

"Although the number of trains arriving has come to a standstill, there are loads of belongings left over from the Hungarian transports," Rachael replied. "We've only just cleared those stored outside, but Mann's reducing the workforce to one hundred and fifty. It's a thousand fewer than the peak."

"What...what about you?" Ludwig asked anxiously.

"I'm good," she replied. "Mann and the SS still need paperwork and gold ingots. Zuzana and I are probably the safest workers in Kanada. For very different reasons."

Rachael was hesitant when she spoke again. "And what about the crematoria SK?" she asked. "Are you safe?"

There was an extended pause.

"You're right," Ludwig replied. "The number of arrivals has fallen. There's only a hundred of us left in the SK. C4's shut down. It's always been unreliable, and the damage caused by the revolt has meant it's going to be permanent. That's why I'm here to demolish the C4 building.

"There are no safe SK workers with Moll around," he added. "He's preparing to demolish C2 and C3, which will mean there'll be only C5 and the incineration pits in operation. Perhaps he'll need fifty men for that. So I've got a one in two probability of surviving the next round of SK selections. That's not bad odds by Birkenau standards."

"And how long will it take to demolish C4?" she asked.

"It's just about finished," he replied. "Perhaps two to three weeks for removing the last bricks and preparing them for transport."

"So..." she murmured. "Will we still be able to meet?"

In the background, the sound of SS guards shouting outside Crematorium 5 could be heard, together with the metallic clanging of the last oven being smashed to pieces in Crematorium 4. Ludwig was vigilantly listening out for a motorbike engine.

"It's going to be difficult," he replied. "Once C4 is finished, they'll lock the compound gate. Working in the other crems will give me no chance of meeting you. I don't think even a huge bribe would persuade Klein to unlock that gate. It's so close to C5, we'd both be spotted."

The excitement of their meeting ebbed away as they realized they faced a period of enforced separation. Their first meeting had been nine months earlier, and since then they had met many times.

"But we must believe we'll meet again!" Rachael said. "We've stayed alive so far, and it's surely only a few weeks more."

"That's true," he replied. "We must plan as if we'll both be here when the Red Army arrives."

"We should agree where we'll meet next," she said. "In one of our barracks. Or at a prearranged spot somewhere between the two."

"I suggest a prearranged spot," he replied. "Who knows if one of us will be moved to a different barracks?"

"Good point," she said. "So how about Lagerstrasse, which is the halfway point between our barracks? It's probably the most likely place where we could meet."

"Agreed," he answered.

"And right in the middle, halfway between the gates of the women's and men's camps?"

"Agreed."

A whistle sounded, and when Ludwig looked around, he saw Klein standing by the rubble of Crematorium 4 and waving at him.

"It's time for me to go," he said. "We can meet tomorrow. There's still work to do here."

"That's good news," she replied.

Although they had agreed to meet the following day, they were reticent about letting go of each other. In Birkenau, thoughts of temporary separation were inevitably transformed into fear of permanent separation.

They moved slowly apart until their fingertips no longer touched. And they went back to work.

CHAPTER THIRTY-FOUR

January 1945

The camp orchestra was formed in 1940 and, depending upon the camp conditions and number of prisoners, was made up of between thirty and one hundred players, most of whom were professional musicians.

Initially, they performed classical music on the weekends for the SS officers and sometimes for their fellow inmates, but the SS leadership soon exploited the orchestra for a different purpose. They were instructed to play German or Austrian marches each morning when the prisoners were leaving the camp in their work groups. Stirring military marches were played to galvanize the prisoners for the hard labor ahead and to drown out the sounds of barking dogs and gunshots. Then the SS demanded the marches were also played when the exhausted workers returned in the evenings.

That day, the orchestra was not playing, and the returning prisoners were met with stony silence. The absence of music was unsettling. The prisoners had grown accustomed to camp routines and knew a change would be a portent of bad news.

Having entered through the main Birkenau entrance, the work groups would be taken to camp B1 or B2. The gates to the two camps were narrow, and if the groups did not move swiftly, the area around the railway platform would become overcrowded. The SS's attempts to restore order would lead to beatings and deaths.

That day, the gates to B1 and B2 remained locked, and the workers were forced to gather in a growing throng wedged between the barbed wire fences. SS guards were standing by, rifles at the ready, facing the crowd, but not intervening.

The prisoners looked toward the railway platform. At a point level with the gates to B1 and B2, a basic wooden scaffold had been erected. Five meters wide, it faced the oncoming prisoners. Four people were hanging there, gently swinging from side to side in the breeze.

With the gates locked and a line of SS guards blocking their way, the prisoners were forced to gather around the scaffold, closer and closer. As they approached, they realized the bodies were naked, female, and covered in bruises and bloody wounds resulting from their treatment at the hands of the SS. They were barely recognizable. Great clumps of hair had been torn away from their scalps, and blue-black bruises cruelly changed the color and shape of their faces. In their nudity, it was clear no part of their bodies had been spared the Nazi interrogation.

Days ago, these women were barely known in camp. Their identities had been kept strictly secret. Now everybody knew their names. Roza Robota, Ella Gartner, Esther Wajcblum, and Regina Safirsztajn were the Union factory workers who had smuggled explosives for the grenades used in the SK revolt. Every day for months, they had smuggled a teaspoonful of gunpowder from the company stores, concealed in their clothing. Despite frequent searches, it remained undetected. Nor were they exposed in the days after the revolt, when it became clear the grenades had been manufactured using Union gunpowder. The women were just four of over a thousand working there.

When 1944 drifted into 1945, three months had elapsed since the revolt, and the surviving members of the SK revolt team started to believe the women would remain undetected, but they were wrong. The SS were ruthlessly persistent and eventually were led to the quartet. Nobody knew the women had been exposed until they failed to return from the Union factory at the start of the previous week. That very day, their fates were sealed.

Plotters, escapees, and those who had supposedly committed crimes, whether guilty or innocent, were incarcerated in Block 11 in the Auschwitz I camp. There, they would be interrogated, tortured and frequently summarily executed. Block 11 was constructed to the same design as the other blocks in Auschwitz, except that the SS had built a high wall around its courtyard, separating it from the rest of the camp. The sounds of firing squads regularly filled the air, but nothing was ever seen.

The remaining members of the SK revolt team were on tenterhooks. Had they been implicated? The poor women were dead, but under the most fearsome torture, had they revealed any of their accomplices? Roza was a long-standing resistance worker with contacts and knowledge well beyond the SK revolt. Nobody was safe.

The prisoners held in Block 11 were executed in the courtyard, and their bodies were rarely seen. Public display of the four women hanging in the center of Birkenau was an attempt by the SS to scare prisoners into betraying their fellow inmates and deterring them from considering other acts of rebellion. Those who looked closely were horrified to see the scale of callous, uninhibited savagery shown by the SS with no quarter shown to the women. Many chose not to look.

The resistance members were both horrified and relieved. They experienced the same horror and revulsion as the other prisoners, but the fact the women had died and not one of them had been arrested could have meant these brave women had not divulged their comrades' names.

SS-Hauptscharführer Moll climbed onto the scaffold, his boots thudding on its wooden planks. His words communicated the usual threats and were delivered with his customary relish. He waved his stick above the crowd's heads, looking like a lion-tamer performing at a cruel circus. Having finished his routine, Moll stepped down and ordered the guards to unlock the gates and herd the prisoners back into B1 and B2.

They were accompanied by the camp orchestra playing the melodious "Erika," one of the Nazis' favorite marching songs.

CHAPTER THIRTY-FIVE

January 16, 1945

The Red Army was closing in. The delays at the end of the previous year had lulled the SS into a false sense of security. They had expected the cold winter to hold the Russians back until early spring, but with a mild winter and token resistance from the German army, the Russians had made swift progress across Poland, and within two weeks, they had traveled from Warsaw to Krakow, seventy-three kilometers northeast of Auschwitz. Once Krakow was taken, they would have an unhindered path to the camps.

SS-Obersturmbannführer Höss had summoned his senior officers to his house for a meeting. Moll noticed boxes lying in the hallway, and how Frau Höss was brusquely giving instructions to the staff. The SS-Hauptscharführer wondered how many of the items being carefully packed into the boxes had come from the Kanada stores. He knew for sure the whitewashed exterior and neatly maintained garden of Höss's home were thanks to the prisoners' labors.

Höss was speaking in a rush, and Moll suspected the camp commandant would leave Auschwitz soon. Moll had always considered Höss to be a competent bureaucrat but not a committed Nazi, and his actions proved it. Moll would remain until he could smell the liquor on the Red Army soldiers' breath. He would rather die a noble death as a Nazi than surrender weakly.

Höss told the officers Reichsführer-SS Heinrich Himmler had given the order to cease the extermination of the Jews and other undesirables with immediate effect. The SS's future efforts had to be concentrated on the destruction and removal of all evidence of the extermination facilities in Auschwitz and Birkenau.

"Haven't we received orders from Reichsführer Hitler himself that the extermination of the Jews should continue?" Moll asked, satisfied to see the uncomfortable look on his superior's face. "He's *the* Führer," he emphasized.

"Yes, but..." Höss paused. "The order from Himmler is more recent and quite specific."

"I'm uncomfortable about disobeying an order from the Führer," Moll insisted.

"The order's clear," the camp commandant continued. "Healthy prisoners are to be marched into German territory, and those not fit to march will be left behind and subjected to special treatment. All records and registers are to be burned. Not taken away, burned. Buildings containing sensitive materials or used to carry out special operations are to be burned and demolished. The topmost priority is the destruction of the crematoria." Höss looked at his pocket watch. "That's it. Those are your orders."

Moll would not allow himself to be distracted by confused orders from the SS hierarchy. The war might have been lost, but he still had a job to do. He had more Jews to kill.

Höss watched the SS-Hauptscharführer leave the house. That dreadful man was going to cause problems, he told himself.

CHAPTER THIRTY-SIX

January 17, 1945

Moll rode his bike to Crematorium 5 to make sure the ovens were operating before moving on to Crematoria 2 and 3, where the ovens had been removed from the incineration rooms, but the manual destruction of the brick buildings had been too slow. He found himself in the invidious position of having too few SK men remaining and not enough time to bring demolition equipment into the camp, but he relished a challenge and intended to destroy the crematoria buildings and kill the remaining SK workers before the Russians arrived.

The SS-Hauptscharführer's bike screeched to a halt by the SS office of Crematorium 3.

"Come here!" Moll shouted at a group of four SS guards, who were loitering in the doorway, smoking cigarettes.

He grabbed hold of a rucksack strapped to the rear of his motorbike, opening it as he walked. Dropping to his knees, he took some sticks of dynamite out of the sack and split them into three equal piles.

"You two!" he ordered. "You blow up C2." He scattered pieces of fuse wire onto the ground. "And you two," he said, turning to the other guards. "You do C3. Use enough explosives to make sure the floor collapses into the gas chamber underneath. I'll be back, and if I find one brick still in place..." He paused. "I'll fucking kill you!"

Moll picked up the remaining sticks of dynamite and put them back in the sack. He climbed on his motorbike, revving its engine angrily before speeding out of the Crematorium 3 compound.

The SS officers were behaving abominably, Moll told himself as he rode away. It was as if they didn't care, but Höss was leaving, and the senior officers were following suit, seeking commissions elsewhere or simply climbing on the nearest train or joining a forced march. The rank and file and junior officers were not given a choice and were ordered to escort the prisoners on the marches. Only the most loyal Nazis chose to remain.

Over recent days, Soviet artillery had lit up the night sky like fireworks and had grown louder as each day passed. More and more of the SS officers disappeared, leaving a smattering of guards on duty around the camp perimeter and in the crematorium compounds.

Moll had work to do. He would not rest until the four Birkenau crematoria were destroyed and every fragment of bone lying among the ashes was ground to dust and buried in the pits.

The SS-Hauptscharführer needed to perform a balancing act with the manning of the SK, keeping enough men to complete the final prisoner burnings and the destruction of the crematoria buildings while making certain not a single member of the SK would survive as witness to what had truly happened in Birkenau.

There were only fifty men left in the SK, split between those running Crematorium 5 and the pyres. Moll intended to have them shot as soon as Crematorium 5 was demolished.

The Administration Office was in flames as Moll rode past it, toward the Auschwitz I exit. Fire was the best way to destroy any documentary evidence and prevent SS soldiers foolishly taking souvenirs or keepsakes that might come to light after the war. There was so much paperwork in different locations, Moll wondered if it could all be destroyed in time and whether the Nazi bureaucracy had become excessive.

Moll had mixed feelings. He was proud of the number of Jews he had helped kill. The Hungarian action on its own had exterminated more than three hundred thousand, but he was ashamed that the war was lost and the SS was withdrawing in such a dishonorable manner.

Standing under the arch of the Birkenau entrance, an SS officer with a long thin face and long thin black mustache was holding a clipboard.

He held up his arm as the SS-Hauptscharführer drew up. He did not know Moll personally but had heard about his reputation. The roar of the motorbike and the maniacal expression on the man's face left the officer in no doubt as to his identity. With only a few days until the rest of the SS staff would be evacuated, it was the wrong time to antagonize this man.

The officer saluted Moll, who reciprocated cursorily.

The officer looked at Moll over the top of his spectacles. "Could I have your name, sir?"

"SS-Hauptscharführer Otto Moll," he replied. "What do you want?"

"I've got orders for you from SS-Obersturmbannführer Höss," the officer replied.

"I've already received my orders!" Moll said dismissively.

"Well, these orders were signed early this morning, sir," the officer said, handing a sheet of paper to Moll. "Very early this morning," he added.

"These can't be for me!" the SS-Hauptscharführer exclaimed. "They say I'm to join a march to Ravensbrück in the morning! I'll need to speak to Höss about this—"

"I'm afraid SS-Obersturmbannführer Höss left the camp this morning, sir," the officer interrupted. "Very early this morning."

Moll had expected Höss to leave quickly, but not that quickly. He grabbed the papers from the thin-faced soldier.

"That bastard Höss!" Moll cried out loud. "He's doing this on purpose because I argued with him in front of the others." He threw the paper to the floor. Höss had even sent him on a women's march as punishment, he thought. No doubt with Irma Grese for company.

The officer bent down and retrieved the document.

"The Ravensbrück march will leave at midday tomorrow, sir," the officer continued, adding tentatively, "Can I presume you'll be attending?"

"An order's an order." Moll nodded.

"Indeed it is, sir," the officer confirmed.

Moll hurriedly mounted his motorbike and sped off, knowing he had less than a day to complete the destruction of the crematoria and make sure there were no members of the Sonderkommando left to tell the Communists what they had seen and done.

CHAPTER THIRTY-SEVEN

January 18, 1945

It was one o'clock in the morning, and SS-Hauptscharführer Otto Moll guessed he would have missed two nights' sleep by the time he had completed his duties in Birkenau and readied himself to march the women prisoners out at midday.

Earlier in the evening, the SS guards had successfully blown up Crematoria 2 and 3, and he would inspect them fully at first light.

As he drove his motorbike back into the Birkenau camp, he noticed Mengele striding out of camp B2e carrying two large cardboard boxes to his car, which was parked on Lagerstrasse. His office was in the barracks nearest the fence, and Moll slowed to watch as two SS guards poured gasoline from a can over its wooden walls before setting it on fire.

As the fire took hold, Moll knew the wide gaps between the timbers would ventilate the building and turn it into an inferno in minutes. The barracks housed the doctor's laboratory and a makeshift sick bay for his patients. Moll wondered if Mengele had removed them beforehand. He suspected not. Everything he wanted, everything he needed, would be in those two boxes. Forget the rest.

In his handlebar mirror, Moll saw Mengele driving off and wondered if they would ever meet again. Mengele was off to Gross-Rosen Concentration Camp, 280 km northwest of Auschwitz, still in Poland, but only 80 km from Germany. By the time the Russians reached Gross-Rosen, Mengele would be back in the fatherland, but that might not be far enough for the doctor. Surely, the Russians would repay the Nazis for invading their land by entering and ransacking Germany in return.

For a few seconds, Moll considered his own situation but decided he would focus on the present. It was clearer and more straightforward.

The fluorescent lamps of Crematorium 5 were the only ones shining in camp that night and were casting grotesque shadows among the nearby trees. In the cloudless sky, the moon cast an eerie light across the camp.

The usual hustle and bustle of the compound was absent. Cattle cars had not arrived in Birkenau for some time, meaning Crematorium 5 was only being used for internal selections. Moll was forced to burn the pits with the remaining logs as fuel and human fat as accelerant.

During the day, the wattle fences had been torn down and thrown on the pyres. Anything flammable was added to the flames—the furniture from the SS offices, paperwork delivered in cartloads from the Kanada stores, and benches from the undressing room. The SS-Hauptscharführer was pleased to be fulfilling two tasks at once: the destruction of the evidence of the SS's activities and the incineration of bodies. He was proud to have carried out his orders so competently.

Moll approached an SS guard who was supervising the burning pits.

"Why have you only got two fucking pits burning?" he asked.

"Not enough bodies, sir," the guard replied.

"But once a pit has been allowed to go out, it takes an age for it to warm up again!" Moll exclaimed. "Idiot!"

"I'm not sure we'll need the other pits again, sir," the guard replied. "The Red Army will be here in a few days."

"But they're not fucking here *yet*!" Moll shouted, his face millimeters from the soldier's. "And why have we got only ten workers here? Where are the rest?"

"I guess they must be in their barracks or the crematoria attics?" the guard answered with a lack of confidence born of fatigue and confusion.

"Considering C2, C3, and C4 have been dynamited, I'm not sure there's much space left in the fucking attics!" the SS-Hauptscharführer raged.

"Ah, that's right!" the guard said, seeming to remember. "That block manager Smizer came along and, seeing we were short of SS guards, offered to escort the unused SK workers back to their barracks. It seemed like a sensible thing to do."

Moll jumped on his motorbike. This was his chance to exterminate the remaining SK members, and Smizer had done him a favor by gathering them all in one place.

As the SS officer sped past B2f, the shining moon highlighted a trail of departing prisoners stretching from the B2d gate toward Lagerstrasse, where the prisoners were being gathered for the marches. Throwing his bike down, Moll barged past the prisoners passing through the B2d gateway. His heart sank when he saw the gate to the walled courtyard of Barracks 13 was open.

The walled courtyard was empty. There were no lights visible in the wooden building except a flickering candle in a kapo's room.

SS-Hauptscharführer Moll burst into the barracks and stumbled in the dark.

"Fucking hell!" he grumbled, rising quickly.

He knew this barracks well, having been there many times before, and his eyes soon grew accustomed to the gloom. Within minutes, he had rummaged among the blankets on every bunk and, apart from four dead bodies, had not found a single living SK worker. They had gone.

The prisoner registers had been destroyed over the preceding days, so nobody could calculate accurately how many prisoners were left in the camp, but when organizing the death marches, the SS officers had estimated a figure of between 50,000 and 75,000. The fifty SK workers would be lost among tens of thousands.

"Fucking hell!" Moll shouted.

Block manager Smizer was withdrawing a piece of paper and a photograph from an envelope when Moll stormed into his room, the draft from the door making the candle flame splutter.

"Where are the fucking SK workers?" Moll asked.

"They've gone to join the marches," Smizer replied calmly, placing the paper, envelope, and photograph on the table next to a scrap of yellowing paper.

"Call me sir when you address me," Moll demanded.

"Sorry, sir," the block manager replied.

Moll detected an insolence in the other man's voice that he had not experienced previously.

"You know full fucking well the SK workers are to be kept away from the rest of the prisoners," Moll snapped. "Who gave orders for this to happen?"

"I did, sir," Smizer replied. "The other barracks in B2d were being emptied, so I let Barracks 13 join them."

Moll was fuming. Reaching down to his belt, he realized he had no baton with which to strike the man. He had only brought his revolver with him.

"You don't have the authority to release those men," Moll said.

"I didn't release them, sir," Smizer said. "I let them join the others. They're still confined within the camp, waiting to go on a march," Smizer added, a thin smile appearing on his face.

"You've done this on fucking purpose, haven't you?" Moll shouted.

The block manager was unmoved.

"You're a traitor!" Moll added. Then it suddenly dawned on him. "You've been a fucking traitor all along, haven't you? In cahoots with the revolting SK workers. You're allowed everywhere in the camp, so you've been passing information back and forth for months!"

Smizer's smile grew wider.

Moll was too angry to continue the conversation. He withdrew his revolver from its holster and shot the block manager squarely in the forehead. The SS-Hauptscharführer turned on his heels and left the barracks.

Smizer's body slumped over the table, his head coming to rest next to the photograph and scrap of paper and his open, glazed eyes staring into nothingness. The blood from the bullet wound trailed down his forehead and crept across the table, pooling around the edges of the photograph of a woman and young girl playing on a beach. The paper lay next to it, upon which some words had been coarsely scribbled in pencil. *Smizer, I checked for you. I found out your wife and daughter have died in Bergen Belsen. Sorry.*

*

By the time the prisoners from the men's camp arrived on Lagerstrasse, Ludwig had made his way to the front of the line, right behind the SS guard who was leading them.

For once, luck seemed to be on his side, and Smizer's bravery in allowing the SK workers of Barracks 13 to mingle with the rest of the men from B2d had brought him to the place where the men's march to Dachau and the women's march to Ravensbrück were both being mustered.

As the numbers of arriving prisoners grew, the watchtower spotlights were switched on, revealing lines of SS guards with their rifles drawn standing in front of the B1 and B2 fences. They did not intervene, but watched, allowing the prisoners to congregate informally on Lagerstrasse.

Occasionally, a searchlight picked out a black peaked cap, which confirmed the presence of an SS officer.

Ludwig had to stay out of the sight of Moll at all costs or he would surely be killed, but his chances were much better on Lagerstrasse than in Barracks 13. He could not let that happen, not when, for the first time, there was no fence between him and Rachael. Ludwig was one of the tallest men in the camp and he contemplated how this attribute would make him conspicuous to both the person he most wanted to meet and the one he most wanted to avoid.

The Pole had not set eyes on Lagerstrasse at night since the day of his arrival, when he had been selected and sent straight to the SK barracks. Now, his head was spinning as the disconcerting searchlights swept by, casting the thousands of prisoners into alternating patches of darkness and light.

With no engagement of the guards and kapos, the prisoners were gathering without direction, but as Ludwig looked toward the camp entrance, the prisoners were actually forming lines as if, even without the SS's screaming, shouting, and beating, they subconsciously knew where to go and what to do.

Ludwig and Rachael had agreed that if they were to rendezvous, it would be halfway between the gates of B1 and B2. This had seemed straightforward to Ludwig, but as the tide of prisoners poured in, this became the most congested area on Lagerstrasse.

Stooping uncomfortably to stay out of sight and listening intently for the sound of a motorbike engine, Ludwig stood and waited.

*

While most of the women who flocked out of B1 drifted toward the main camp entrance, Rachael walked straight ahead. She was tired but determined. The surrounding women were starving and weak, and she took pains not to knock them off their feet as she strode on.

Rachael accidentally bumped into a woman, who was wearing a black coat and a black headscarf, and dislodged a morsel of bread from her hand. The woman dropped to the ground, groveling to retrieve the precious food, but let out a despairing moan when it was trampled into crumbs by the swarm of feet surrounding her.

The Dutch woman took her by the arm and lifted her up. There was barely any weight to lift, and the arm felt like a fleshless bone. The nighttime temperature was well below freezing, and Rachael wondered how long this woman would survive outdoors on an SS march. Perhaps a day or two? And yet this woman preferred the prospect of a march to remaining within the Birkenau fences.

The woman wearing black was speaking a language Rachael did not recognize or understand, but the way she drew her pinched fingers toward her mouth showed she was pleading for food.

"Wouldn't it be safer and warmer inside your barracks?" Rachael asked, pointing to the women's camp.

Not comprehending, the old woman continued to gesture toward her mouth.

Rachael pulled her coat tightly around her shoulders and drew closer to the woman, who appeared fearful, stopped begging, and let her hands drop. As she did so, Rachael's hands flew out from within her coat and placed a chunk of stale bread in the woman's fingers. The woman looked down in surprise and then glee, holding the bread close to her chest as if it was a cherished belonging, before nodding at Rachael and disappearing into the crowd.

Rachael had had two days to prepare for their imminent departure. SS-Unterscharführer Mann had been genuinely distraught at the thought of being separated from Zuzana and had shown little interest in the sheds' activities, except Shed 1, where he continued to monitor the gold collections, even though they were becoming progressively smaller and lighter. He was not bothered, or did not notice, that Rachael and many of the Kanada women were arriving for work wearing considerably fewer clothes than normal and departing swollen by several warm layers, which they shared with the other women in Barracks 19. Within two days, a significant proportion of the women in Barracks 19 had a set of warm clothes and shoes.

Although the food in camp was almost exhausted, Mann continued to order rations for Kanada, the more nutritious elements of which he allotted to Shed 1 where Zuzana was then working. Mann had insisted on her transfer.

So, as Rachael made her way across Lagerstrasse that night, she felt almost warm with a thick pullover and woolen coat included in her layers and two pairs of socks worn inside her sturdy boots. She had torn a hole in the coat lining and filled it with a supply of bread she had collected over those days. The inside pockets concealed two thermos flasks of precious, clean water. Her heart sank when she thought of the woman in black and her solitary piece of bread. Perhaps it would be her last meal.

However, Rachael knew all her efforts would be meaningless if she did not find Hannes. And Ludwig.

Halfway between B1 and B2, the number of women dwindled, and the crowds comprised predominantly men. Rachael stood on tiptoes to see if she could spot Ludwig looming above the other men as a searchlight passed by, but to no avail. Although she was desperate to find him, she told herself he would be easier to locate once the sun was up and the crowds were settled. So she stood still, tucked her hands back in her pockets, and waited for sunrise.

*

There was a clear sky as the orange sun rose above the arched entrance to Birkenau, but it had been bitterly cold throughout the night, and bodies lay everywhere across Lagerstrasse, scattered among the living, who had remained standing. The frozen ground was only for the dead.

Over the intervening hours, Rachael had drifted in and out of sleep, and was awoken by the SS guards, who had been standing in front of the fences, stirring into action and ordering the kapos to remove the corpses. The cursing and the beatings began. A shot rang out somewhere among the tens of thousands of prisoners who were squeezed between B1 and B2.

The redhead shielded her eyes from the sun and noticed the gate to Birkenau lay open. The SS officers and guards were darting around in front of the entrance building, barking orders at the prisoners. Within thirty minutes, straight columns of people stretched from the camp entrance to the far end of Lagerstrasse, where Crematoria 2 and 3 once stood. The ranks of women occupied the side of the sector next to the women's camp. Beyond the fence, a few women were standing outside their barracks, watching silently. It seemed as if the vast majority of the B1 prisoners had gathered on Lagerstrasse.

Without the camp orchestra drowning out any noise, the sounds on Lagerstrasse were amplified. The shrill order of an SS guard coursed through the sector like an echo in a cavern or a cathedral. The shuffling of thousands of feet on the frozen ground was like a dull drum roll. Somewhere in the distance, a dog barked, and it felt as if the hound was right beside them.

Ludwig raised his head deliberately to scan his surroundings. He bent and stretched his neck to ease his stiff, aching muscles. He had an uninterrupted view across Lagerstrasse; there was no sign of Moll, and he was reasonably sure that, unless he had fallen asleep without realizing it, the SS-Hauptscharführer's motorbike had not passed nearby.

If Moll was supervising the women's march to Ravensbrück, then Ludwig needed only to join the men's march to Dachau undetected, and he would leave Birkenau alive. The men outnumbered the women, so his march would be an enormous group. Ludwig told himself literally to keep his head down, stay anonymous, and he would survive.

Ludwig scoured the horizon again. A commotion was taking place at the front of the men's ranks, a movement of bodies he could not figure out. He watched closely, and it became clear. The men were being arranged into five lines and were moving toward the camp exit. The Dachau march was beginning. It would take a substantial period of time for all the men to pass through the archway, but Ludwig could not afford to be left among the less densely populated ranks of men at the rear where he would be easier to spot. He needed to be concealed in the tightly packed center, and preferably before Moll arrived.

Ludwig's heart throbbed. Not stronger, but weaker, like the flickering beat of a tiny bird. The pressure of locating Rachael and finding a safe place in the crowd weighed heavily upon him.

The Pole made his way to a point between the gates of B1 and B2 and looked around for Rachael, but he was surrounded by men and only caught glimpses of the dirt gray headscarves of a few women. On the point of shouting or waving his cap above his head, he was made to pause by the sound of a distant roll of thunder. As he listened, it grew louder until he recognized the sound of an engine. There were several motorbikes in Birkenau, but he had grown accustomed to the threatening roar of Moll's. Glancing up, he watched the SS-Hauptscharführer riding along the path running between the ruins of Crematoria 2 and 3. The prisoners were scattering before him, those too slow to take evasive action being knocked down or pushed sideways.

The crowds were thinner there, but the motorbike was still forced to grind to a halt at regular intervals, whereupon Moll would shoot his pistol in the air and scream words that were undecipherable from that distance, although Ludwig could well guess what those words were.

The crowd of women became denser the farther the motorbike drove, and Moll's shouting and firing in the air to clear his path became more frequent. When he drew level with the B1 gateway, he was less than a hundred meters from the stooping Ludwig, who had kept the SS-Hauptscharführer in sight and was confident he was concealed among the mass of faces, which were watching the motorbike's progress, but Ludwig's fear of Moll ran deep, and being that close was nerve-racking. He was haunted by the fear that the SS officer would suddenly ride in a different direction, scattering the crowds and driving straight into him, rooted to the spot. One bullet, and it would be over.

Another shot rang out from Moll's pistol, followed by screaming and wailing. Ludwig looked but could not see the raised pistol. Another shot rang out, and Moll's motorbike edged forward.

The prisoners were thrown into a panic as soon as the first bullet felled a woman obstructing the motorbike, and they tried to flee through gaps in the crowd which did not exist. Those running in the opposite direction found themselves face-to-face with the terrifying electrified fence of B1, some kneeling on all fours so they would not topple onto the barbed wire.

The second shot created a narrow pathway between the prisoners but forced more women toward the fence. Those who were lucky put out their hands, and their figures landed in relative safety on the concrete fence posts. The rest put out their hands with no chance of survival. Some fell over those crouching on the floor and tumbled into the wire.

Working in the crematoria SK, Ludwig had dealt with the dead or those quietly awaiting their so-called shower. In all his time in Birkenau, he had never heard a sound more mournful than the desperate wailing of the women prisoners snagged on the wire.

*

Rachael was sure she would spot Ludwig towering above the other prisoners, but she did not. There were so many people on Lagerstrasse, it seemed inconceivable he was not one of them. Unless a mishap had befallen him.

And here she was, a few hundred meters from the camp exit and the end of the horrors of Birkenau. And the impending arrival of the Red Army. And the end of the Nazis' reign of terror. And her brother was waiting for her in Dachau. Hopefully. All her good luck seemed to have been stored up and presented to her as one gift. If only Ludwig was there with her.

They had promised each other to do their utmost to survive. At first, her sole focus had been on being reunited with her brother. Then the tall, gentle giant had appeared by the Kanada fence and entered her life, guiding and comforting her through the torments she had suffered. She realized she needed to survive for him as well. As she watched the lines of prisoners walking out of the camp, she felt a tug-of-war in her heart, between leaving for her brother in Dachau and staying behind for her love in Birkenau. Her stomach knotted so tightly she could hardly breathe.

She argued with herself that Hannes had survived Birkenau for months and must have been fit and healthy enough to be sent to Dachau. So surely, he could survive for a short while longer? When the Red Army liberated the camp, she would be swiftly reunited with him, but she reminded herself her brother was not yet a teenager and his young mind and body had suffered the same torture as the adults. How could she presume his physical or psychological state?

After these moments of agonizing deliberation, Rachael concluded she had to join the march to Dachau. It was a men's march, but fit and able women were allowed to take part. Just like the men, if they lagged behind, they would be shot.

She hoped Ludwig would arrive on Lagerstrasse before the Birkenau gates were locked behind them. If he missed the march, he would know where she had gone. If he missed the march and was still alive.

When the motorbike drew level with Rachael and its rider started shooting, the mass of women surged, pushing her toward the center of Lagerstrasse, closer to the men's lines, which were more tightly packed. So tightly packed she could barely move, never mind search for Ludwig.

Rachael was still determined to find out whether Ludwig was there, so she removed her headscarf and waved it above her head. She had not spoken loudly for months, and her body was weak, so when she shouted "Ludwig," a hoarse, unintelligible wheeze emanated from her mouth. Closing her eyes, she told herself to concentrate. She breathed deeply to invigorate her lungs and coughed firmly to clear her throat.

"Ludwig, Ludwig!" Her voice rang out above the heads of the crowd, making her cough violently and drop her upraised hand to her mouth.

SS-Hauptscharführer Moll watched the women fleeing out of his path. Parting like the Red Sea, he thought to himself and smiled.

Just as he was about to twist the motorbike's handlebar throttle and accelerate away, a call went up in the crowd. Did he hear the name "Ludwig"? Somewhere in this camp, there were fifty SK workers, many likely to be on Lagerstrasse at that precise moment, and one might be Ludwig Albin. Moll glanced to his left and saw a ghostly horde of emaciated faces, but no sign of Albin's head jutting into the sky. The SS man dearly wanted to kill the remaining members of the SK, but he had been ordered to accompany and supervise the women's march and could not afford the time to wade into the crowd to seek the Pole out. He would ride to the front of the women's lines and fulfill his duties there. With that, he revved the bike's engine and sped toward the narrow gap between the women before it closed up.

*

Ludwig's wish had come true when Moll's motorbike did not stop until it reached the camp entrance, but the SS-Hauptscharführer had left his gruesome mark behind: the moaning of traumatized prisoners and a sickening, greasy, burning smell, which Ludwig knew well.

The Pole was certain he had heard a voice and eagerly scanned the faces in front of him, but the women looked the same, with pale, drawn features and gray headscarves tied tightly around their heads. The early morning sunshine made their pale skin whiter and the gray lighter...until he caught a flash of red out of the corner of his eye, like a single beacon on a jet-black night. He looked excitedly in that direction and started walking. Inexorably, his bulky frame created a path through the prisoners like a snowplow.

Rachael saw the crown of Ludwig's head rising above the crowd.

"Ludwig!" she cried out.

"Rachael!" he murmured in disbelief, seeing her face for the first time without a screen of wire separating them.

She could barely move through the densely packed crowd, but Ludwig looked as if he was striding unhindered.

When they finally faced each other, she offered him her hand, which he accepted. They stood like innocent teenagers, staring at each other and smiling, neither knowing what to do next.

"I saw your hair," Ludwig mumbled, shy and unprotected without the fence between them. "Your beautiful hair."

Rachael blushed, aware of the surrounding prisoners looking on.

"And I saw your head!" she replied.

It was Rachael who moved first, stepping forward and putting her arms around his barrel chest. Ludwig was reticent, then reciprocated, bending forward and placing his arms around her shoulders. They squeezed each other tightly. She felt protected by this warm giant of a man, and he marveled at the loveliness of this brave and smart woman in his arms.

They stayed in their embrace for a few moments, then Rachael spoke.

"We'd better get into the lines for the Dachau march," she said. "Dachau's where we'll find Hannes. I can feel it in my bones."

As he squeezed her, she was comforted. She tried her best to conjure up her brother's face in her mind, but it was blurred. She squeezed her eyes shut and thought of Hannes's seventh birthday on the day in 1940 when the Nazis entered Amsterdam, and his features became sharp and clear, and she smiled at the image of his breathless happiness as he described his new pedal bike. There were no bikes in Birkenau, just the threatening noise of the SS officers' motorbikes.

The couple walked off together, still holding hands, Ludwig extending an arm to clear a path for them.

*

SS-Obersturmführer Andreas Müller had been told the first part of the march to Dachau was to the railway station in Wodzisław Śląski, a town lying over seventy kilometers away. Then, the surviving prisoners were to be loaded onto cattle cars and transported to Dachau. No further formal communication was forthcoming.

"There're plenty of different routes and trains that lead to Dachau," Müller's commanding officer had said glibly. "You'll find a way. My suggestion is to take any train that is going broadly toward Dachau. Remember! The aim of the march isn't getting the prisoners to Dachau, it's getting them away from Birkenau. And quickly."

Müller had been stunned when the sun had risen that morning. As he was standing beneath the Birkenau arch, the female and male prisoners were stretched across the length and breadth of Lagerstrasse. There was hardly a patch of ground visible. The railway track extensions and the new platform were completely covered. Even the largest Hungarian transport had only occupied half of Lagerstrasse.

And three-quarters of those present would be under his supervision on the Dachau march.

The SS-Obersturmführer recalled the words of his superior and decided to leave straight away. The march was due to begin at midday, but the sooner they departed, the sooner Birkenau would be emptied.

Müller approached the SS guard at the gate.

"Open the gate," he ordered.

"Yes, sir!" the guard replied. Pulling a set of keys from his uniform pocket, he unlocked the gates and pushed them wide open.

The SS officer had been given no instructions about how to manage the march, not even the number of guards he would need or, more importantly, would be made available. He removed his cap, scratched his head, and smoothed his blond hair back into place. His hand rested on his pointed chin, which sat at the end of his long, narrow face.

Replacing his cap, he walked back to the columns of prisoners.

"What the fuck are you doing?"

Müller recognized Moll's voice. He had spotted the SS-Hauptscharführer at the head of the columns of women preparing to leave for Ravensbrück but had deliberately not engaged with him. His reputation preceded him. Although both men were leading a march,

Moll's rank was one higher than Müller's, so the SS-Obersturmführer showed due deference.

"Excuse me, sir?" Müller replied.

"Why the fuck are you opening the gates?" Moll demanded. "It's not midday yet."

"There are so many prisoners here," Müller said. "I thought it would be more efficient if the marches departed at different times." He gestured toward the gate. "I'm not even sure both groups would squeeze through, sir."

"I can squeeze the fucking Jews anywhere," Moll sneered. "Anyway, what makes you think you can go first?"

"By all means, you can take the women first," Müller said. "It's your choice, sir."

"No, you go first," Moll answered, suddenly and surprisingly accommodating. "The women can wait. I'll…I'll watch the men leaving."

Müller did not dwell on his superior's change in mood but walked up to one of the SS-Untersturmführers who were assigned to his march.

"Right, you can take the first group," Müller said.

"How many in a group, sir?" the officer asked.

"How many?" Müller replied. This was his first prisoner march, and he was not sure. He had ten SS-Untersturmführers and had been told the Dachau march comprised 10,000 prisoners.

The superior officer thought for a few seconds.

"Okay. Ten officers take one thousand prisoners each. We need one guard for every hundred prisoners. So each officer has ten guards, and we need a hundred guards in total. The Jews will walk in rows of five, which will require twenty rows for each guard. Please count them through."

"Understood, sir," the other officer replied. "But taking a hundred guards might leave the later marches short."

"So be it," Müller said. "That's for somebody else to deal with. We'll be long gone by then. For now, let's get this march going. Please take out the first group immediately. I'll inform the other officers of their orders."

"Yes, sir!" the officer replied, turning away to summon the nearest ten guards.

*

Rachael and Ludwig were standing in the third and middle line of the march bound for Dachau, having squeezed their way to a point halfway to the front. His strength had cleared their passage through the masses.

It had been eerily quiet during the freezing night, but as the sun climbed in the sky, the prisoners seemed to awaken as well, and a murmur rose among them.

"Where *is* Dachau?" somebody asked.

"Near Munich, I think," the reply came.

"Is that nearer to home?"

"It depends where home is."

"France."

"Yes, Munich's much closer to France than Birkenau."

"What about the Netherlands?" Rachael asked.

"The Netherlands is a little nearer, but there's a lot of Germany to travel through before you reach home. If you survive Dachau, Switzerland's the nearest place of safety."

"We'll go to Switzerland," Rachael whispered to Ludwig. "We'll find Hannes, go to Switzerland, and return to Amsterdam when the war's over!"

*

Well before noon, SS-Obersturmführer Müller watched the SS-Untersturmführer lead the first prisoners through the Birkenau archway.

"Get moving!" the SS-Untersturmführer bellowed, thrashing his baton against the metal bars of the gate. "Stay strictly in your lines. If you don't stay in line, you'll be punished. If you fall behind, you'll be shot on the spot. Don't think you've escaped from Birkenau. This march will be worse, you Jewish bastards!"

The prisoners shuffled after the SS officer but from the start appeared to be struggling. Many of them added a longer stride or an extra step to keep up.

Ludwig held Rachael close to his side, away from the guards who had taken their places along the length of the column. The guards who had observed them watchfully during the night were in full voice and action, shouting obscenities at the prisoners, often at close quarters. It was a routine the guards had practiced every day during roll calls and with the work groups and on selection duty and in every interaction they had with the prisoners.

Silence reigned where the other prisoners were waiting to leave. After thirty minutes, Ludwig and Rachael nervously moved forward. Even though they did not know what the march had in store for them, at least they were on the brink of leaving Auschwitz-Birkenau after more than a year of hell.

Ludwig's senses were sharpened, listening intently for any unusual sound above the shouting of the SS guards and searching for the unforgettable, leering face of Moll near the Ravensbrück prisoners.

Suddenly, Ludwig heard the bark of a dog. He felt Rachael shiver by his side.

"Is everything okay?" he asked her.

"I thought I heard Grese's dog," Rachael replied, not raising her head.

"Don't worry," he replied. "There are lots of dogs in the camp, it's unlikely to be Grese's."

Ludwig continued to watch.

The arched brick gateway to Birkenau was flanked on either side by office buildings. A door to one of these opened, and a woman stepped out onto Lagerstrasse, followed by a substantial German shepherd dog on a leash.

Rachael had told Ludwig about SS-Oberaufseherin Grese, but he had never seen her. As the men's lines advanced, he was close enough to see her clearly. Her blond hair, illuminated by the morning sun, and her facial features were as striking as Rachael had described them, and contrasted with the gray dullness of her SS uniform. There was an emotionless and callous intensity in her face, which Rachael had warned him about, but it still made him shudder.

"It's her, isn't it?" Rachael asked.

"Yes," he whispered in reply.

Although concealed within a crowd predominantly comprising men who were taller than her, Rachael felt as if she were standing alone in the center of Lagerstrasse with Grese staring directly at her. She could not prevent herself from surreptitiously peering through the gaps between the heads in front of her until her gaze fell upon the female officer. Rachael's fingers probed the edges of her headscarf to make sure no strands of red hair were protruding.

The SS-Oberaufseherin's dog barked loudly and repeatedly.

"The dog can smell me!" Rachael whispered.

"Don't worry! It can't smell you. You smell as bad as the rest of us," Ludwig reassured her, before adding, "We're almost out of Birkenau."

Rachael saw the shadow of the entrance building creeping toward them as they approached. It was true, they were almost there.

As the couple drew level with the front row of the women's march, Ludwig took a sharp intake of breath. A motorbike lay on the grass between the prisoners and the building. At the same moment, SS-Hauptscharführer Moll exited the same doorway as Grese, pulling on his black leather gloves as he did so.

Ludwig desperately hoped Moll would be preoccupied with supervising the Ravensbrück march, but no; Moll walked past the columns of women, stopped near to the exit gate, and scrutinized the Dachau march as it passed.

Suddenly, Moll sprang forward, plowed into the moving lines and returned, dragging a prisoner by the coat collar. The SS officer threw the man to the floor, and Ludwig recognized Filip Toszka. With speed Ludwig knew well, Moll drew his revolver and shot Toszka dead.

When the shot rang out, the dog barked uncontrollably and, straining at its leash, pulled its owner toward the site of the incident. As Grese approached Moll, the dog was only a few meters from the prisoners, who continued to walk but squeezed closely together to keep as far away from the animal's jaws as possible.

It slowly dawned on Ludwig that the prisoners were walking too slowly. Even with the exhortations of the SS guards, the men and women were starving and so fatigued they could not march out of the camp. They could barely walk. Moll was left with plenty of time to watch them pass. Every single one of them.

"Stand up straight, you fucking Jews!" Ludwig heard the familiar shout and knew he was done for. He couldn't go back, only forward. He couldn't run; Moll wouldn't even need his bike to catch him. Every step closer to the Birkenau exit was a step closer to his death.

"What's wrong?" Rachael uttered in surprise as Ludwig removed his arm from around her shoulders and gently, but firmly, pushed her away. "What's wrong, Ludwig?" she repeated.

Ludwig kept his head down but watched Moll examining the prisoners as they passed. He almost felt a sense of relief and release when Moll's gaze locked on him. The SS man's eyes bulged with glee, and he broke out into a broad smile.

"Ludwig Albin!" Moll smirked. "I've caught you, you fucking Polish bastard!"

The prisoners surrounding Ludwig shrank back. They would surely reveal them both to Moll. And Grese.

Ludwig stepped in front of Rachael and pushed her carefully, but firmly away, letting another prisoner fill the place she had vacated. He yearned to turn around to speak to her, to say how he felt and to say goodbye, but even the briefest glance behind might have betrayed her, so he looked straight at Grese. She returned his gaze with mild amusement.

Without taking his eyes off Grese, Ludwig pushed through the last two lines, with each step making sure a prisoner filled the gap he created until he found himself standing in the open space in front of Moll, Grese, and the barking dog. He sensed the lines of prisoners shuffling toward the gate. He closed his eyes and, in his mind, watched Rachael passing through the Birkenau gateway. A wave of relief surged through his body. He remembered their meetings by the barbed wire and their first embrace. He pictured the narrow houses and canals of Amsterdam and Rachael teaching the schoolchildren.

SS-Hauptscharführer Moll raised his pistol with delight. Another member of the SK would not live to tell his tale. As Moll made to squeeze the trigger, the Pole stood up straight, puffed out his chest and smiled at SS-Oberaufseherin Grese. Moll was confused. The Pole, seconds from death, had a blissful smile on his face.

*

Rachael's mind was a blur. Hardly had she crossed the threshold of Birkenau than she heard the gunshot. She was filled with a catastrophic sense of loss, but the terrible rhythm of Birkenau took over. The footsteps of the prisoners, the shouting of the guards, the beatings, the shots fired, the pain of hunger, the indescribable fatigue, and the fear of death pummeled her loss into the recesses of her mind.

Within an hour, hunger overtook Rachael. Afraid that the other prisoners would beat her and steal her food, she was careful not to reveal her supply. Bending her head close to the inside pocket of her coat, she rummaged for a piece of bread. Her fingers grasped something like a length of string, which she withdrew. It was the dandelion Ludwig had given her.

The flower lay listless in her palm, crushed and withering but with petals still marked by patches of bright yellow. The loss of Ludwig rose like a tidal wave in her mind, threatening to drown her. He was gone, and she briefly contemplated throwing the flower to the ground but paused and tucked it back inside her coat pocket.

There was a tug on Rachael's coat sleeve, and she turned to see Zuzana Kováčová, looking frightened and vulnerable. A number of women had joined the Dachau march, but Rachael was surprised to see Zuzana. She had assumed SS-Unterscharführer Mann would have ensured her safety.

Rachael pulled the Czech woman close and placed her arm around her shoulders. Zuzana responded by putting her arms around Rachael's chest. They walked on, silently, clinging tightly to one another.

Gradually, as the hours passed, the hope of finding her brother emerged, like a blooming yellow flower, and her determination to find him grew with every step she took.

EPILOGUE

January 27, 1945

It had taken three hours for the Soviet soldiers to remove the landmines that the fleeing Nazis had laid close to the camp entrance, so it was midday by the time Major Anatoly Shapiro of the 322nd Rifle Division of the Red Army stood before the Auschwitz gate. He removed his cap, revealing his thick, dark hair before peering upward to survey the gray steel archway that spanned the entrance.

"Arbeit Macht Frei. What does that mean?" the major asked his translator, who had been a permanent presence by his side over the previous twelve months.

"Work is liberating, sir," the translator replied.

"I'm not sure how a prison is liberating," Shapiro said. "Let's see what sort of work's been done here." He took a step forward before calling over his shoulder, "Colonel, are we sure there are no more SS soldiers around?"

"The camp's been cleared, sir," came the reply.

"Very well," Shapiro said, striding up to the unlocked gate and pushing it open.

The cobbled path into the camp was covered in a mosaic of brown mud and patches of recently fallen snow. There was not a soul to be seen. As the major advanced, there were brick barracks on either side. He approached the door to one, beckoning the translator to follow.

The smell outside was strong, but the stench inside was stinging, making Shapiro throw his gloved hand over his nostrils. The smell was indescribable. He considered walking straight out, but his men had to inspect scores of similar barracks, and he needed to set an example.

A small group of prisoners walked toward him, appearing from the shadows like moving skeletons. They bent low before him.

"We're not Jews! We're not Jews!" they pleaded, terrified.

Shapiro could not comprehend why these poor, emaciated souls were so keen to tell him they were not Jews.

"It doesn't matter whether you're Jews," the major replied via his translator. "We're the Russian Army. The Nazis have gone, and we're here to free you."

Shapiro had expected a more jubilant response to the news that their Nazi oppressors had departed, but as he made his way farther into the barracks, he understood why. The degradation, squalor, and stench grew as he walked among the bunks. Naked bodies lay on bunks, smeared in blood and excrement. Those in bunks and alive could barely move, not even to turn their heads to see their saviors.

The prisoners' clothing was so threadbare it seemed translucent, and many of them had no shoes, just strips of material wrapped around their feet. Later that day, Shapiro would be reminded of this sight when standing in front of a Kanada shed, staring aghast at an enormous pile of shoes, the top of which had toppled onto the building's roof.

The Red Army had been forced into retreat when Hitler's army had invaded Russia in 1941, but after Stalingrad had been reclaimed in 1943, the Soviets recovered lost ground and progressed into Eastern Europe in 1944. They had experienced victories and defeats and the deaths of many of their compatriots. When they arrived in the nearby town of Krakow, neither Shapiro nor his men knew the true purpose of Auschwitz. They were soon to discover that their worst experiences on the battlefield did not compare to the vision of hell presented to them in the camp. They were bombarded with horror in every corner, in every room, in every building.

The Soviet soldiers scrabbled in their pockets to find pieces of chocolate to give to the prisoners. It took the Red Army twenty-four hours to find out the prisoners were so severely starved their digestive systems were dangerously compromised. The consumption of solid food like chocolate could make them sick or even prove fatal.

By the time Major Shapiro reached the western edge of the Auschwitz-Birkenau camp, the few words spoken by the survivors had drawn him a crude picture of its true nature. An accomplished soldier, aged thirty-two and in rude health, he was well acquainted with the nervousness felt before a major battle and how to overcome it. But as he approached the trees that shielded Crematoria 4 and 5, he had a sense of foreboding he could not shake off.

At first, the scene seemed almost idyllic, the dark tree trunks contrasting with the pure, glistening snow, and with birds singing from the treetops, but as he made his way along the path, the landscape opened out in front of him, and the two destroyed crematoria came into view. Haphazard piles of brick and a splintered roof section jutted out like a jagged mountain range above the tall, uncut grass.

The SS had made sure there was no sign of the machinery used to carry out their deadly work. All that remained of Crematorium 4 were bricks, a roof that had collapsed and split on the floor below, and some contorted strips of steel. Shapiro spotted part of a rubber seal, still attached to a metal door hinge, and a section of wire mesh.

In his mind, he had told himself the SS must have planned their flight from Auschwitz well in advance and would have ceased operations weeks ago to give them enough time to demolish the crematoria. He smelled the familiar odor of dynamite lingering in the air. He bent down to pick up a brick from among the debris. One side was burned.

But another smell pervaded, which Major Shapiro did not recognize. It was caustic and yet sickly sweet. And it smelled like burning, but not the burning of bricks and timber.

The major looked at the snowfall surrounding his feet, and something caught his eye. The major scooped up a handful of the snow and saw that it was, in fact, off white. He prodded the lump with his finger. A frozen crust had formed on its top, and on its surface lay hundreds of tiny black specks, which, when he gently blew on them, flew into the air like dust in a storm.

And suddenly, Shapiro felt claustrophobic. The ash was choking him, filling every cavity in his lungs, sticking to his tongue, clawing at his throat. Everywhere. He threw his hand to his mouth and ran. He went only a few meters before retching violently, then berated himself for splattering the snow with vomit.

Ashes in the snow, he thought. Ashes in the snow.

HISTORICAL NOTE

Most of this novel takes place in the period from November 1943 to January 1945. In little more than a year, between 600,000 and 750,000 prisoners were murdered in the Auschwitz-Birkenau extermination camp.

The speed and scale of the slaughter are almost beyond comprehension. Probably the starkest example of this is the fate of the Hungarian Jews. The first mass transport left Budapest on May 14, 1944, and by July 9, official figures showed 350,000 of a total of 434,000 Jews had been gassed and incinerated in one of the four Birkenau crematoria or five recently dug pyres. This equates to an astonishing murder rate of 6,500 human beings every single day, seven days a week.

The SK revolt in Birkenau is a factual event, taking place in early October 1944. It was a partial success, with Crematorium 4 being seriously damaged and some prisoners escaping. The revolt participants exposed themselves to huge risks and were ultimately all killed, including the four women (Roza Robota, Ester Wajcblum, Ella Gartner, and Regina Safirsztain) who smuggled gunpowder from the Union factory.

It was three members of the crematoria SK (Marcel Nadjary, Zalman Gradowski, and Leib Langfus) who buried their written testimonies in the Birkenau ground. Nine of these "Scrolls of Auschwitz" were recovered close to Crematoria 2 and 3 between 1945 and 1980. As proof that the world continues to learn more about the horrors of Auschwitz, in 2017, modern digital techniques recovered the text of one of Marcel Nadjary's scrolls, which had been damaged and illegible since its discovery in 1980. Again, members of the SK took significant risks in obtaining the writing materials to produce and bury the scrolls.

Remarkably, the scrolls were discovered and in a legible condition (eventually). They provide invaluable testimony to the horrors and crimes committed in the four Birkenau crematoria. Full transcripts are widely available in translations.

The Sonderkommando Photographs are the four blurred photographs that were taken secretly by a member of the crematoria Sonderkommando and exist because of incredible risks taken and bravery shown by several people: Greek prisoner Alberto Errara, who took the photos; those who got hold of the camera (probably a Leica) and smuggled it into the Crematorium 5 compound; those who stood guard to ensure the photographer had a clear view to take the pictures undisturbed; and finally, those who smuggled the roll of film out of Birkenau, hidden inside an empty toothpaste tube.

Two photographs were taken from inside the Crematorium 5 gas chamber, showing the burning cremation pyres outside, together with SK workers and piles of bodies. The third photograph depicts a group of naked women being herded toward the gas chamber from the woods close to Crematorium 5. The fourth shows the tops of the trees and proves the difficulty of taking photographs secretly and with the camera held at waist level. These images are the only known pictures of the actual extermination process at any Nazi camp and provide irrefutable evidence of the SS crimes in the mass murder of Jews, Sinti, and many others.

The role of the Sonderkommando (SK) has attracted a great deal of discussion over the intervening decades. These were the Jews who helped other Jews remove their clothes before escorting them into the gas chambers and then dragging their lifeless bodies to the furnace halls and incinerating them. Sometimes, members of the SK had to deal with the bodies of their own friends and families. There has been a school of thought suggesting that the SK was collaborating with the Nazis in the murder of fellow Jews in exchange for better living conditions. Although living conditions were better (more food, less crowding, improved hygiene), they were marginally so, and the SK were isolated from the rest of the camp prisoners, suffering the same mortality rates as the other prisoners.

SK members did carry out resistance activities (the Auschwitz scrolls, the Sonderkommando photos, and the Sonderkommando revolt). All the prisoners in Auschwitz-Birkenau were physically and mentally beaten by the Nazis and were usually starved from the moment they stepped inside their first railway cattle car. It was enormously difficult to contemplate revolting against well-armed SS soldiers. Also, the SS reprisals after any acts of resistance were always brutal, and the capture of one rebel would often lead to ten arbitrary executions amongst the prisoner population.

Attitudes to the members of the SK have softened in recent years, given the almost impossible position the SS put them in.

The SS leadership was cunning in obliging Jews to take on roles which, at first glance, seemed to help them but were in fact merely making the SS process for persecution and murder run more smoothly. In the Netherlands, the SS achieved this by manipulating the Jewish Council. In Birkenau, this included the SK, who engaged with fellow prisoners but never directly killed them (it was always an SS soldier who administered the Zyklon B).

The kapos were in a similar position to the SK members. The SS preferred non-Jews as kapos, but when Jews were appointed, the SS expected the same level of brutality from them. The SS would often select kapos who were criminals or who had an animosity toward Jews. Jewish kapos beat other Jews to death. There has been discussion since 1945 about the extent to which kapos had any realistic option but to behave as they did, since any reticence on their part would lead to their own execution and replacement.

With both the SK members and the kapos, judgment of the cruelty inflicted by Jews on other Jews is tricky, especially in the light of the ever-increasing amounts of postwar information being uncovered.

The Political Department Identification Service ("Politische Abteilung Erkennungsdienst") took the official photographs in the Auschwitz-Birkenau camps, which included portraits of the prisoners who had been tattooed and registered for hard labor.

SS-Hauptscharführer Bernhard Walter was the director of the service and instructed his assistant, SS-Unterscharführer Ernst Hofman, to take the 193 photographs that became known as the Auschwitz Album. The images were taken in the summer of 1944, at the height of the transportation of the Hungarian Jews, when the railway tracks had been extended into the main Birkenau camp.

Fifteen copies of the album were made, the photographs arranged in sections with handwritten headings: "Arrival," "Women's Arrival,"

"Selection," "Post Selection fit-for-work men," "After Disinfection," "Workers," "Entry into camp," "Belongings."

The album shows the huge numbers of Jews being unloaded from the cattle cars. Several pictures show two trains, one stationed on the recently added second track.

Perhaps the most blood-chilling photos in the album are those of the selection process with five lines of prisoners stretching into the distance and an SS officer casually pointing to the left for hard labor or to the right for death. In the background, crowds of Hungarian Jews are walking the few hundred meters to Crematoria 2 and 3.

Some photographs were taken from a distance, but many were taken at close quarters, and the faces of those men, women, and children who were soon to be gassed are clearly visible, as were the cattle cars crammed to capacity.

One section of the album that does not have a heading follows the progress of those who had been selected for immediate extermination. Predominantly women, older men, and children can be seen walking along the paths leading to the Crematoria 4 and 5 sector, where they sit or stand among the trees, unaware that the crematoria, and death, are a few hundred meters away. There are no signs of stress or agitation on any of their faces.

The scenes among the trees are the last part of the extermination process that the SS took photos of. None were taken of the undressing, gassing, or incineration processes. One can only assume even the SS could not bring themselves to film those horrors.

It is not clear why the Auschwitz Album was produced. It has been suggested the SS wished to prove how orderly and efficient their selection process was, omitting the horrors of the gassing and incineration of prisoners. Or it might have been intended as a training guide for future camps. Irrespective of the reasons, the SS hierarchy was aware of the incendiary nature of the album's contents and ordered all copies to be destroyed. But a Jewish survivor, Lili Jacob, happened upon a copy in an abandoned barracks in the Dora concentration camp, a sub-camp of Buchenwald. Presumably, an SS officer who was fleeing Auschwitz in haste via Dora left his copy behind by accident. It became a vital piece of evidence of the existence and scale of the Birkenau extermination process.

*

Rudolf Höss, born in 1901, joined the German army at the age of only fourteen and became its youngest non-commissioned officer at seventeen. In 1923, he was convicted and jailed for murder.

Höss joined the SS in 1934 and grew a strong admiration for Heinrich Himmler. He wrote a report recommending the building of a camp in Auschwitz.

Having gained experience in other camps, in summer 1941, Höss was sent to Auschwitz by Heinrich Himmler to implement the Final Solution, the extermination of the Jews of Europe. It was Höss who implemented the prisoner selections on the railway platforms and the building of the crematoria and large gas chambers in Birkenau, together with the testing and introduction of Zyklon B gas.

Höss was removed from Auschwitz in 1943, possibly because of an affair with a female prisoner. However, he was reappointed in May 1944 to deal with the imminent arrival of the Hungarian Jews.

After the war, Höss went into hiding but was discovered and arrested in 1946 while working as a gardener. In his memoirs, Höss did not admit any culpability, choosing to blame those below him (subordinates and kapos) and those above (Hitler and Himmler). An American psychologist who interviewed Höss confirmed he had the absence of empathy and emotion of a psychopath.

In March 1947, he was tried and convicted of war crimes. On April 10, he returned to the Catholic Church and took communion. Two days later, Höss finally admitted to having "sinned gravely against humanity" and pleaded for the forgiveness of God and the Poles (but not the Jews). He expressed similar sentiments in his last letters to his wife and children. It is open to debate whether the man who played such an integral part in the murder of millions of people did finally acknowledge and repent his crimes against humanity or was simply reacting to his imminent death.

Höss was hanged on April 16 within the Auschwitz camp, with a priest in attendance.

SS-Hauptscharführer Otto Moll was born in 1915, joining the SS aged twenty. He was blinded in his right eye in 1937 during a serious truck accident. Some experts have suggested the head trauma he suffered might have contributed to his subsequent behavior.

Moll's first role in Auschwitz in 1941 was managing one of the most gruesome activities in the camp, the digging of mass graves. Coinciding with the return of Rudolf Höss, he was put in charge of all the Birkenau crematoria in mid-1944. At the time of the transportations of the Hungarian Jews, his behavior was especially cruel. He would torture men, women, children, and babies, often throwing them onto the pyres alive or pour burning oil over them.

Moll was captured and put on trial in November 1945. He was found guilty of fatally shooting numerous prisoners and was hanged in May 1946. There are many eyewitness reports of Moll's cruelty, all highlighting his extreme brutality and inhumanity.

Although SS-Hauptsturmführer Josef Mengele plays a minor role in this novel, the so-called Angel of Devil is one of the most infamous SS officers who took part in the Final Solution. He arrived in Auschwitz-Birkenau in 1943, where he performed a variety of experiments, particularly on twins, dwarfs, and pregnant women. He was actively involved in the selection process on the ramps.

Mengele avoided capture after the war and found refuge in Argentina (his wife refused to accompany him). Perpetually in fear of being apprehended, he moved frequently, dying in Brazil in 1979.

SS-Oberaufseherin Irma Grese is perhaps the most infamous female member of the SS. She frequently attempted and failed to join the SS during her teenage years until, finally, she was transferred to Auschwitz in March 1943, aged twenty. She started working as an assistant in the mailroom and worked her way through the SS ranks. Her nicknames included the Blond Angel of Death, the Hyena of Auschwitz, and the Angel of Hell. Several prisoners attested to her physical beauty, and she was known to have had sexual relations with men and women among the SS and prisoners. She reveled in the pain of others and was directly responsible for many deaths and acts of cruelty, including setting her starving dog on prisoners and actively taking part in selections and medical experiments.

Grese was arrested, tried, and found guilty of war crimes in November 1945. She was sentenced to death and was hanged on December 13, 1945, aged twenty-two, the youngest SS camp guard ever to be executed by hanging.

In this novel, SS-Unterscharführer Franz Mann and the prisoner Zuzana Kováčová are loosely based on SS-Unterscharführer Franz Wunsch and Helena Citronova.

The Heroine of Auschwitz

Wunsch was only twenty years old when he arrived in Auschwitz in 1942 but was soon promoted to be head of the Kanada stores. He also took an active part in the selections, both on the railway platform and at the gas chambers. Witnesses testified he adopted the standard SS approach of brute force and deception to gain the cooperation of the prisoners. Some said his behavior became less cruel when, later in 1942, he started an affair with the twenty-year-old Czech prisoner, Citronova.

Because he was kind to her, Citronova regarded Wunsch as a human being, not a cruel SS officer. Although he was besotted with her, the feelings were not reciprocated, as she abhorred the thought of being involved with a member of the SS.

Wunsch certainly made her life in Auschwitz more bearable by providing a job in the Kanada stores and making sure she received improved food and clothing allowances. In one instance, Wunsch saved Citronova's sister, who had been selected for the gas chamber. Although Citronova often handed her extra rations to her fellow prisoners, many were jealous of the benefits and safety she enjoyed because of Wunsch's attention.

As a young woman surrounded by death and degradation, it is difficult to judge Citronova's behavior. Their relationship was never sexual, but the other prisoners clearly knew of Wunsch's infatuation with the Czech woman by the regular gifts she received. If nothing else, perhaps their relationship allowed them a fleeting glimpse of a better world away from Auschwitz.

The two were separated when the camp was liberated. Wunsch went to live in Austria, and Citronova, having found her hometown destroyed, moved to Israel. Over the subsequent years, she rebuffed Wunsch's frequent attempts to make contact. However, she provided testimony at his trial in 1972, confirming that he had had been kind to her but not condoning his actions as an SS officer. Wunsch was found not guilty because of lack of documentary evidence, although eyewitness testimony confirmed his presence during the gas chamber killings. Wunsch died in Austria in 2009 and Citronova in Israel in 2007.

When the Red Army was closing in on the Auschwitz-Birkenau camp, and the SS realized they could not murder all the remaining prisoners, they organized a series of cruel death marches in the period between January 15 and 27, 1945. Approximately 56,000 prisoners were forced on these marches to destinations such as Dachau, Ravensbrück, Bergen-Belsen, and Mauthausen. In freezing winter conditions, the starving and sick were forced to walk tens of kilometers and were then crammed into railway freight cars. Many died en route through starvation or exposure. Those who lagged behind were shot dead by the SS.

Marchers were given a tiny ration of bread and sausage prior to departure, but there was no provision for food during the march. Prisoners ate snow and other scraps off the ground. Local villagers were forbidden by the SS from helping, at pain of death.

Approximately 15,000 of the marchers died prior to reaching their destinations.

ACKNOWLEDGMENTS

Firstly, I am indebted to Gary Dalkin, who has continued his indispensable editorship, keeping both me and my work balanced and coherent. Thanks also go to Nicky and Richard, who have read and given constructive feedback on draft manuscripts.

I would like to thank Estelle and Michelle at TAUK Publishing and Phil at Novel Websites, who helped me share Rachael Kisch's story by transforming tens of thousands of words into immaculate ebooks and paperbacks. I'm also grateful to Linda and Liz, who have guided me through the labyrinth that is book marketing and strategy.

Thanks go to Karen and Alex, who have continued to support me as I pored over mountains of papers and books, leaving a never-ending trail of untidiness behind me. Special thanks go to Alex for her fantastic work on the camp map. Pippa, the cat, has remained impervious.

The encyclopedic knowledge of the staff at the Auschwitz-Birkenau State Museum made my two research trips to the camps enlightening and gave me a true insight into the scale of the harrowing events that took place there.

I wanted to thank all of you who read *The Thirteenth Child* and have said so many kind words about it. You provide the pick-me-ups whenever my writing pen runs dry. I sincerely hope you stick with me through the next stages of Rachael's journey.

My unending thanks go to the incredibly brave people who inspire me to tell their stories. Some of you survived, and many did not, but your deeds in the face of unimaginable adversity live on and provide a vital message for future generations. Never forget.

ABOUT THE AUTHOR

Mark is best known for writing enthralling historical fiction novels that take place during World War II. He's particularly interested in those actual events and characters that are generally less well-known but still represent compelling and moving human stories.

His thorough research gives his readers a vivid insight into the people and places of the time, and his plots provide compelling and emotional stories.

A number of Mark's Dutch Jewish ancestors were murdered by the Nazis in Auschwitz and Sobibor, and it is preserving the memory of those poor souls which drives him to research and write about those difficult times as a reminder to future generations.

Mark has also produced several award-winning short stories.

His debut novel, *The Thirteenth Child*, was shortlisted for the 2024 CIBA Hemingway Award for 20th century Wartime Fiction and has been a Kindle number one bestseller several times. It forms part of the series *The Rachael Kisch Trilogy*.

Mark lives in the North of England, where he spends most of his time writing and researching with a patient black-and-white cat for company.

Mark would love to hear from you via:

TikTok – mdm82442
Facebook – www.facebook.com/MarkdeMezaauthor
Website – https://markdemeza.co.uk/

ALSO BY THE AUTHOR

The Thirteenth Child
Part of The Rachael Kisch Trilogy

TAUK Publishing is an established assisted publisher for independent authors in the UK.

With hundreds of titles including novels, non-fiction and children's books, TAUK Publishing is a collaborative-based team providing step-by-step guidance for authors of all genres and formats.

To sign up to our newsletter or submit an enquiry, visit:
https://taukpublishing.co.uk/contact/

For one-to-one advice, consider scheduling a Book Clinic:
https://taukpublishing.co.uk/book-clinic/

Connect with us!

Facebook: @TAUKPublishing
Twitter: @TAUKPublishing
Instagram: @TAUKPublishing
Pinterest: @TAUKPublishing

We love to hear from new or established authors wanting support in navigating the world of self-publishing.
Visit our website for more details on ways we can help you.

https//taukpublishing.co.uk/

Made in United States
North Haven, CT
30 July 2025

71114843R00152